Murder in Plain Sight

Natasha Orme

First edition 2025

ISBN 978-1-7394505-6-4 (paperback)

ISBN 978-1-7394505-7-1 (ebook)

Also by Natasha Orme

The Jason Hunter series
Murder in the Fast Lane
Murder Has a Price

Non-fiction
Travels with My Child

To Dad, for being the real life Jason Hunter.

THE GUNMAN

LEICESTER SQUARE, LONDON

Sunday 29th May

The crowd below thrummed and swelled like a living thing and people were crammed into every corner.

It was busier than usual, the weekend throng making the already busy square almost unbearable. Slow moving crowds had become immovable masses.

Sunday. Why did it have to be a Sunday?

Blacked-out barriers lined the square, separating the red-carpet celebrities from the riff raff. But from his vantage point, he could see it all.

The uninvited general public were climbing on stone benches, and craning their necks to get a better view, some holding cameras on selfie sticks extended as far as they would go in the hope that they'd be able to glimpse a celebrity.

Stern-faced security personnel stood unwavering at intervals around the perimeter with several more guarding the entrance to the premiere.

At the very back of the square, the more reserved were stood apart from the main crowd and watching the live stream from huge plasma screens.

Inside the barriers, he could see the celebrities posing for photos and stopping to sign pieces of paper thrust in their faces. A few even stopped to take a selfie or two with adoring fans.

The evening air was warm without being stifling. Royce Gill and Maiti Preston – the two biggest names in the movie – posed together, Royce's arm casually slung around Maiti's waist. Keneder Owen stood on his own, an air of superiority around him.

And there he was.

Alfonso Torres.

The arrogant prick walked the red carpet as if he owned it. He probably did; the man was wealthy enough.

The whole movie was a sham anyway. An expensive piece of propaganda designed to show him in a more favourable light. But Alfonso Torres hadn't come to own Formula One by chance. No, the man had tricked and cheated and blackmailed his way to the top in the most despicable of ways.

That wasn't why the gunman was here though.

No. He was here because Alfonso Torres had pissed off the wrong person.

He'd finally tricked and cheated and blackmailed the wrong person.

And that person had a score to settle.

The L115A3 sniper rifle was already assembled and ready. Peering through the telescopic sight, he watched as Alfonso Torres paused for the camera, his face stony and immovable. Keneder Owen, his on-screen counterpart, meandered over to join him and the pair posed for yet more photos.

He wanted to get this over with. Get the job done and move on. But the instructions for the contract had been explicit. He needed to wait for Alfonso to have had his moment in the spotlight. His imminent death would have a big impact on the success of the movie. He may even be painted as a martyr, a good guy, all his misdeeds glossed over by the media. Or maybe they'd discover what the bastard had done. Maybe some journalist or other would dig deeper and find the dirt. Either way, he needed to time this perfectly.

Fergus Navarro, the final big celebrity name, walked out and the fans went wild. Even from where he hid, he could hear their screams.

Alfonso Torres smiled, but it was more of a grimace, the look completely insincere.

Almost time.

He checked his breathing. Followed his target through his scope and waited for the right moment.

All the celebrities were on the red carpet. And now they were lining up for group photos; Alfonso Torres was in the middle, Keneder Owen on his left, Maiti Preston on his right and Royce Gill and Fergus Navarro at each end.

They smiled, posed, repositioned clothing and posed again. Maiti Preston smiled and tipped her head back slightly as she laughed – at what, he didn't know. Nor did he care.

The group extricated themselves from one another and began to move further along the carpet, towards the exit where the premiere of *The Last Lap* waited for them.

He pressed his finger lightly on the trigger, pulling it halfway. This was it. He inhaled through his nose and slowly exhaled through his mouth, just as Alfonso Torres turned and glanced over his shoulder.

He pulled the trigger the rest of the way, felt the sharp recoil in his shoulder as his muscles tensed to hold the weapon in place.

On the red carpet, the bullet slammed into Alfonso Torres' forehead. His head snapped back with sickening ferocity and his body crumpled into a heap on the floor.

Then the screaming began.

Chapter 1

Jason Hunter

Casino de Monte-Carlo, Monaco

Monday 30th May

I walked into the grand 19th-century hallway, with huge diamond chandeliers hanging from the ceiling and soft lighting throughout. It was magnificent. Everywhere I looked there was opulence and grandeur. Music thrummed from somewhere in the building and raucous laughter spilled out of the games hall. The space was filled with people coming and going, and waiters with champagne circled the room. I could see that most people had indulged in at least a few.

In fact, I swept my eyes around the room and guessed the guys in the suits stationed at strategic entrance and exit points were probably the only ones who were sober. I counted at least eight.

Unsure what do with myself, I moved further into the room, spying the slot machines and gambling tables through the main archway on the other side. It was meant to be the party to end all parties. A celebration of the Monaco Grand Prix being over for another year. A place where all the wealthy came together to let off some steam.

Stacey James, world-famous Formula One driver, had broken records this year. As well as being the first female in Formula One, she was showing everyone exactly what a woman could do; win. And it was exhilarating to watch. Not least of all because she lived in my house, slept in my bed, and filled my every waking thought.

Being a divorced dad of two in my mid-thirties, the term 'girlfriend' felt too juvenile. But we also hadn't officially labelled our relationship. And I wasn't sure how I felt about that.

Since taking Stacy on as a client when she couldn't shake her stalker, we'd been through a lot together. Her body double had been murdered in Budapest while standing in for her on the podium, and that had triggered a whole chain of events I know Stacey still struggled with.

Somewhere along the way, the boundaries of our professional relationship blurred. I'm never usually so unprofessional, but there was something about her; her sassiness, her strength, her take-the-world-by-the-balls attitude. God, I loved the woman.

And that's why I was here, walking into the biggest casino in Monte Carlo at nearly one in the morning, looking for Stacey.

Last year, I'd been hired by popstar sensation Iris Mccleary to provide security for her UK tour. Specifically, to put some distance between her and any over-excited fans. My idea to provide a female-only team – an idea I'd gotten from Stacey – was a big win and Iris loved her security team.

For her upcoming world tour, Iris had only wanted one person on the job: yours truly. While I was flattered by her complete faith in me – let's face it, the business needed the steady income – her insistence that I handle *every* little detail was time-consuming and meant I often had late nights and awkwardly timed meetings.

I'd been stuck in a Zoom meeting to discuss the US leg of her tour. The venue management team was proving to be tricky to deal with which had resulted in some last-minute rescheduling of meetings, working to California's time zone and me jumping on a last-minute flight out of London to be here.

A waiter flitted by with a tray of champagne flutes. I plucked one up and looked around for some familiar faces.

I had no idea where Stacey was. Her stunning blonde hair would be easy to spot, but failing that, someone like Aldric St Pierre, her long-time friend and mentor, would probably be able to point me in the right direction.

I nodded to Jackson Yang, a tall, broad-shouldered guy I knew from Stacey's security team, who stood sentry on the edge of the room. His eyes widened and his lips started moving, speaking into the almost invisible headset he wore.

His eyes flitted around the room nervously as he continued to speak into the headset. I frowned. What was he looking so on edge about?

He gave a firm nod and then swiftly closed the distance between us.

"Boss, we have a problem."

Chapter 2

JASON HUNTER

CASINO DE MONTE-CARLO, MONACO

Monday 30th May

"What's happened?" I rasped, and then winced. I hated the sound of my voice these days. After dragging my sorry ass from a burning warehouse 7 months ago, it had never been the same. There'd been an explosion, and in the chaos that had followed, I'd headed back into the flames to drag Bill Cooper, Stacey's ex-boyfriend and gun-for-hire, to safety. The cost of which had been my voice. I'd spent nearly a week in the hospital recovering from emergency surgery when Alek Gromov, the Russian crime boss, had tried to strangle me to death for double-crossing him. It's safe to say my poor throat had been thoroughly wrecked.

The damage had been extensive; I'd likely suffer from shortness of breath for the rest of my life, which made my gym visits particularly difficult. But the raspiness, like I'd smoked fifty a day for my entire life, was meant to have improved by now. And it had. It was definitely better, but part of me worried it would never fully heal.

"You need to speak to Sam," Jackson said and gestured down the hallway, away from the crowds.

Without waiting for my reply, he strode off and I followed. An iron knot had formed in my stomach and I felt sick. Something in my gut was telling me this was going to be bad.

We turned left, walked past the 'Authorised personnel only' sign and up a set of carpeted marble stairs, the sound of revellers getting quieter the further we went.

We reached the top of the stairs and Jackson turned right. As we rounded the corner, the sounds from the gaming room almost disappeared, a strange quiet settling around us. At the end of the corridor was an ornate door made from solid wood. Stationed outside were two men in suits, each with an earpiece. I knew where we were going.

The guy on the right nodded at me, then turned and opened the door.

Inside, the room was dimly lit. I could just about make out the elaborate designs on the ceiling and the vintage wallpaper on the walls. But the main feature was the bank of security screens along one wall, glowing in the dim light.

A glass touch-screen table was set up in the middle of the room where at least five men stood, pouring over what looked to be a map of the casino. They all looked up at my entrance and I immediately recognised Sam.

Abandoning their conversation, Sam strode over. At 6'4", Sam dwarfed even me. He was a huge unit of a man, wide as well as tall with dark blonde hair and observant green eyes.

"I've been trying to call you," he said, his voice gruff and, dare I say, angry. I don't think I'd ever heard Sam angry. He was always calm and collected, a man of few words. No matter the storm, I was always confident he could weather it, but the look on his face made the knot in my stomach tighten painfully.

"I–" Pulling my phone from my pocket, I looked down at the screen to see the little airplane symbol in the top left corner. "I thought I'd taken it off airplane mode," I said.

"Stacey's missing."

My head snapped up.

"What?" I could feel my heart racing in my chest as panic closed in.

"She's missing," Sam repeated.

"How is that even possible?" It came out more strangled than I intended. I cleared my throat and tried again, but my voice was still too raspy.

"I don't know. That's what we're trying to figure out."

I could feel it then, the overwhelming fear as it came crashing down. After everything we'd been through together, after everything I'd done to keep Stacey safe, this is what it came down to.

I took a breath and grounded myself. Stacey could be in real danger and letting myself go to pieces now wouldn't help anyone, least of all her.

"Tell me everything," I said and strode over to the table.

"I escorted her to the ladies' toilets. I was posted outside, but she didn't come back out. I went in to check on her and she was gone."

"How long?"

"How long what?"

"How long until you went in?"

"About 15 minutes."

I nodded. A reasonable amount of time. Not that I doubted Sam. He was the best I had.

"And tell me what we have here," I said, gesturing to the table in front of us.

It was unlike anything I'd ever seen. The glass top was opaque and finger sensitive. It currently showed the floorplan of the casino, with the gaming rooms outlined in red.

"Phillippe Moreau," said Sam, indicating the man opposite, "is Chief of Security." Dressed in a well-tailored black suit and bow tie, Phillippe inclined his head to me. He was in his late fifties, with a head of silver hair, and deep lines on his face. "Show him," said Sam.

Phillippe tapped on the table and the floorplan moved, zooming in on the main entrance.

"We know that Stacey came in through these doors at 10.07pm. She went into the games room with Aldric St Pierre and stayed there, playing at the tables until 11.42pm," he said, his French accent thick but his words clear. The floorplan zoomed out again and Phillippe showed me where the games room was in relation to the entrance. "That's when Sam escorted her to the toilets." He traced his finger along the table, indicating the route they took. He double tapped on the corridor outside the toilets and a CCTV camera recording opened up to show footage of Stacey entering the toilets.

He pressed the double arrow to fast forward the footage that showed Sam standing guard outside, and then slowed it back down again at 11.59pm to show Sam checking his watch and then knocking on the toilet door. He waited a moment before opening the door and entering.

I watched the seconds tick by, knowing that no matter how many times I watched the footage, the outcome would be the same; Stacey wasn't in there.

Sam reappeared on screen, talking urgently into his earpiece. Even on the grainy footage I could see the thunderous expression on his face. He walked briskly down the corridor and Phillippe tapped on the other end of the corridor, opening up a second camera feed where Sam emerged into the main atrium and looked around.

He stood sentry for a moment before walking back down the corridor. I knew what he was doing. He would need to stand sentry outside the ladies' toilets to prevent anyone else from entering or leaving. He needed to secure the scene until others could arrive to help with the search.

And sure enough, the rest of his team arrived a moment later. I watched as Sam gave instructions to two of the guys – one of them being the young Jackson Yang I'd met on the way in – and then gestured for the third to follow him.

They headed to the main atrium and Sam gave more instructions. The two men split up and began searching the crowd for a particular blonde-haired racing driver.

Phillippe stopped the footage and looked up at me. "Sam alerted my team that Stacey was missing at 12.06am and we did a sweep of the entire building. The perimeter has been locked down; no-one is allowed to enter or leave without ID verification."

I glanced down at my watch. That was less than half an hour ago.

I cursed the delayed flight, the difficulty traversing the streets of Monaco with so many people here to watch the Grand Prix and then the stop at my hotel to get changed. I hadn't wanted to fly in my suit, but I hadn't had time to change before I'd headed to the airport. I should have changed in the car. I should have done a lot of things. Maybe then I would have been here in time to prevent Stacey from going missing.

Chapter 3

Jason Hunter

Casino de Monte-Carlo, Monaco

Monday 30th May

The tension in my chest, curled around my heart and squeezed.

Stacey was missing.

It was stupid, really. So unbelievably stupid. The worst part? The security team had been right there. They'd done everything by the book; they'd been right outside. So how the hell had Stacey managed to walk into those toilets and disappear?

I couldn't let my thoughts spiral. Couldn't let the panic consume me. I could feel it sitting in the pit of my stomach, making me sick. Between that and the weight in my chest, I couldn't breathe.

Get a grip. Stacey needs you.

I swallowed. I needed to look at this as in impartial outsider. Needed to treat it like I would any other client. It was my job to keep Stacey safe, always had been. And I'd failed, yet again. But that kind of thinking wouldn't get me anywhere.

"So, she goes into the toilets and doesn't come out."

Sam nods.

"Any other entrances or exits to the toilets?"

Sam shook his head. "Main door is the only one."

"Actually," said Philippe. I turned to look at him. He was frowning. Leaning over the table, he tapped a few commands and returned to the original floor plan. He tapped again and a keyboard opened up in front of him. A few commands later and a login box appeared in the centre of the table demanding a password.

I hadn't been introduced to the other men in the room, but they all stood in silence, watching Philippe. He entered the password and was then prompted to place his hand on the table for scanning.

Security protocols complete, the floorplan reappeared with an overlay of markings in blue.

"What's this?" I asked.

"There's a series of secret rooms in the casino. These," said Philippe, indicating two rooms that were coloured grey in the original plan, "are in use. Reserved for dignitaries, the Royals and any other high-profile players. But these," he indicated several more rooms that hadn't appeared on the original plan, "are no longer in use. They're mostly used for storage, and they haven't been open to the public in years."

"But none of them are connected to the toilets," I said, unsure where he was going with this. It wasn't surprising to see there were hidden rooms in the casino. Even the New York subway had its hidden stations. But as I looked more closely at the floorplan, I noticed other markings. Not rooms, but ... passageways? There was one leading right to the ladies' toilets. "What are these markings?" I asked.

Phillippe was still frowning. "They're corridors connecting rooms."

"This—"

"Connects to the ladies' toilets."

"So, you mean to tell me that someone could have taken a different way in and out?"

But Philippe was already tapping on the screen.

The next moment, another CCTV stream opened next to one of the hidden games' rooms. Phillippe rewound the footage to the time Stacey went missing and we held our breath as we watched it play in double speed.

The room was mostly empty, except for one corner that was stacked high with sheet-covered furniture. The walls were covered in wooden panelling and in excellent condition for somewhere that had clearly been shut off from the world.

The time stamp in the corner said 11.50pm as part of the wall opened. Slowly at first, almost like the hinges had rusted shut and whoever was opening it was having to battle against unseen forces. Then, two figures emerged into the room; one was Stacey James, tall and elegant in her midnight blue dress, her blonde hair braided over one shoulder. Behind her was a man, and the moment I saw him, my heart sank.

He was about the same height as Stacey and completely ordinary looking. But I'd recognise his face anywhere. I'd trained him myself. I'd taught him everything he knew about how to protect someone, how to keep them safe. Which made him dangerous; he knew the tricks of the trade and our inside secrets. He'd been one of my own guys. Vetted just like all the others, but somehow Liam Harvey had slipped through the net.

I could feel a snarl slip up the back of my throat as I watched Liam, grab Stacey around the top of her arm, and roughly pulled her through the room. The gun dangling from his fingers told me why she wasn't struggling.

"How the bloody hell was he able to get in?" I snapped. "And with a weapon?"

Phillippe was still frowning. "I don't know," he said. "We'll need to follow his movements. Locate where and when he entered the premises. He should have been searched."

I turned to Sam.

"This is a big problem."

He gave a single nod. He knew. I didn't need to tell him how much of a shitshow this was. Liam was dangerous. Obsessive and dangerous. He'd stalked Stacey for months before becoming part of her security team when she'd hired me. He'd managed to worm his way into the team of guys that she'd hired for the specific purpose of keeping her safe from him. It was a cruel joke. And the fallout had left her traumatised.

She'd been seeing a therapist for months now, trying to process the anger and pain. But Liam had escaped. I'd had the chance to catch him, but at the time, Stacey had been trapped in the Lamborghini sportscar Liam had stolen and then crashed. So I'd had to make a choice; catch Liam or save Stacey. It was an easy decision. And one I definitely didn't regret. The only downside was that Stacey had been living in fear of Liam returning for over a year.

He'd even gone so far as to send her postcards after each race. Each one featured a tourist hotspot in the city where she'd been. It had pissed her off as much as it had terrified her. And DI Hayley Irons had done everything in her power to track him down. But keeping tabs on him across international borders was proving difficult, especially when he kept changing locations.

And now he was here.

Chapter 4

Jason Hunter

Casino de Monte-Carlo, Monaco

Monday 30th May

Phillippe's fingers skittered across the table as he brought up a number of different camera feeds to track their movements through the casino; we needed to know exactly where they went and at what time.

They emerged into the main games room where crowds of people squeezed between slot machines and gambling tables, not a single person stopping to look up at the ornate and priceless paintings hanging up, the intricate mouldings adorning the walls, and the dangling chandeliers.

Liam and Stacey easily blended into the crowd, slipping into one of the staff corridors less than a minute later. That's when I realised how well he'd planned this, why he'd chosen to ambush her in the toilets; not only was there an exit route from the toilets, but he was able to get her through the main floor without drawing any attention. And the staff entrance was the perfect escape route – it would be less guarded, and no-one milling around with prying eyes.

Liam's hand, and the gun it was holding, were casually tucked into his pocket as he strode down the corridor, but Stacey still didn't fight.

Why wasn't she shouting for help? Why wasn't she struggling? What had Liam said to her to make her go willingly?

I could feel the fury rippling under my skin. He must have threatened her. And I dreaded to think exactly what that threat might have been.

Phillippe, already one step ahead, was pulling up the cameras from the corridor. Staff in neatly tailored black trousers and waistcoats with white shirts and bow ties bustled up and down the corridor, barely paying them any attention.

"Where does that corridor lead?" I asked.

Without looking up, Phillippe replied, "Offices and staff rooms, mainly. But it does have a private exit."

Of course it did. Liam had planned this far too well. I was willing to bet there was an unknown car parked in one of the staff bays as well.

"I take it there's parking out back?"

"Not really." Phillippe shook his head and continued bringing up more camera feeds; one showed them further down the corridor, one near the exit, and one coming out into the night air.

Once they were out of sight of any staff or members of the public, Stacey suddenly started to fight back.

So the threat he'd made had been about those nearby.

And Stacey, being Stacey, wouldn't have wanted to put any innocent lives at risk, even if it put her in more danger. If the circumstances hadn't been so grim, I would've almost smiled at how far she'd come from the cocky, arrogant Formula One celebrity I'd first met nearly two years ago. But then I couldn't forget that it was Liam who'd changed it all. It was Liam who had tormented her to the point where she felt broken. And it was Liam who had her now.

I watched as she wrenched free from his grasp and used all her strength to knee him between the legs. Liam twisted at the last second, and she caught him in the thigh. It didn't have quite the same impact but all the training Stacey did to keep fit for her races worked in her favour as Liam went down. She didn't hesitate to slam the heel of her hand into Liam's face, watching as the blood spurted from his nose.

Good girl.

The self-defence lessons I'd given her were paying off. And although there was something that felt dangerously like hope fluttering in my chest, I knew this still wouldn't end well.

Before Stacey could pull away, Liam backhanded her across the face, and she crumpled. He wiped a hand across his face and looked at the blood before lifting the sleeve of his jacket to try and staunch the bleeding.

I really didn't want to see what happened next.

Stacey scrambled to her feet, her dress already torn, and Liam grabbed a fistful of her hair, yanking her head back. I could see the pained shout on her lips. He held her steady, pressed the gun into her back, and spoke into her ear.

Stacey's body went rigid and, with a quick look around the empty area, Liam led them over to an unmarked white van.

I pointed to the van, opened my mouth, but before I could say anything, Phillippe was typing away.

"I only have access to cameras on the premises."

Frustration rippled through me and I opened my mouth, but Sam interjected.

"Where are the police?"

I threw him a glance, grateful he'd intervened. I don't think I could trust myself to be professional and not explode at Phillipe.

He gave me an ever-so-slight nod.

Sam had been one of my first hires. And by far the best one I'd ever made. He was my right-hand man for everything. And the only one

I trusted to keep Stacey safe. Ironic considering the current situation. But Sam knew the score. There was no way he could've known Liam would have planned it so well. No one had been told about the secret passages. It was clearly an oversight on the casino's part, and one that I would raise hell about. But first, we needed to get Stacey back.

"On their way. I've alerted them to the situation."

"Right," I said. The helplessness I felt made me jittery, and I couldn't stand still, couldn't sit in this room and wait for the police to arrive. Monaco wasn't a big country, and I knew it was heavily policed, but who knew how long it might take for them to arrive? How long it would take for them to get up to speed, to follow after the unmarked white van? With every second that ticked by, the chances of finding Stacey before dawn were slipping away.

"Here's what we're gonna do," I said, looking to Sam. "You and me, we're gonna follow the van. We know it headed towards Port Hercule, so we can start there. See if anyone saw anything."

Sam nodded and Phillippe looked like he was about to object.

"I'm not gonna sit around and wait." I glanced at the paused footage on the table in front of us and then looked down at my watch. "We're already nearly 45 minutes behind them. It only takes 30 to get to Nice Airport, not that I think he'll head out that way. Too easily traceable."

"He's gonna stick to the roads. It's too noticeable to go by boat. He'd have to be checked in and out of the harbour. Too easy to follow," said Sam.

Phillippe gave Sam an appraising look, as if he was seeing him in a new light. "But not impossible," he said. "Port Hercule is just one of the harbours in Monaco. The main one, yes, but not the only one. Is he likely to have help?"

I opened my mouth to say 'no', but something stopped me. My stomach churned. Was Liam acting on his own?

I thought back to all the instances where our paths had crossed. Like the confrontation in the office of Alek Gromov's outrageously lavish mansion. Liam had been caught between blackmailing Gromov and profiting from the arms deal between Gromov, an American, and Adam, my old boss and the original owner of Hawk Security. By the time I'd arrived, Liam had killed both Adam and the American – I never did find out his name.

And then there was the time he'd manipulated the anonymous gunman who'd killed Stacey's body double on the podium at the Hungarian Grand Prix. He'd deliberately intercepted communications for his own twisted games.

While I didn't doubt Liam was a sole operator, I couldn't confidently say that he hadn't roped anyone else in to help. He was a master at manipulating others, and he wasn't above using blackmail, threats, and bodily harm to get what he wanted.

So perhaps they *had* fled via one of the harbours. It was the most efficient and direct route out of the city. He could easily get to the next port and then disappear by land. He just needed a cover to do it. Some poor unsuspecting boatman held at gunpoint, just as Stacey had been.

My blood ran cold.

They could be anywhere.

Chapter 5

JASON HUNTER

CASINO DE MONTE-CARLO, MONACO

Monday 30th May

I had no idea what we were hoping to achieve. I just knew that I had to be doing something. *Anything.* I couldn't sit around waiting.

Phillippe assured me the police would be arriving within 10 minutes, but even that felt too long. I shuddered to think what Liam might have done during the time he'd already had.

The plan was simple: while Phillippe got the police up to speed on the situation, we would head down to Port Hercule and speak with the maritime police. The alert had been sent out nationwide so no doubt they were already on the lookout. With any luck, they'd have a half-decent camera system in place. If we could catch Liam on CCTV, we'd know with certainty that this was his route out.

If we didn't... Well, I didn't want to think about it.

Sam climbed into the passenger seat of the black Bentley he'd arrived in with Stacey just a few short hours earlier. Grabbing the fob from the valet dressed in the impeccable mint green uniform complete with golden lapels and a Pershing cap, I slipped behind the steering wheel.

The silence sat heavy between us as I put the car in gear and drove away.

"Boss," said Sam.

I glanced over at him, but he was staring resolutely out of the windscreen.

"Don't say it," I said.

"I have to."

"No, you don't."

Sam didn't reply. But I could feel he wanted to. Could feel the words on his lips.

"We might not—"

"I know, Sam," I snapped. I didn't need him telling me we weren't likely to find them. That we weren't likely to magically find Stacey safe and well at Port Hercule. It was a long shot that we'd find any evidence that they'd come this way. And I didn't want to hear it. But I knew what he was doing. Sam was the most grounded person I knew. He was level-headed, calm, and stoic. He wouldn't be doing his job if he wasn't reeling me in when I needed it. When he could see me spiralling, it was his job to keep me tethered to the here and now. And I hated to admit how much I relied on him for that.

"By the time the police are up to speed, it could be another 20 minutes, maybe more." I paused, made the turn in the road and took a deep breath. "If there's any chance he's taken her by boat, then I want to be at Port Hercule looking at whatever evidence they may have. Tracking them by land would take too long; at least this way we can rule it out."

From the corner of my eye, I saw Sam glance at me and then back to the road.

"As long as you know it's unlikely. You going rogue right now wouldn't help Stacey. Or me," he added.

I nodded.

I knew what he meant.

When Adrianna, my ex-wife, had been kidnapped last year, I'd gone 'rogue', as he put it. I'd gone off grid and hadn't thought to bring Sam with me. And had almost gotten myself killed in the process. I hadn't been completely stupid though; I'd called Bill Cooper for backup. And the guy had saved my bacon.

But this. This felt different. This wasn't blackmail or manipulation. This was an out-of-control obsession. And the cost of that might very well be Stacey's life.

My grip tightened on the steering wheel as I once again fought to keep the panic at bay. I couldn't breathe properly. The knot tightening in my chest was like a crushing weight I just couldn't escape. My whole body locked tight, and I could feel the ache in my jaw from where my teeth were clenched.

"Boss," said Sam, his voice low, laced with warning.

I exhaled and relaxed my grip, easing my foot off the accelerator as we approached the next turning far too quickly. I slammed my foot on the brake, and Sam's hand shot out to brace himself on the dashboard.

"Sorry," I mumbled.

I let out a long, steady breath, and we drove the rest of the way in silence.

We drove past the entrance to Port Hercule and followed the road as it curved around the right-hand side of the harbour. Remnants of the weekend's racing still lined the streets where the day before, Stacey had battled against the other racers for another shot at the championship title. Having won last season, she was feeling the pressure, trying to keep her crown against those trying to knock her from her pedestal. Barriers, fencing, and grandstands were everywhere we looked and would be for another three weeks as teams worked hard to dismantle them, returning the city to normality.

"At the end, on the right," said Sam.

I slowed the car a little more as we continued down the side of the harbour, past restaurants and convenience stores until I spotted a large 'Police Maritime' sign sitting above a concrete archway.

I slid the Bentley into a parking space opposite, not caring about the huge, stencilled letters on the floor that spelt POLICE. Climbing out of the car, I turned to see a small, two-windowed shop front with 'Police Maritime' in big bold letters above the doorway. An illuminated sign jutted out in the covered walkway between the concrete arch and the front door. The light in the walkway flickered from the overhead strip lighting.

It looked like the dodgy back-alley office of a shady private investigator, not home to the police force of one of the richest countries in the world. Yellowing blinds hung limply in the windows, and the white paint peeled around the door frame. It was eerie. And it didn't fill me with confidence.

We'd only taken a few steps from the car when the door to the office swung open and we were greeted by two armed police officers.

"Phillippe Moreau called ahead," said one of them.

Good.

I glanced at the convenience store next door, the Red Bull tables and the rack of postcards in the window. A man stood on his own, leaning against one of the waist-high tables, smoking a cigarette and watching us with interest.

Not a conversation I wanted to have in public.

I nodded my understanding and approached the two men, the one who had spoken gesturing for us to enter.

Chapter 6

JASON HUNTER

MARITIME POLICE HEADQUARTERS, MONACO

Monday 30th May

Inside, the office was surprisingly busy. A waist-high counter stood at the front of the room, made of cheap, yellowing wood, and a bored-looking receptionist sat behind it, a headset digging into her untamed curls.

Part of the counter had been flipped up, allowing us to move past the receptionist – who didn't even glance in our direction – and into the main hum of the room. The space was crammed with desks, at least half of which were occupied. I guessed that the race weekend meant everyone was pulling double shifts.

We weaved through the desks and followed the two officers through a door at the back into a bright room filled with computer screens.

Double desks filled the room, each with multiple computer monitors. Some showed radar screens with small blinking dots, others were live camera feeds of the harbour. Along the back wall, there were more desks and more screens, these mounted on the wall all the way up to the ceiling, with four screens working to create one picture. Maps of the harbour and charter plans were up and being discussed by more armed personnel.

Down the right-hand side of the room, the wall was lined with shelves. A few box files were stacked at the far end, but they were mostly empty.

A man stood in front of the wall of screens with his back to us. Dressed in black laced boots, combat trousers and a thick black roll-neck sweater, he turned to face us as we entered, and I realised it wasn't a man, but a woman with close-cropped hair and a muscular build.

"Jason Hunter," she said, taking a step forward and offering a hand. "Bridgette Johnson. Capitaine and Head of Maritime Police for Monaco's Port Hercule."

"You're American," I said, surprised.

She smiled. "I am indeed."

I didn't know why it took me by surprise.

"This is Sam Thornton," I said, gesturing to Sam's silent presence beside me. "My Head of Security Operations." She looked Sam over once and gave a curt nod.

"Phillippe called and updated me on the situation. We're currently tracking down the details of all the boats that left the harbour within the last hour. If the guy – Liam, is it?"

I nodded.

"If he had help, the boat could have left anytime within the last 24 hours and waited further along the coast, just offshore."

My stomach dropped. I hadn't thought of that.

"But let's start with the more obvious escape route and go from there. We've accounted for 90% of the boats that have left and been able to confirm the number of passengers on board. I have someone checking the list of who's moored in the harbour to see if anyone's missing."

She gestured to a man hunched over a computer in the corner. Before him, one screen was a map of the harbour, and the second looked like registration details.

"Right," I said, suddenly feeling at a loss. The adrenaline that had been coursing through my system until now felt like it was about to drop me off the edge of a cliff. "What can we do to help?"

"In all honesty, not much. We're working as quickly as—"

"Capitaine!" We all looked over at the guy in the corner.

Bridgette marched over, firing off questions in rapid French. I glanced at Sam who shrugged at me.

Now stood behind the desk, Bridgette was bent at the waist, looking over the guy's shoulder as he pointed to one screen and then the other.

She patted him on the shoulder and turned back to us.

"We might have a hit."

She patted the guy on the shoulder again, said something in French, and then returned to the centre of the room.

"*Sunset Voyager* is missing," she said to those assembled in the room. "Berth schedule has them in port until Wednesday. It's a short-term berth, which means they're unlikely to have left early."

I frowned.

"The long-term stays don't care about the extra money, they just want the reservation. The short-term berths are more money-conscious. They rarely leave early," she added, clearly for my benefit. "It's a 50-footer, registered under a company called KYS," she continued, addressing the room again.

"KYS?"

She turned to look at me again. "It's not uncommon to have a boat registered under a company name."

"I get that," I said, waving her explanation away. "KYS, as in 'Keep You Secure'?"

Bridgette looked over at the guy who'd been checking records. He shook his head. "KYS Ltd," he said, his accent thick.

Maybe I was making connections where there weren't any. KYS was our biggest competitor in the security space. Had been for years. But they focused more on providing security systems; cameras, alarms, that kind of thing. They did have a personal security department, but it was small. Most of the time, our biggest clients were also clients of theirs. Even Mickey, my ex-wife's new husband who had been murdered in his own home, had installed KYS systems in his penthouse apartment.

Was 'Keep You Secure' their business name, but KYS Ltd their legal trading name? I needed to look into this when I got back home. It wouldn't help me now, but what if they were somehow connected? What if Liam was somehow connected to KYS?

I didn't like it.

It felt like too much of a coincidence.

And I didn't like coincidences.

Chapter 7

JASON HUNTER

MARITIME POLICE, MONACO

Monday 30th May

"CCTV confirms *Sunset Voyager* left at 12.30am. We're approximately—," Bridgette Johnson looked down at the watch on her wrist, "—60 minutes behind them."

She began giving orders in French as various teams sprang into action, heading out the door.

"You two, with me," she said in English, pointing to Sam and I.

I nodded, and we swiftly followed her out of the door and back through the main office. As we went, she grabbed two high-visibility coats from a rack, handing one to me and the other to Sam. Then she grabbed a third and stuffed her arms into it, shrugging it over her shoulders and zipping it up with practiced ease.

The coat was thick, warm and weatherproof, the kind fishermen wore out to sea. Considering I was still in my tuxedo, the additional layer was more than welcome. She stopped behind the partition that separated the reception desk from the rest of the office, slid open a cupboard door, and pulled out several life jackets.

"You're gonna need these," she said, handing one to each of us. I didn't hesitate in slipping the life jacket over the bulky coat and clipping it into place, pulling the straps until it was as tight as it would go.

She gave a final nod of approval, grabbed one for herself, and led us out into the night air.

The guy smoking the cigarette at the convenience store next door still stood leaning against one of the Red Bull tables. His eyes went wide as he saw the maritime police pour from the shabby office front. Bridgette barrelled past, turned right and headed to the red police boat moored alongside the edge of the harbour, stepping into it with ease and setting it bobbing gently.

A second officer stepped onto the boat and immediately turned towards the motors as Bridgette turned and held out a hand.

"We're going to follow out as far as we can with the control room providing directions. But 60 minutes is a long time, and it's unlikely we'll be able to catch up to them. The GPS has been switched off, but we'll head for the last known location and hope we get lucky."

Thankful I wouldn't have to deal with clambering around on one of the floating jetties, I ignored her hand and stepped onto the boat, Sam following close behind. The boat rocked violently from the added bulk, and I turned to look at him in surprise. He shrugged his shoulders, a small smile playing on his lips.

As the engine of the boat roared to life, and Bridgette started talking into the radio, coordinating with the control room, that familiar sense of dread started creeping over me.

Holding on to the rail of the standing shelter where Bridgette took up the wheel, I watched as she expertly manoeuvred us out of the berth and headed towards the open ocean.

"The patrol boats are too slow," she shouted over the noise of the engines and the water lapping at the sides of the hull as the boat slowly built-up speed. "This little thing is much faster, but we won't be able to go too far from the coast. Too dangerous."

I nodded but I wasn't really listening. We were doing something, and that felt like the right thing. I knew it was unlikely that we'd find them. She'd already pointed out that Liam had a 60-minute lead. How much could we really catch up to them? How long would it take? I doubt he would be taking it easy.

He knew I'd come after him.

Chapter 8

Jason Hunter

Somewhere in the Mediterranean Sea

Monday 30th May

After an hour of speeding through the water, we reached the last known coordinates of *Sunset Voyager* before beginning to methodically search the surrounding areas, moving further and further out as we went. It wasn't the high-octane, high-speed chase you saw in the movies. Instead, I was frozen to the bone, my fingers painfully numb and a small muscle about halfway down my back was spasming violently.

I didn't complain though. Didn't say anything. It felt like I deserved it. God only knew what Stacey was going through. Had Liam thought to give her something to keep warm?

Bridgette had said *Sunset Voyager* was a 50-foot yacht. That meant there would be enough space on board for at least a couple of bedrooms – or 'staterooms' if you wanted to get technical. I wasn't a boating man, had never been interested in being on the water, but I'd suffered through a couple of trips where clients had insisted on hosting parties on board their latest purchase. They were always a security nightmare and I'd do everything I could to persuade them to host their party somewhere else. They'd never listened, of course. Why would they? They were hiring me to keep them safe, not tell them how to live their lives. And if they wanted to party on board a 100-foot yacht, then they bloody well would.

Without warning, Sam stood up.

He lifted a finger and pointed into the inky blackness.

"There," he said.

I'd been staring out at the black sea for far too long. I couldn't be sure that what he was pointing at wasn't just a figment of my imagination. But sure enough, something was bobbing in the water ahead of us.

The single search light mounted to the standing shelter only illuminated a short distance in front of us, and even then, its beam wasn't strong enough to cut through the thick darkness that threatened to swallow us whole.

Bridgette was speaking rapidly in French into her radio, checking the readings behind the helm, and relaying them to the control room.

We neared the boat, but there was no sign of life on board, and I didn't know if that was a good thing or not. There were no lights, no hum of the engine.

Bridgette told the officer to cut the engines, and we sat on the water, observing.

After a moment, she brought the radio to her lips and said, "Attention, *Sunset Voyager*, this is the Monaco Maritime Police. We are carrying out an investigation that involves this vessel. If anyone is on board, you are ordered to respond immediately on channel 16. Failure to comply will result in further action. Over."

She repeated the message in French and then we waited, the radio and the yacht unnervingly silent.

Reaching up to the ceiling of the standing shelter, Bridgette unclipped the speaker microphone, flicked the switch next to it and spoke into the handset.

This time, her message boomed across the waves.

"*Sunset Voyager*, this is the Monaco Maritime Police. If there is anyone on board, identify yourself immediately. We have reason to believe this vessel may be connected to Liam Harvey, who is considered dangerous and may have a hostage. Comply with our instructions and ensure the safety of everyone on board. This is your final warning before further action is taken."

Again, she repeated the message in French and then paused for a response.

When none came, she said, "*Sunset Voyager*, this is the Monaco Maritime Police. You have failed to respond to multiple attempts to communicate. We are now preparing to board the vessel. If anyone is on board, you are advised to comply immediately to ensure the safety of all parties. This is your last warning."

She re-holstered the loudspeaker microphone and watched the boat for any sign that someone might be on board. But there was nothing. And it was unnerving.

"What next?" I asked.

"We board the boat," she said, her eyes still focused on *Sunset Voyager*.

"What?"

"Well, not you."

"Shouldn't we—"

"The patrol boat is on its way. When it arrives, we'll board, search it, and see what we can find. My gut tells me they're long gone. But we can't make that assumption."

"And if the boat is empty?"

She turned to look at me then, the search light mounted above the standing shelter casting an eerie glow. I could only see one half of her face, and I didn't like the sombre look there.

"If the boat is empty, we'll need to return to the marina."

Chapter 9

Jason Hunter

Somewhere in the Mediterranean Sea

Monday 30ᵗʰ May

The boat wasn't empty, but there was no sign of Liam or Stacey.

Bridgette Johnson and several officers from the patrol boat boarded *Sunset Voyager*, swiftly cleared the top deck, and then descended to the lower deck. Huge spotlights mounted on the patrol boat lit up the area, giving us a clear view of the 50-foot yacht.

A short while later, Bridgette emerged onto the top deck with someone in tow.

It wasn't who I was hoping it would be. It wasn't even the son of a bitch who'd taken her.

No, it was a man named Michel DuPont, the yacht's skipper.

The guy was in bad shape. Battered and bruised, they'd found him in the galley, hog-tied with a gag in his mouth.

Now dressed and warm, he sat in the galley of the patrol boat, cradling a hot drink in both hands. I sat opposite him, my hands wrapped around my own hot drink. Sam sat next to Michel, a steady presence but also conveniently blocking any exit. Bridgette sat to my left.

The boat we'd piloted out was now being taken back by a couple of the officers who'd been on board the patrol boat, allowing us all to warm up, but more importantly, to understand what the hell had happened on board *Sunset Voyager* in the last few hours.

Michel's English was pretty good, but the trauma of the last few hours had left him shaken and incoherent, so he was rambling in French and Bridgette was making notes.

Another police officer stood sentry at the end of the table, listening to the conversation, acting as witness, and occasionally supplying us with fresh drinks when the mugs were empty.

Finally, after what felt like hours, Michel DuPont fell silent.

Bridgette looked down at her notes.

"Mr DuPont here was sleeping onboard *Sunset Voyager* last night, as he often does when visiting Monaco, when two people boarded the boat without his permission. Based on the descriptions he's given, I can confidently say that those two people were Liam Harvey and Stacey James."

I watched Michel's face as Bridgette walked us through his testimony of events. But Michel wouldn't, or couldn't, look at me. Instead, he simply stared into his half-empty mug.

"Liam was agitated, and Stacey was bruised. Mostly on her face, which corresponds with the fight Phillippe Moreau saw on the Casino de Monte-Carlo's CCTV, right before Liam forced Stacey into the van." She let out a heavy sigh. "He threatened Mr DuPont with a gun, at which point, Liam Harvey forced Mr DuPont into the galley of the yacht and tied him up."

"Where—?" I blurted, but Bridgette lifted a hand to silence me.

"He believes Stacey was led into one of the staterooms and tied up as well. He could hear her shouting regularly throughout the trip. They left the marina pretty quickly, and he has no idea where they went. After a while, Liam came down into the galley and asked Mr DuPont how to turn the GPS tracking off. When Mr DuPont wouldn't tell him, Liam beat him, pretty savagely by the state he's in.

"That's when Mr DuPont told him how to disable the GPS. He's unsure how long Liam piloted the yacht for, but eventually he cut the engines, and retrieved Stacey from whichever room he'd put her in. His best guess is the master cabin based on where the shouts were coming from. Apparently, she put up one hell of a fight as he tried to get her off the yacht."

A small smile twisted my lips, even if it was tinged with an all-consuming sadness. Of course she would fight, in the middle of the sea, with nowhere to go. My girl would fight with all she had. And she wouldn't stop fighting him. She'd either die or get free. There was no alternative.

And that's what scared me most.

Chapter 10

JASON HUNTER

LONDON OFFICE

Thursday 9th June

"Sporting Director Eden Schneider has confirmed that Stacey James will not be racing at this weekend's Grand Prix in Azerbaijan. This morning, he appeared at a press conference and issued a statement saying that her whereabouts are still unknown. Speculation—"

I swiped the remote from my desk and muted the TV.

Leaning back in my chair, I let out a whoosh of air and stared out of the window.

It had been nearly two weeks since Liam had taken Stacey. Two weeks where I'd felt like I was going insane.

I'd done everything I could to try and find her, but nothing had materialised. Not even a hint of where she might be, whether she was even still alive. The permanent knot in my gut ached.

After returning to the Port Hercule marina with Michel DuPont in custody, Bridgette Johnson had questioned him again before handing him over to the police department. Phillippe Moreau, Casino de Monte-Carlo's Chief of Security, had been present and was acting as liaison between the casino and the police department.

Satellite imagery had confirmed a second boat had been waiting for Liam and Stacey near where we'd found *Sunset Voyager*, but the GPS on the second boat had been deactivated a long time ago.

So where did that leave us? Blindly searching international waters for a vessel of unknown origin.

After a few days and very little progress, I had no choice but to return to the UK. The business needed me, the kids needed me, and life had to go on, even if it was crippling me.

Of course, the kids had found out before I could tell them. It had been plastered everywhere; all over the news channels, all over social media, and all over the front cover of newspapers and magazines. I should have called Adrianna as soon as we'd brought DuPont to shore, should have told her what was going on, but some stupid, hopeful part of me had thought that maybe if I held out a little longer, I wouldn't need to tell them such horrible news.

A knock on my office door pulled me from my thoughts. I turned to look as Lucy popped her head in.

"How you doing?" she asked.

I gave her a small nod. She spoke to me in that horribly sympathetic tone that everyone seemed to be using on me, and it was driving me mad. Sam seemed to be the only one treating me as he always did.

Lucy came in and closed the door behind her.

"No news then?"

I shook my head and turned to look out of the window again.

Lucy was my PA, and had worked for me for nearly ten years. She had chin-length platinum blonde hair that was always meticulously in place and bright blue eyes that missed nothing.

"I'm sure you'll find her," she said quietly. I looked at her. It was unusual for Lucy to be so placating. She was normally kicking my ass and telling me to get on with things, but this felt different.

"No, you aren't," I said with a sigh.

She opened her mouth to say something else and then closed it.

"I'm sorry, Jason."

I leaned forward onto my desk and dropped my head into my hands.

"I know," I said. "I know you are. So am I."

Lucy didn't reply.

I looked up.

"I guess there's a reason you needed to see me?" She winced, and I hated myself for being so blunt, for being almost cruel, but I'd given up caring.

"I've just had a call from the Mayor's Office." She hesitated.

I frowned. "What is it?"

"Well, he's booked a meeting. Wants to speak to you."

"About what?" I asked in disbelief. Last year, the office of Mayor Robert Britland had taken a dislike to me. Mostly because London's wealthiest and most powerful people thought I had some pretty damning evidence against them. At the time, I didn't. But that didn't stop him from playing dirty. He had drugs planted in my office and then sent the Met narcotics division after me. I didn't want to think about what the consequences might have been if I hadn't called Alek Gromov.

Gromov was an old client of mine. He'd hired me around the same time that Stacey's body double, Gemma, had died at the Hungarian Grand Prix. An awful moment in history that seemed to trigger everything that followed. Gromov was as slippery as he was rich. He was untouchable. And he financed Stacey's biggest rival in Formula One, Dima Volkov.

I hadn't wanted to call the Russian bastard, but I'd had no choice. I needed someone with power and influence who could act fast, and I'd run out of options.

The joke was on me, though, because I was then indebted to Gromov – he owned me. And when I double-crossed him, he tried to kill me. Not once, but twice.

Thankfully, he was currently rotting away in HMP Belmarsh. And I hoped he stayed there for the rest of his miserable life, but knowing my luck, the snake would find a way out. And then I'd be in deep, deep shit.

"He's requested our security services."

I was speechless. Of all the things I expected Lucy to say, that was not one of them. Especially after the threats that I'd received from Mayor Britland. He'd even gone so far as to warn off my other clients. It had worked for some, and not for others.

Vance Cherry, Iris Mccleary's manager, had called me to let me know. He'd seemed positively delighted that I'd pissed off the Mayor of London, which only seemed to work in my favour. Iris Mccleary's tour was still ongoing and her female-only security team were doing an excellent job of being discreet yet effective.

"Why would the Mayor of London need us?" He had the whole Metropolitan Police Service at his disposal; was that not enough?

Something told me this was a power play of some kind, I just didn't understand how.

"I-I don't know," Lucy stammered. Actually stammered. I don't think I'd ever heard her sound anything less than bold and blunt.

"What's going on?"

She frowned.

"What do you—?"

"Never mind. Fine. I'm guessing you've scheduled the meeting in my diary?"

She nodded. "For this afternoon."

"Today?"

That would explain why she'd come in to see me. Well, that and the fact that he was a bloody unusual client. Lucy had been in the office when the police had come storming in to search the place. She'd been here when one of the cops had pulled out a bag of powder, claiming they'd found it on the premises. All bullshit, of course. But I'd never forget the look on her face. The trust that wavered, for just a second.

"Thanks, Lucy," I said. "I'll take a look at the meeting notes." I turned to the laptop open on my desk, a clear dismissal. I just wanted to be on my own.

"Jason," she said, her voice quiet.

I looked up.

"I'm worried about you. Is there anything—"

"Unless you know where Stacey is and you can bring that damn bastard to justice—or better yet, let me beat the living shit out of him, there's nothing you can do, Lucy." I hadn't realised I'd raised my voice until I'd run out of breath and everything went quiet.

That's when I saw it. A cold look passed over Lucy's face. It was like I was watching a wall go up behind her eyes, and I inwardly swore at myself.

What a fucking prick.

I rubbed at my eyebrows with my left hand, hoping I could erase the last few seconds from history. But when I reopened my eyes, I could see the damage had already been done.

"If there's anything else you need, you know where I am," she said, ever the professional. She turned on her heel.

Ah shit.

"Lucy—" I called out, but she'd already left my office, closing the door behind her.

I watched through the glass wall as she swiftly crossed the office and disappeared down the corridor towards the kitchen. I slammed my fist down on my desk with a grunt of frustration.

I was acting like a complete twat, and I knew it. And yet, somehow, I couldn't control myself.

The whole Stacey situation was eating away at me. And what was my response? To push people away and behave like a prick, as if that would magically make things better. Talk about self-sabotage.

I leaned down and pulled open the bottom drawer on the left-hand side of my desk, flipping up the false bottom with practised ease. Inside the hidden compartment lay a burner phone, two fake passports, and a Glock 17 handgun.

Chapter 11

Jason Hunter

London office

Thursday 9th June

I scooped up the phone and closed the compartment, ignoring the lump of black metal that felt like a safety net as well as a hangman's noose.

The contents of the drawer had grown with my paranoia over the last year. And considering the current circumstances, rightly so. Before all this started, I would never have thought I'd go so far as to acquire an illegal weapon. I'd always done things by the book. Always. But if the last year had taught me anything, it was that no one else did. Especially not the bad guys.

As long as I didn't have the gun in the house, I could compartmentalise. Kind of.

I switched the phone on and waited impatiently for it to load up, connect to the network, and tell me if I had any messages.

A little red notification appeared in the corner of my WhatsApp, and I quickly opened it.

There was only one conversation in the app's history. The only person I ever used this phone to contact.

The message was simple:

Call me. I have news.

With shaking fingers, I tapped on the contact's blank profile and hit call. He answered on the first ring.

"What news?" I asked, skipping the niceties.

"I found the guy who met them," said Bill Cooper, his voice clear despite the music in the background.

"What? Where?"

It took him a moment to answer, and I heard the faint clink of a glass. That was when I realised; he was drinking.

"A little place called Varazze, just over the Italian border," he said.

"How?"

"Asking around."

I knew what that meant. Bill Cooper was notorious in the wrong circles for the wrong reasons. His military history was hard to get hold of, some kind of secret service. Despite the information I did have access to, I still didn't have a complete picture on him. My best guess was that he was part of an elite team that was brought in when all other avenues had failed.

How he'd managed to have a relationship with Stacey, I really didn't know. But with everything going on in her life, and Bill Cooper gaining a reputation for doing others' dirty work, I'm not surprised Stacey broke it off. She'd told me that it was to focus on her career, and that was the last we'd spoken of it.

I hated relying on Cooper, hated having him still in her life. But we'd come to an uneasy truce and he was proving to be a bloody valuable asset. The cost? His methods were often shady, dangerous, and people most definitely got hurt.

But I was done playing by the rulebook.

"And?" I asked impatiently. "What did he say?"

"He was paid a large sum of money, in cash, to meet a boat in the middle of the night. Co-ordinates were sent via radio. He rocked up, collected the passengers, and came back to the marina in Varazze."

"Then what?"

"I'm working on it."

"Where's the guy now?"

"Indisposed."

"Don't kill him," I warned.

There was a long pause on the other end of the line before Cooper said, "This isn't my first fucking rodeo."

"I know, I know. I just don't want you making any stupid mistakes. I want to find her too, remember. But if you go killing anyone who might have information, we're gonna be pretty screwed."

"I know what I'm fucking doing."

Was he slurring his words? Maybe it was just my imagination.

"I know you do. I'm on edge, alright. This is doing my head in." I paused, unsure what else to say. I desperately wanted to fly out there and help, but the last time I'd suggested it, Cooper had bitten my head off and said he didn't need a babysitter. And I knew I'd just get in the way. "Keep me updated," I finally said, and hung up.

I was instantly on Google Maps, looking for Varazze.

It was quite far up the coast from Port Hercule, more than a 2-hour drive. And I kind of admired Liam for the way he'd planned it out. Not only had he executed a near-perfect extraction, he'd made a good job of covering his tracks, too.

Varazze wasn't too far from Genoa, the centre of the Italian Riviera. I didn't know much about the city, but a little exploration on Google told me it was known for its maritime history, food, and art.

Liam couldn't have risked docking in a large marina where there would be stringent rules and regulations, or a village where he would draw too much attention. Varazze, a municipality of Genoa, was a good-sized town, allowing him to remain anonymous and slip under the radar. Except he'd failed to consider one thing: I had Bill Cooper. And Bill Cooper was like a fucking bloodhound.

Chapter 12

Jason Hunter

London Office

Thursday 9th June

I spent the next hour spiralling further and further into the black hole that was the internet. I walked the virtual streets of Varazze, looked up its history, and familiarised myself with the marina, but I kept coming back to the same question over and over again: where had Liam gone next?

It would be a while before Cooper had another update. Daytime drinking never went well, and this was all clearly taking its toll. I was still surprised. Cooper didn't strike me as the type to be so reckless. In fact, everything I knew about the man told me this was very out of character. But then, how well did I really know him?

At least we had made *some* progress. It felt like a huge leap forward. But instead of offering clarity, it just created more questions. No doubt, Cooper would do everything he could to track Liam down. And I wouldn't be surprised if he left a few bodies in his wake.

My non-burner phone vibrated on my desk, but I ignored it.

After a minute or so, it started vibrating again, and this time it wouldn't stop.

I glanced at the screen to see the name *Hayley Irons* and instantly picked it up.

"It's been a while," I said, none too kindly.

Liam had kidnapped Stacey, and when I'd called Hayley asking for her help, I'd been given a bunch of bland excuses as to why she couldn't. Since then, she'd kept her distance. Of course, the Met police had been involved. They'd been very good so far, but Hayley was a friend. I'd thought I could count on her.

"Can you meet me? For a coffee?"

I paused. Part of me wanted to say no. But I knew I needed her. Stacey needed her. And after everything she'd done for me over the last few years, I owed her that at least.

"I have a meeting in half an hour. I can meet you afterwards at The Crown. It's a pub just down the road from the office."

"Sure, that works." She hung up, and I stood up for the first time in hours, pocketing my phone. I walked out of my office and over to Lucy who was typing away furiously at her desk.

"This meeting with the Mayor," I said.

"Mmm-hmm," she said, not pausing for even half a second as her fingers flew across the keyboard.

"He coming here?"

"Yes," she nodded, still not looking at me.

"He say why?" I asked.

Now she did stop, and the clacking of the keys went quiet. "He wanted to talk about our security services. That's all he would say."

"Just seems odd. Why the hell would he come here?"

She shrugged her shoulders.

"He was pretty insistent on it, actually. And he wanted to see you today."

I frowned.

"Do we have an information file on him?"

"Not really," she said. "I can start one, but I doubt we're going to find anything other than what's in the public domain."

"True," I said, only half listening.

Chapter 13

JASON HUNTER

LONDON OFFICE

Thursday 9ᵗʰ June

I knew the face of the man sitting opposite me. It was hard not to, given that it was constantly plastered across the city of London. New waste disposal initiative? This man's smiling face. Carbon-neutral buses? This man's smiling face. Tackling street crime? This man's smiling face. Increased rent taxes? This man's smiling face.

But right now, he wasn't smiling.

Mayor Robert Britland was in his late fifties with short, greying hair. He had a serious face, a high forehead, and thin lips. And when he did smile – as demonstrated by his many awful billboard campaigns – his teeth were artificially white.

There was nothing about this man that made me trust him.

His well-fitted suit was navy blue, as was his tie. He was bland to look at, but I knew that it was only a front. And I wasn't going to take any chances.

"Mr Mayor, it's nice to meet you in person."

He gave me a thin-lipped smile and interlinked his fingers in his lap.

"I must admit I was a little surprised," I continued, but he didn't react. "I wouldn't have thought you'd be in need of my services. Surely, it's the responsibility of the Metropolitan Police to provide security if it's required?" He didn't rise to the bait. "And I really wouldn't have thought you'd be coming to me. I could easily have come to Downing Street if you had concerns over your safety. It's common for high-profile individuals to request a third party to conduct a security audit. We do them all the time."

The thin-lipped smile reappeared and there was a menacing glint in his eye.

"Mr Hunter, I've heard so much about you," he said.

I wasn't surprised he'd deflected my question. I really wasn't expecting him to answer it. But I needed to at least lay the groundwork. The whole situation was ludicrous. Why the hell was the Mayor of London currently sitting in my office, and what the hell did he want?

I let out a sigh.

"What is it that you want?"

"Ah, to the point. I like that."

He paused, and I waited.

"I've had concerns since the recent arrest of Alek Gromov," he said. I frowned. "It turns out several of my most trusted – shall we say – *advisors* were on his payroll, and they've compromised the security of my team. The Metropolitan Police are investigating the issue, but until then, I need to know I have a team I can trust."

I resisted the urge to roll my eyes.

I didn't for one second buy his story. Advisors? More like cronies. And I was willing to bet that they were on Gromov's payroll because Gromov was in Britland's pocket.

Mickey had been murdered because he had a memory stick. A very valuable memory stick that held all the information about a huge fraud ring. It had contained all the numbers, dates, transactions, and evidence needed to put some very powerful people behind bars.

I found myself in possession of the memory stick, coincidentally around the same time that Mayor Britland's office suddenly took great interest in my business.

That only told me one thing: the mayor was dirty.

"So, what?" I asked. "You need a new security detail?"

"Exactly."

"What's wrong with this one?" I asked, nodding my head to the two guys positioned outside of my door, and the two others on the other side of the office by the lifts.

"Like I said, it's all about who I can trust," he said, this time flashing me one of those billboard-famous smiles. It was even more hideous in real life.

"This wouldn't have anything to do with Alfonso Torres being murdered on the red carpet, now, would it?" I asked.

"What are you talking about? Why would it?" The smile slipped from his face, replaced by a frown.

Oh, he was convincing all right. But he was still a snake.

I leaned back in my chair and couldn't help the smirk that spread across my face.

"Very well, Mr Mayor. I'll need to know your budget and operational requirements, and I can draw up a proposal for you. Should be ready in a couple of days."

"Today," he said.

His urgency turned my smirk into a smile.

Scared. The Mayor of London was scared.

"Today, then," I said.

Chapter 14

SAM THORNTON

LONDON OFFICE

Thursday 9th June

Sam stood in the office kitchen, making himself a coffee. With Stacey missing, Sam felt like a loose end. He'd split his time between checking in with the other teams, as any Head of Security Operations should do, and keeping tabs on Jason.

This meant regularly running errands and inserting himself into the boss's life wherever he could. There was no denying that he was worried about Jason. His frantic energy and lack of focus showed that he was teetering on the edge. Understandably so.

Sam added half a teaspoon of sugar and slowly stirred his coffee.

It was a rare moment of quiet for him. He never usually indulged in coffee, but he'd been up most of the night trying to reorganise Iris Mccleary's tour team after one of them got sick.

He loved working with the all-women teams, but it was like they had something to prove, and they pushed themselves way beyond their limits, which meant that when one of them went down, there was a pretty big hole to fill.

He wished they would check in with him more often. No, not more often. They checked in regularly enough. He wished they could be more honest with him. He never knew if the 'all okay' actually meant everything was okay or if it was just a cover-up.

"You okay, Sam?"

Sam looked up to see Lucy standing in the doorway of the kitchen, a small frown creasing her forehead.

"Yes," he muttered, turning away quickly.

Lucy made him nervous. For no reason other than he thought she was perhaps the most gorgeous person he knew. Gorgeous, confident, and not afraid to put others in their place if she needed to. He'd seen her take Jason down a peg or two over the years. He could feel his cheeks redden as she walked in and began rinsing the two mugs she carried.

"How's boss man doing?" he asked, still stirring his coffee.

"I'm not sure, if I'm honest. It's hard to tell. One minute I think he's okay and then the next he's biting my head off or has completely missed a meeting because he's too absorbed in God knows what."

It was Sam's turn to frown. He wasn't sure how long they could let this go on for. Jason might be the boss, but he was also a friend.

"I'm just hoping he doesn't put his foot in it with the mayor. That's the last thing we need."

"What are you talking about?"

"Oh, I assumed he'd told you."

"Told me what?"

"The mayor requested a meeting."

"When?"

"He's in there now."

Sam dropped the spoon into the sink, not bothering to wash it up, scooped his mug off the countertop, and headed down the hall.

"Bye then," he heard Lucy mutter, and could almost hear the eye-roll he was sure came with it.

Halfway down the corridor, he spotted Mayor Britland and Jason shaking hands outside his office before the mayor turned on his heels and headed towards the lifts on the other side of the open-plan office. Two men in black suits followed.

Sam stopped next to Jason as he gave a final, friendly wave.

"What the hell was that all about?" asked Sam.

"It looks like Mayor Britland is in some serious shit, and the fucker needs our help."

Chapter 15

JASON HUNTER

THE CROWN , LONDON

Thursday 9th June

"Sorry, what?"

I took another sip from my beer and placed it on the table between us before replying.

"Mayor Britland has contracted me to provide a protection team," I said. I glanced around the pub, a force of habit more than anything. The place was packed with early finishers and tourists. We'd been lucky to get a table.

"Why the hell would he do that?" asked Hayley, stunned.

I filled her in on the conversation I'd had with Britland earlier.

"Bloody hell," she said when I finished.

"Well, we know Alfonso Torres was a name in that fraud ring," I said. "He was laundering millions through those NFTs. Why else would he have been murdered in broad daylight, at a public event?"

"We don't know for certain that's why he was murdered," she said. "And I can't talk about an open case with you."

"So, you are dealing with this one?"

"I may have pulled a few internal strings to be put on the case. I'm sure you agree, the MO sounds awfully familiar."

I took another sip of my pint, savouring the cool feel of the bubbles on my tongue. She wasn't wrong. First Gemma, then Mickey. A sniper shot at a public event was a calling card we'd seen before.

"Britland is involved in this somehow. I just don't know if he's the ringleader or a co-conspirator," I said.

"Well, leave it to the police to find out," she said with a warning look. I rolled my eyes. "I mean it, Jason. Don't go meddling."

I held up a hand as if I were mortally offended.

"I would never—"

"Let me stop you there," she said. "You have bigger things to worry about right now."

I looked down at the half-finished pint in front of me, trying very hard to keep the emotions at bay.

"Any news?" she prompted gently.

"No," I said.

We were both silent.

"We may have found where Liam docked the boat, but nothing concrete yet."

"We?" she asked.

I looked up at her and then across the room at the busy pub. Despite being in a fairly secluded corner, I still felt far too exposed. I hadn't wanted to have the Britland conversation in the office, but having it in public didn't seem like the smartest idea either. And I should have seen this coming. Of course, Hayley would ask about Stacey. It was inevitable.

"Who's we?" she prompted.

She wasn't letting me off the hook this time.

"Cooper is tracking her down," I sighed, knowing what was about to come next.

"Cooper?!" She almost shouted, then glanced around and lowered her voice. "Are you fucking insane?"

"Not insane. Desperate," I shot back, and then coughed. My throat felt raw and raspy.

"Jason, you could end up in prison just for associating with him, for crying out loud. And I'm not even exaggerating here. The guy is *bad news*."

"Don't you think I know that?" I said. "Let's not forget he also saved my life last year."

"That doesn't mean you owe him anything," she said.

"I know, I know. But Stacey is in real danger. Liam is unpredictable and who knows what he's doing to her." I shuddered.

Hayley reached across the table and took my hand.

"I'm sorry I haven't been around much lately," she said, squeezing my hand.

I took a breath and nodded. "I know, not your fault."

"There's not much anyone can do, really. It's down to the Monaco police to investigate. When was the last time you spoke to the FCDO?"

I could feel the despair rising again. She was right, I knew she was. I'd spoken to the Foreign, Commonwealth and Development Office countless times since returning to the UK, and they were liaising with the Monaco police as best they could, but it was frustrating that there was so little progress. And if Cooper was right, Liam had taken Stacey into Italy.

The right thing to do would be to alert the Italian authorities and pass the information along to the Monaco police. But a small part of me just didn't trust them to follow up properly, or worse, completely bungle the investigation. And I didn't want them getting in the way of Cooper doing his thing. The fewer police involved in that region, the better, especially if he was leaving a trail of bodies.

It would only be a matter of time before someone discovered the boat. And then we'd have no choice.

"Jason, don't go doing anything stupid. Talk to the police. Tell them what you know." She lifted her glass and drained it. "I need to go," she said. "This Alfonso Torres mess is kicking all of our asses." She stood up and gave my shoulder a squeeze. "I'll check in with you in a couple of days. If anything changes – and I mean anything – you call me."

I nodded and morosely drained the rest of my drink before ordering another.

Chapter 16

JASON HUNTER

LONDON OFFICE

Thursday 9th June

It was gone 5pm by the time I managed to drag myself away from The Crown and back to the office. After Hayley had left, I couldn't resist the temptation of drowning my sorrows. It seemed easier than going back to the office to face the emptiness that seemed to roll through me day and night.

"Have you been drinking?" asked Lucy, shock written all over her face.

"I might have had one or two," I said.

"Well, for God's sake, I hope you've got your wits about you. There's a visitor in your office."

I let out a long groan. "Who the hell is it now?"

"Miroslava Gromov."

Her words were like a slap across the face.

"Miroslava Gromov?" I asked, dumbfounded. "What does she want?"

Lucy shrugged. "No one tells me these things."

"Isn't it your job to find out?"

She scowled at me. "I can't help it if people won't tell me anything," she snapped and stormed off.

Well. I deserved that.

I looked towards my office, feeling like I'd had a bucket of ice water dumped over my head. *What the hell was Alek Gromov's wife doing in my office?*

Honestly, I'd had enough of today.

Taking a deep breath, I walked across the office.

"Stop," said Lucy, reappearing in front of me.

Like a naughty schoolboy who'd been caught out, I halted.

She held out a pack of mints. I took one, thanked her, and continued walking.

I paused with my hand on the door to my office, took another deep breath, and pulled it open.

"Mrs Gromov," I said, not even faking the surprise. "What are you doing here?" I inwardly winced at how raspy my voice must sound to her. I didn't like how obviously different it was. It was a permanent reminder of what had happened. And it was worse knowing it was her husband who was responsible.

She stood up and turned to face me.

The last time I had come face to face with Miroslava Gromov, she'd been haughty and dismissive. It had been at their Hampstead home where I'd met Gromov for lunch, back when he'd been in a wheelchair and recovering from emergency surgery after being shot. Back when he was trying to keep me on side, and before everything went to shit and I became the target.

Just like the last time I'd seen her, Miroslava Gromov was dressed in enough jewellery to fill a bank vault, with tight-fitting trousers, sky-high stilettos, and a top that showed far too much cleavage for my liking. She was at least twenty years younger than Gromov, and her face looked to be immobile from what I could only guess was an awful lot of cosmetic surgery and Botox. It was hard to tell, considering her makeup was layered on so thick, but I wasn't sure her facial muscles could actually move.

"Mr Hunter," she drawled, her Russian accent thick and heavy.

No trace of the arrogance I'd come face-to-face with on our last encounter.

I gestured to the chair she'd been sitting in. "Please," I said.

As I walked around my desk, there was a light knock on the door, and Lucy popped her head in.

"Can I get either of you a drink?" she asked.

"A water," said Miroslava, her eyes fixed on the view out the window. The sun was beginning its slow descent for the day, but it was still light enough to see across the London skyline.

I gave Lucy a small shake of the head and she disappeared, closing the door behind her.

We sat in silence for a few moments, both of us looking out the window.

"I didn't know who to speak to," she said, turning to look at me. I met her gaze.

"What's happened?" I asked.

She took a deep breath. "Alek is in danger."

I frowned. "How? He's in Belmarsh prison."

"They are coming for him. He does not have much time."

"Who's coming for him? What are you talking about?"

"I need you to go and see him. Talk some sense into him. Warn him."

Lucy reappeared, interrupting our conversation, and I didn't dare say anything with her in the room in case Miroslava decided to stop talking. Something weird was going on here. It was clearly a day for it, first with Mayor Britland and now this.

Once Lucy left the room, I tried again. "I need you to start from the beginning and tell me everything."

She reached forward, picking up the glass of water and taking a tentative sip before placing it back on my desk.

"I have had messages," she said, struggling to find the words. Or maybe just struggling to articulate herself. It was painful to watch. The woman was clearly on edge and terrified. Her hands wouldn't sit still in her lap, constantly fidgeting with the rings on her fingers.

"What do the messages say?" I asked gently.

"They say Alek will die if I do not give them what they want."

"And what do they want?" My god, it was like pulling teeth. I desperately wanted her to spit it all out because the tension was killing me. No, it wasn't killing me, it was giving me a goddamn headache. *Or maybe that was the three afternoon pints.*

"I do not know," she said. "I do not know what they want. They say he has it, but I do not know what *it* is." A tear slipped free and began to track down her left cheek.

"Do you have these messages on your phone?"

She jerkily nodded her head before looking down at the pink handbag at her feet. Pulling it up onto her lap, she began to rummage through the contents. Having found her phone, she unlocked it, found what she was looking for, and then handed it across the desk to me.

I scrolled through the texts and my heart raced.

You have something that doesn't belong to you. Return it. Or Alek Gromov dies.

Alek's life is in your hands. Think about your next move. Find the drive.

This is your last warning. No police. No stalling. Find the drive or Alek Gromov dies.

Your time is up, Miroslava. You have until midnight.

This was a big fucking problem.

"We need to show this to the police," I said.

Her eyes went wide with panic. "No. They said no police."

"I know they did, but Miroslava—"

"Call me Mira."

"Mira. If Alek is in trouble, the prison needs to know. They can put him in isolation, increase security..." I trail off as my brain kicks into overdrive. If Alek's life really was in danger, it was a big, big problem. I needed to speak to Hayley. And we needed to act fast. "Have you replied to any of these messages?" I asked.

She shook her head. "I-I do not know what they are talking about," she said, tears running freely down her face. She was clearly terrified, and I could understand why. This was scary shit.

"Right," I said, trying to work through what we needed to do next. "We need to speak to DI Irons. I know the messages said no police, but she'll be able to inform the prison and keep Alek safe. And then we're going to arrange an exchange. Reply to the messages asking where and how to deliver the flash drive."

"What?"

"Trust me. Well, trust DI Irons. The moment we tell her, she'll be taking over, and rightly so. We need some professionals handling this."

Mira nodded.

Chapter 17

Jason Hunter

London Office

Thursday 9th June

Lucy was sitting with Mira in my office while I nervously waited by the lifts. Hayley would be here any second, and I needed to speak to her first.

A ding announced the lift's arrival, and the doors slid open. Hayley was dressed in the same jeans and Converse as earlier with a casual shirt rolled up to her elbows.

I led us into the smaller of the two conference rooms and closed the doors.

"I literally saw you a few hours ago. This better be good, Jason," she grumbled.

I hadn't been able to tell her much on the phone. Past experiences had made me cautious, and I really didn't need her flying off the handle.

"Miroslava Gromov is sitting in my office."

Hayley's eyes darted to my office, where you could just about see the two women sitting in the chairs opposite my desk.

"She's been receiving threatening text messages from an unknown number—"

"Threatening how?"

"They say Gromov will die. They want the USB."

She frowned.

It was Hayley I'd handed the USB stick to over 7 months ago, right before Gromov had tried to blast me alive in an abandoned warehouse. He'd come for me after his plan had failed, and that's the only reason he was locked up. The guy was a master at manipulation and had been dodging the FSB – as well as our own police – for years.

"So they clearly don't know you gave it to me."

I shrugged.

"What?" she asked.

"Maybe. Or maybe they're just making it look that way so we let our guard down."

Her frown deepened and she crossed her arms. "That sounds like paranoia," she said.

"Or maybe they're just looking for an excuse to kill Gromov," I suggested.

"What are you talking about?"

"First Alonso, now this. Feels like too much of a coincidence if you ask me," I said.

"So, what? They're scaring Miroslava Gromov half to death with a deal they know she can't deliver on just so they can kill Alek?"

"Stranger things have happened," I muttered.

Hayley went quiet.

***

"Will you stop fidgeting," hissed Lucy.

"Sorry," I mumbled, bringing the chair to a stop.

It was late, and everyone else had gone home. It was eerily quiet in the office now, the lights dimmed to just the few desks where we sat. Lucy was sitting at her usual place, I was in a chair at the desk to her right, and Sam stood leaning against the nearest wall, his hands in his pockets.

"She's been in there for nearly an hour," I muttered.

"You're like a child." Lucy's fingers didn't pause as they flew across her keyboard. She was always so poised and unflustered. Like, seriously. Did nothing make this woman stumble? My mind flashed back to the horror on her face the day that the office had been raided by the police. The same day they'd tried to frame me for drug possession, and I'd had to call in Gromov as an emergency bailout. Yeah, that day she'd been flustered.

"What could possibly be taking so long?"

I looked over at Sam who just shrugged his shoulders.

Through the glass front of the office, I watched as Hayley stood up. She tapped the screen on her phone a few times and then put it to her ear as she opened the door and walked out into the open-plan area.

"Yes. Teams need to be on high alert. Is isolation possible?"

"Do you want to—" I muttered to Lucy, gesturing at Mira who sat with her face buried in her hands.

"Of course," she said, and instantly abandoned her typing. She grabbed a box of tissues she kept in one of her drawers and went into my office, closing the door behind her.

"So?" I asked when Hayley finished her call.

"I've alerted the prison. They'll do what they can to keep Gromov safe, and I'll be investigating who's sending the threats."

"What took so long?" I asked, gesturing to where Lucy now sat with a comforting hand on Mira's arm.

"She wasn't very forthcoming to start with. She's always been told not to talk to the police, so we can't really blame her. Especially when one of the texts explicitly says not to speak to me. Once we got past that, I wanted to make sure that I had all the information."

"Such as?"

She rolled her eyes at me.

"Jason, how long have we known each other now? I'm not going to discuss the details of an open case."

"But you just—" I said.

"I only said exactly what you already know," she said, a small smirk lifting the corner of her lips.

Now it was my turn to roll my eyes.

"What next?" asked Sam.

I'd almost forgotten he was there.

"I do my investigation, and we hope that the prison can keep Gromov alive," she said, but there was a niggling voice in the back of my mind that told me it wasn't that simple.

Chapter 18

Alek Gromov

HMP Belmarsh, London

Thursday 9th June

Something was happening in the prison. Electricity buzzed in the air. The prison staff were on high alert and many had been relocated to a different area to deal with whatever was happening.

A fight, most likely.

They weren't uncommon in this hellhole. Put all the most dangerous people in the country under one roof and you're bound to have issues.

Alek sat in his cell, reading a book. And it wasn't just any book, but one of his favourites, *Zuleikha*. And better yet, it was in his native Russian.

While money couldn't get him out of this nightmare, it certainly could make life a tiny bit more comfortable, and he was using it to his full advantage.

Opposite the bed was a small writing desk and a chair. A narrow cupboard hung on the wall above the pillow of his bed, and a sink was mounted at the other end of his cell. Thankfully, he'd been able to secure one of the newer units, which at least had some semblance of cleanliness. It was basic, yet functional.

The viewing window of his cell door slid open, and the familiar face of one of the guards peered in.

"All good?" he asked.

Alek nodded and returned to his book.

He'd noticed the guards seemed to keep a particularly close eye on him, but it didn't bother him as much as he thought it would. It was often the only time he ever saw another living being. And he'd built some good rapport with a few of them. This young guard included. Stevens was his name. He was far too smiley for someone who worked in a prison, but his cheerful demeanour didn't seem to cause any issues, and if anything, the prisoners liked him all the more for it.

The noises seemed to be getting louder. Whatever commotion was going on, it was getting closer.

Alek looked at the door again and frowned. It wasn't like any sound he'd ever heard in here before. Raucous yelling, grunting, and... shouts of pain?

Stevens' face had disappeared from the viewing window and Alek cautiously stood up to investigate. He took a step forward and then another before there was a thud against the door. Alek froze. This wasn't good.

A few long moments of fumbling and the lock of the door clicked.

Alek had dreamed of the door opening more times than he could count. Of being able to simply walk out of this place as a free man. He'd dreamed of the look on that bastard Jason's face when he once again evaded justice. What he hadn't dreamed of were the three large men who now stood in the doorway to his cell. All of them were smiling.

"Hello Alek," said the one in the middle. "It's so nice to finally meet you."

Chapter 19

JASON HUNTER

HOME

Thursday 9th June

I closed the front door behind me and the quiet dark of the house instantly enveloped me, sucking me in. For half a heartbeat, I expected to see Stacey appear from the living room, dressed in the loungewear she favoured when she was at home.

I'd never known someone to look so damn good in a pair of sweatpants and a cropped tee, but my god, she was gorgeous. Is. Is gorgeous. My heart contracted at the thought. I wasn't giving up. I couldn't. She was out there somewhere, alive. I just knew it.

Walking through the living room and into the kitchen, I flicked the lights on and dumped my bag on one of the seats at the kitchen island.

I stood, immobile, my hands on the edge of the kitchen worktop, my eyes fixed on a dip in the floor. And I let the emotions I'd kept at bay all day wash over me. The anger, the hurt, the frustration, but more importantly, the guilt. The guilt for thinking she'd be here, the guilt for forgetting for even half a second that she wasn't.

Spinning on my heels, I let out a roar and swiped my hands across the counter, sending everything crashing to the floor. Crockery smashed and glasses shattered. The mug tree landed with a thud, several of the mugs breaking.

I sank to the floor amidst the chaos, not even caring that sharp pain sliced through the palm of my hand as I did the one thing I hadn't done in a very long time.

I cried.

Chapter 20

STACEY JAMES

LOCATION UNKNOWN

Thursday 9ᵗʰ June

It was a small room. Basic, but comfortable. A simple wooden-framed bed was pushed up against the far wall, and a chest of drawers stood against the other. From here, she could see them both clearly in the moonlight that filtered through the window.

She sat in the corner on the floor, her knees pulled up close to her chest. It was far from comfortable, but at least here she could see the whole space. And more importantly, she would be hidden from view should Liam make a middle-of-the-night visit.

It wouldn't be the first time, and at least from here she'd be able to take him by surprise.

She'd seen almost the entirety of the house by now, except for one room that was kept locked, and the basement. But she'd seen enough horror movies to know that you should never go into the basement. Something in her gut told her that if she went down there, she wouldn't be coming out alive. And staying alive was her number one priority right now.

For her first few days here, she'd fought like hell against Liam, against the walls, the door, and even the window. She'd shattered a few of the small panes of glass before Liam had tied her to the bed for three days straight. And that's when he'd started beating her.

Every time she stepped out of line, he'd attack her mercilessly. But it wasn't like when he'd grabbed her from the casino. No. Now she was weak and she couldn't fight back.

Couldn't even fight him off when he abused her body in ways she would never be allowed to forget.

She swallowed hard, trying to rid herself of the memories of Liam's heavy body pressing down on her, the memories of him... entering her. She shook her head, desperately trying to dislodge it. She cradled her arm closer to her chest, wincing from the pain.

Today, after having managed to slip from the house, she'd discovered the place surrounded by empty farmland. She didn't even know which country she was in, let alone which direction to run in. But desperation drove her and she'd run with everything she had down the dirt track that led away from the house.

But Liam had been right behind her. He'd caught up with her before she'd even made it a few metres past the property line, and it had been the worst beating yet. She could almost taste his anger in the air. She was sure he'd broken her arm. Not that she was going to be telling him that. She didn't need him knowing where she was weakest. For now, she'd bear the pain, do what she could to protect it, and then maybe try again in a few days.

A tear slid down her cheek as she thought of Jason. Of the wonderfully kind, gentle, and loving man she'd found. Of the life they'd started to build together. But more than all of that, she held onto his spirit. Because she knew that somewhere out there, the stubborn bastard would be looking for her, and he wouldn't give up. No. He'd come for her.

In the meantime, all she had to do was stay alive.

Chapter 21

SAM THORNTON

LONDON OFFICE

Friday 10th June

"Where's the boss man?" asked Sam. He was looking through Jason's glass-fronted office, but it was clear he was talking to Lucy.

She looked up from her keyboard and glanced into the office before looking back at Sam, frowning.

"I actually thought he was with you," she said.

Sam scowled and before Lucy could say anything, he was heading back towards his own office at the other end of the corridor, the office that had once belonged to Adam.

"He's going to miss his meeting with Royce Gill!" she called after him.

Pulling his phone from his pocket, Sam dialled Jason's number, only to be met with his voicemail.

"Fuck's sake," he muttered and grabbed his keys from the top drawer of his desk.

Back in the main office, he headed for the lifts.

"I'm going to Jason's," he told Lucy.

She nodded, worry lining her face.

"What should I tell—?"

"Move it to this afternoon and I'll handle it."

Lucy nodded.

In the basement garage, Sam jumped into his old Land Rover and drove to Jason's townhouse, praying that nothing had happened to him.

All was quiet when Sam parked up nearly half an hour later. It wasn't a long commute, but the traffic had been a nightmare. A quick glance at the fuel tank on his dashboard made him once again think about swapping his old trusty Land Rover for something more fuel-efficient. But he'd grown up with Land Rovers. His dad had had one, and some sentimental part of him just couldn't give that up.

A quick glance up and down the street confirmed nothing out of the ordinary.

Sam had texted Adrianna just as he was leaving the office in the hope that she knew where Jason was, but the message that flashed up on his phone screen told him Jason was definitely AWOL.

He pocketed his phone and climbed out of the car, locking it behind him before crossing the street and climbing the few steps to the front door. He slammed his fist on the door a few times, hearing the sound echo on the other side, before leaning over the railing to peer through the window on his left.

It looked straight into the living room, everything as neatly organised as normal. He took in the bookcase filled with books on the wall to the left, next to where the TV was mounted above a unit, one sofa up against the wall on the right, another at a right angle and acting as a divide between the living room and the kitchen.

The kitchen. His eyes widened at the devastation he could just about make out over the top of the sofa. Everything had been swiped from the countertop and lay shattered on the floor.

Panic began to crawl up his throat.

Taking a deep breath, he lifted his hand to knock again, just as the door swung open.

In front of him stood a very dishevelled, very hungover Jason.

"What?" Jason said, squinting up at him as if he hadn't seen daylight for a week.

Without a word, Sam barged past him and into the house. He needed to secure the place, and Jason was clearly not in any fit state.

"Whoa, whoa, what's going on?" he asked.

"What happened to your kitchen?" Sam asked, scanning down the hallway before walking into the living room.

"I—I—" Jason stammered.

Sam paused and turned around.

"What. Happened. To. Your. Kitchen?" Sam enunciated each word like he was talking to a child.

"It's a long story," Jason muttered, waving a dismissive hand in the air and turning to head up the stairs.

He'd seen Jason stressed, angry, frustrated, and at his wit's end, but he'd never seen him like this. Broken.

"You've got five minutes to put on some clothes and grab your gym bag."

"I'm not in the mood," he said without even pausing.

"Is that what you'd tell Stacey?"

He stopped, one hand on the bannister and a foot on the first step.

"Don't—" he said, his voice lethally calm.

"I mean it, Jason. Pull your shit together. This isn't you."

Chapter 22

JASON HUNTER

OFFICE GYM

Friday 10th June

My shoulders burned. My arms ached. I could feel the sweat trickling down the back of my neck. My hands were wrapped and up by my face in a protective stance as I bounced from one foot to the other.

Sam slowly circled on the other side of the mat, his hands out in front of him, each one gloved in a boxing pad.

I had no idea how long we'd been here. Or how many punches I'd made. Sam had taken them all without a word.

It was working, though. With each punch, I felt the tension in my body dissipate. Slowly, it was being replaced with something more familiar, something I recognised, something I could work with. Focus.

I threw another combination of blows, and then another. The ache was good. It had been a while since I'd worked like this, and I could feel the muscles down my back working hard as I threw all of my anger and frustration into every hit.

The gym was quiet. It often was in the middle of the morning. A couple of people were on the weightlifting machines at the other end, while someone else was practicing what looked like yoga. No, maybe Pilates?

My breathing was laboured but steady. With each breath out, I felt stronger, more determined.

This is what Stacey needed.

She needed me to be me. Not to wallow in my grief. Not to drown in self-pity. She needed my strength. My resolve. My determination. And my God, I felt determined.

I gritted my teeth and pushed through a few more combinations before relaxing my stance and rolling my shoulders.

"You good?" Sam asked.

I nodded and walked over to the edge of the room where I'd dumped my water bottle. Sam joined me as I took deep gulps of water. I patted him on the shoulder as he drank from his own water bottle.

"Thanks."

He wiped the water from his mouth with his arm and gave me a long, hard look before nodding his head just once.

"I'll see you back upstairs," I said and headed over to one of the treadmills.

It felt like a fog was finally lifting, and I could see clearly again.

Stacey was out there somewhere, and she needed me. Needed me now more than ever.

The monotonous thud of my feet as they hit the treadmill was soothing. And I kept going, putting one foot in front of the other, letting the sound wash over me and drown out everything else.

The gym was on one of the middle floors of the building, with views over the street below. I watched as people walked past the shops and cafés that lined the pavement, or lingered at bus stops and taxi ranks.

Everything was continuing as normal.

Chapter 23

JASON HUNTER

LONDON OFFICE

Friday 10th June

"Do you not answer your bloody phone?"

My head snapped up. I'd been working on the mayor's protection plan and had been making good progress. It was the first time I'd felt focused in weeks. I looked across my office and through the floor-to-ceiling glass wall. Almost every head in the office also looked at the figure currently marching past their desks.

Detective Inspector Hayley Irons was on a warpath. And she was heading straight for me.

I stood up, but before I could even move out from behind my desk, she'd stormed into my office and slammed the door behind her. I winced.

"I've been calling you," she yelled.

I held my hands up in surrender. "What the hell is going on?" I asked, my voice rising defensively.

She stood behind the two chairs facing my desk, her hands gripping the back of them as her knuckles turned white.

I frowned.

"Hayley, what the hell is going on?" I asked more gently.

She looked down at her hands as if they somehow held the answers, but her vicelike grip didn't let up on the chairs.

"There was a riot at Belmarsh."

"A what?"

"Well, 'riot' is a strong word for it. There was an incident. A bunch of inmates got into a fight. Prison staff intervened, and the inmates turned on them. They think it was a co-ordinated attack."

I felt sick.

"Co-ordinated how?" I asked, knowing I wasn't going to like the answer.

Slowly, she looked up at me. And that was when I noticed the pallor of her skin. The dark circles under her eyes.

"Gromov is dead," she said.

And there it was. That bubbling rage in the pit of my stomach. I could feel it clawing its way up my throat, begging for release.

I gritted my teeth and turned to look out the window.

I slowly ran a hand over my face, hoping the motion would be able to keep it all from spilling out. I stopped, my hand over my mouth, my fingers clenching hard along my jawline. I could feel it. The need to smash anything and everything within range. As if that would somehow help me regain control. As if that would somehow change what had happened.

I forced myself to take a breath and then dropped my hand, turning to face Hayley.

"Tell me everything," I said.

She opened her mouth and I knew she was going to protest. It was an ongoing investigation. She couldn't tell me everything. Wouldn't risk her job like that.

"Don't fuck with me, Hayley. I think we're well past that now."

She bristled at my tone and her eyes narrowed.

"I know your pissed, Jason. Trust me, I'm not exactly happy about it either, but that doesn't give you the right to speak to me like that."

I held her gaze, letting the emotions roiling inside of me run rampant.

"Are you kidding me right now?" I almost shouted. "Things have been going from bad to worse since you showed up. I literally handed you the most dangerous fraud ring in history on a silver platter and what have you done about it?" Before Hayley could reply, I ploughed on. The floodgates had been opened and I was powerless to stop them. "Nothing. That's what. Absolutely fucking nothing. Two of them are fucking dead! But that's not all, is it? The most dangerous people in the city are left to do whatever the hell they want. And if you'd done your job in the first place, Liam wouldn't still be out there!" I yelled, jabbing my finger in the direction of the London skyline.

The silence that followed was deafening.

Hayley straightened, releasing her grip on the chairs and adjusting the denim jacket she wore today.

"Say how you really feel, eh, Jason?"

"Hayley, I—"

But she was already turning on her heels and walking out.

"Hayley!" I called after her, coming out from behind my desk and following her into the main office.

She marched over to where the elevators were and instead of waiting for one, she yanked open the stairwell door to the right and disappeared from view.

That's when I noticed everyone quickly averting their gazes. My office clearly wasn't soundproof. *Shit.*

I turned to see Sam standing by my open office door, a mug in one hand, the other slipped casually into the trouser pocket of his well-tailored suit.

"I'm only going to say this once more," he said, in a tone I don't think I'd ever heard him use. It was as threatening as it was menacing. "Pull your shit together, Jason. Before it rips you apart."

Chapter 24

JASON HUNTER

LONDON OFFICE

Friday 10th June

The moment I closed the office door behind me, I felt the sickening rush of shame.

Feeling the eyes of the office bore into me through the glass wall, I yanked the door open and marched down the corridor to the men's toilets. I needed a moment of privacy.

In the toilet, I flicked the lock for the main toilet door and leaned against it, my breathing coming fast and heavy. There was a burning in my throat. Sinking to the floor, I let my head drop into my hands and didn't stop the heaving silent sobs that wanted to escape.

Hot tears ran down my cheeks as I gasped for air but I was sick of holding it all in. I was sick of trying to pretend everything was okay.

I'd been trying to channel my energy into finding Stacey. But the frustration and helplessness had just been building with every passing day, every passing hour.

I couldn't go on like this.

Sam was right. It was going to rip me apart.

Chapter 25

JASON HUNTER

LONDON OFFICE

Friday 10th June

The office had been unnervingly quiet since Hayley had stormed out. And I couldn't blame them; it was awkward.

Zack, my Head of Marketing, had cancelled our meeting, as had Roman, my Head of Training.

I got the message loud and clear.

Lucy appeared at my office door an hour or so later, her face full of sympathy as she asked if I needed anything. I shook my head.

"No thanks, Luce."

She gave me a small smile. "Let me know if there's anything I can do," she said softly.

Her gentle kindness almost broke me again.

"Sam's meeting with Royce Gill."

Ah shit. I'd completely forgotten. The movie star had called me a few days ago to book a meeting, and it had completely slipped my mind.

"Alright. Thanks, Lucy," I said, and she left.

I'd tried calling Hayley several times. The first few attempts rang out and then they started going straight to voicemail. She'd either blocked me or turned her phone off. But I understood. She didn't want to speak to me. I wouldn't want to speak to me if I were her.

Looking at my laptop screen, it felt like a lifetime ago that I was pulling together the security plans for Mayor Britland. It felt so foreign and unimportant right now.

I assumed Hayley, or maybe someone from the prison, was speaking to Mira Gromov, telling her that she'd no longer be able to visit her husband in prison. That she'd never be able to see him again. I wondered if she blamed herself for not finding the USB drive. Or for speaking to the police when she'd been explicitly told not to.

Turning on the TV mounted on the far wall of my office, I flipped to the news channel where, sure enough, a reporter stood outside Belmarsh prison. The ticker tape along the bottom said a fight had broken out in the prison, causing numerous injuries and several fatalities.

So Gromov hadn't been the only target then.

There was a possibility that he'd simply been in the wrong place at the wrong time, but experience told me those kinds of coincidences didn't exist.

It was strange, though. If Gromov was a target, were the perpetrators the same people who'd taken out Alfonso Torres? It certainly wasn't a sniper that had done the job. Perhaps a bribed inmate? Or even a guard?

I opened Google search and typed in 'Alfonso Torres murder'. Millions of search results popped up, the top ones all from major news outlets. I scrolled through a few of the articles, and they all mostly said the same thing. But the further into the search results I got, the more speculative the content became. We'd left the realm of factual news reporting and had ventured into conspiracy theories.

Some were completely crazy, blaming aliens and an unknown human species that lived in the tunnels underneath London. One said that it was mind control, whilst another mentioned government conspiracy. Not that far off the mark, really.

The more I scrolled, the more I read. It was pretty entertaining seeing all these wild ass theories floating around with zero evidence to support them.

And that's when I spotted it.

A lone comment that stood out from all the rest.

Feels a bit like that time someone tried to take out that Formula One driver.

My heart skipped a beat.

Someone had made the connection.

I frantically scanned the replies, but no one seemed to be paying the comment too much attention.

Picking up my phone, I dialled Hayley's number, which went straight to voicemail. *Right.* Leaving a voicemail, I took a screengrab of the comment and saved the URL. Not trusting my emails, I sent them both over to Hayley using WhatsApp.

A single tick appeared in the bottom right corner of the message, telling me it had been sent. But a second tick – the one that would tell me it had been delivered – didn't appear. So, Hayley's phone was switched off. *At least she hasn't blocked me.*

WhatsApp app disappeared and a number flashed up on my screen. It was a local London number, which wasn't unusual. We did a lot of business within the city of London. But I knew that number.

I ignored the clench of my stomach as I answered the call.

"I thought I made myself clear when I said I wanted to see your proposal by the end of yesterday?"

Even through the phone, I could tell the mayor had clenched his teeth.

"Something came up."

"Not good enough," he spat. "I need your teams in place by tomorrow."

"Tomorrow? That's not possible. I need to finalise the proposal, and the paperwork needs to be processed."

"Tomorrow, Mr Hunter. It's not up for debate. I have a press conference, and I need your personnel to ensure my safety." He wasn't quite shouting, but his voice was definitely raised.

"I will email the proposal across to your office in the next few hours," I said.

"No," he replied, far too quickly to be casual. "Send it directly to me."

"Of course," I replied, a small sense of smug satisfaction creeping in. The mayor didn't even trust his own PA.

Chapter 26

BILL COOPER

VARAZZE, ITALY

Friday 10th June

Cooper woke with a start. His head was pounding and his tongue felt as dry as the desert. He unstuck it from the roof of his mouth, which felt like it had been packed with sawdust.

My god. How much did I drink yesterday?

Squinting, he looked at the bright sunshine streaming in through the curtains. He'd been out for a while then.

He pulled himself up into a sitting position and looked around the room. It was basic, with just a chest of drawers against one wall and the bed he was in, the metal frame creaking under the uncomfortable mattress.

There was a bathroom just down the hall, which was in desperate need of some upkeep. The bare stone walls were cold and uninviting, and the crumbling brickwork could be seen through some cracks in the plaster.

He'd rented the apartment from a guy he'd met at the local tavern. He just needed somewhere cheap and secure, and the apartment did the job.

The previous day had been rough. After he'd phoned Jason, he'd downed several more drinks. He'd started with a grappa – or two, maybe, he couldn't really remember – before asking the barman if he had any whiskey stashed away somewhere.

And somehow he'd woken up here, in his room.

Memories of yesterday came flooding back to him. He'd found the guy who'd been on the second boat in Liam's grand escape plan. Found him and beaten the absolute living shit out of him in the hope he'd spit out the information Cooper needed.

But the guy had known very little. Liam was too good at covering his tracks, which made him question how much they really knew about the guy. He'd already dodged Jason's background checks once; who knew how many skeletons might be in that closet. And he really didn't want to find out.

It was thoughts of Stacey that had sent him to the bottle.

Groaning, he stood up and begrudgingly made his way to the bathroom, where he had a cold shower. Emerging into the warm June sunshine 20 minutes later, he felt a lot more human.

He rolled his shoulders and stretched his neck before walking down the street in the direction of the marina.

Varazze might have been a medieval town once upon a time, but it definitely didn't feel like one anymore. He knew there was a cobbled old village somewhere closer to the town's centre where you could see the original medieval wall that had kept the village safe from outsiders, but here it felt like that was a million miles away.

The streets were clean and tidy, lined with pastel-coloured buildings in shades of yellow, pink, and orange. Trees and colourful plants intertwined themselves around the fencing that divided the public pathway from private property, and the place felt cheerful.

Further down, the left-hand side was taken up by a construction site where two apartment blocks were half built.

A few locals smiled in greeting as they walked past and said, "*Buongiorno.*"

He grimaced each time and gave them a small nod of his head, muttering "*Buongiorno*" in return. The Europeans were far too friendly for his liking, especially in a small town like Varazze.

He could just about see the masts of the yachts in the marina poking above the foliage lining the road, and within a few minutes he was walking along the waterfront. He liked how the pontoons were open and unguarded there. It made things a lot easier. If he'd been back home in the UK, there would be security gates accessible only by keycode.

At the end of the pontoon, he took the right branch and walked as far along the pontoon as he could until he reached the final boat. He guessed it to be around 40 feet long. The hull was red, but the paint was flaking off, and Cooper could see why the owner had jumped at the chance to make a little extra cash.

Without hesitating, he stepped aboard the boat and made his way down to the master stateroom. Opening the door to the room, he saw the owner, bound and gagged. The man, still fully clothed, whimpered. He was stretched out like a starfish, his ankles and wrists linked to the four corners of the mattress. And huge black bruises were beginning to appear on the visible skin.

Well, at least the restraints had held. Knots good enough to make even a seaman proud. Cooper smiled to himself.

"Hello Matteo," he said. "Now, where were we?"

Chapter 27

Jason Hunter

London Office

Friday 10th June

Keen to avoid the wrath of Mayor Britland and whatever hell that would unleash, I did my best to push all thoughts of Varazze and conspiracy forums to the back of my mind as I pulled together a detailed outline of how we could provide the mayor with the protection he so desperately wanted.

It reminded me a lot of how I'd originally met Gromov. How he'd sauntered into my office, demanded a security detail, and then ended up in hospital with a bullet in his shoulder when we hadn't been quick enough to get things operational.

I wasn't planning on making the same mistake twice. Even if the mayor deserved whatever was coming after him.

There was a knock at my office door, and I looked up to see Sam.

"Come in," I said, gesturing to one of the chairs.

He gently closed the door behind him and sat down opposite me.

"All okay?" he asked.

"Yeah, just finalising this proposal for the mayor," I said, waving a hand at my computer as I leaned back in my chair.

"You spoken to DI Irons?" he asked.

I shook my head and let out a long breath. "She's turned her phone off, won't answer any of my calls."

He gave a single nod of his head but didn't say anything else.

"How was the meeting with Royce?" I asked.

"Good," he said. "Pretty basic. Got spooked after the Alfonso Torres murder so wants to be cautious."

"Understandable," I said. "Although if this sniper is coming for him, there's probably not much we can do."

My poor attempt at a joke fell flat. Sam dipped his chin but didn't reply.

And so we sat in silence for a few moments.

"Is Richard in?" I asked, cringing as I said it. Richard was my least favourite person in the business, but he was my Operations Manager. And if I wanted to get this proposal across to the mayor today, I'd need Richard's input.

Sam nodded.

Great.

Neither of us spoke.

"I appreciate your help," I said.

"I know," he replied and got to his feet. "Anything I can do?"

"Turn back time?" I gave a half-smile, but Sam didn't return it. "Maybe speak to Hayley? See if she got my message. It could be important."

He gave me a brief nod and left.

Chapter 28

JASON HUNTER

LONDON OFFICE

Friday 10th June

Richard's door was half open. I knocked and opened it a little wider.

The room was light and airy, with a potted plant in one corner and a large single-seat chair in the middle of the room, facing the desk where Richard sat, his head bent.

He looked up from the plans scattered across his desk and waved me in.

"Hey, Jason. How can I help?"

"I've just sent you an email for a new proposal. Can you take a look and sign it off, please?"

"Yes, of course."

"Catch is, I need it done today. Preferably now. It's for Mayor Britland, and he's hounding my ass to get it sorted by the end of the day."

He frowned.

"Mayor Britland?"

"It's a long story," I sighed.

"Yeah, no problem." He gathered up the plans he'd been looking at and stacked them to one side, pulling his laptop towards him as he said, "I can take a look now."

"Appreciate it," I said and left him to it.

As I walked down the corridor back to my own office, my phone vibrated in my pocket. I pulled it out but I didn't recognise the mobile number on the screen.

I answered the call, pressed the phone to my ear but before I could say anything, a familiar voice cut me off.

"Jason. It's Robert Britland."

Oh my God, this guy was on my case. Did he not know how to be patient?

"I've just given your proposal to my Operations Manager for approval, Mr Mayor."

"Yes, great. I have a more pressing issue."

He sounded... distracted somehow. And not at all like the cool, calm, and collected man who had sat in my office just yesterday.

"I have a press conference this afternoon and I need an emergency team to be present," he said.

This afternoon? That was way too short notice.

"I thought the press conference was tomorrow?"

"It's been brought forward," he said through gritted teeth.

"Has something happened?" I asked, reaching my office. I closed the door behind me and stood for a moment, wondering if my day was about to descend into chaos.

"No, nothing like that. As I said before, I'm not sure that my current team is meeting requirements. I'd much prefer to have a third party fill the position in the interim."

"Right. And how many do you need on that team?"

"Normally, I have a team of two for these things, but maybe we need four just to be on the safe side?"

Okay, so he was definitely panicking. And that made me wary.

I crossed my office to grab a notepad and pen.

"And what time is this press conference?" I asked as I started scribbling notes.

"4 o'clock."

I wrote that down and then glanced at my watch. "That's in less than two hours," I said. The man couldn't be serious.

"Yes, I know. Less than ideal. You don't need to tell me. Look, can you do it or not?"

I made some mental calculations. Sam wasn't on rotation at the moment, what with Stacey – my stomach tightened at the thought of her – not being here. And then there was me. I'd have to check who else wasn't on rota, or if any of our casual staff had availability. Turnaround time would be pretty tight.

"I can guarantee two. Myself and my Head of Security Operations will be there, but I can't guarantee a full team of four."

There was a momentary pause before Britland replied, "It's better than nothing." And he sounded almost resigned.

"Where is the press conference?"

"HMP Belmarsh. I expect you know where that is."

"Of course." My mind was whirring. This clearly had something to do with the riot that had broken out. Maybe it had something to do with Gromov, too.

"I'm meeting with the Governor beforehand, so I'll meet you there."

"No problem. You have my number," I said.

He hung up. I looked down at the notes I'd scribbled down.

What the hell was going on?

Chapter 29

Jason Hunter

HMP Belmarsh, London

Friday 10th June

The press conference was being held in the open area in front of the prison's main entrance, right where the vans would normally arrive when transporting the high-security prisoners. Not an ideal location. In fact, far from it. The area was too exposed, and the far side was lined with trees, making it impossible to completely secure the place.

Mayor Britland stood to my right, a few steps behind the temporary podium where he was currently shuffling his papers and getting ready to speak. Sam stood on the other side of him, and I knew he wasn't happy about the situation either.

We'd tried speaking to the prison's Press Officer, but she was having none of it and insisted the press conference be held here. She stated that the prison needed to be in any and all photos that were taken to emphasise the message that Mayor Britland would be delivering.

I'd fought the urge to roll my eyes.

Between Sam and the mayor stood the Governor of HMP Belmarsh, a ferocious-looking woman with her hair pulled back into a neat ponytail. She wore a tight-fitting pencil skirt and a matching blazer. Her square-framed glasses made her look more like a stern librarian than a prison governor.

In front of our small group stood a cluster of reporters. At least twice as many as I was expecting. They'd jostled each other to get to the front until prison security staff had pushed them back. Now they were surreptitiously trying to lean as far forward as they could without stepping over the boundary that had been put in place to keep them at bay.

I scanned the rows of faces, looking for any that were familiar and mentally cataloguing the rest.

A hush descended over the group as the mayor stepped up to the podium, placing his papers in front of him and looking out at the assembled crowd.

"At approximately 8pm on Thursday 9th of April," he began, "an incident broke out at HMP Belmarsh, involving several inmates who tried to overpower the prison staff on duty. Additional staff were deployed to deal with the incident, and those responsible were detained."

The reporters were watching with rapt attention, some holding microphones and others filming on their phones. I glanced over at the few designated press photographers loitering at the edges of the group, their camera lenses trained on the mayor.

"During this time, there was a second incident." Mayor Britland paused before continuing. "An inmate was attacked in his cell and unfortunately died."

The reporters erupted into questions. They surged forward and I braced myself to intervene.

"Step back!" shouted one of the prison staff, holding up a hand in warning.

Prepared for the outburst, the mayor waited patiently. He was nothing if not professional, and he knew that this would happen.

The death of an inmate was always big news, especially when caused by other prisoners. The media outlets would turn this into a feeding frenzy, and I knew the governor would be the first sacrifice.

A strong breeze ruffled my hair and tickled the back of my neck, reminding us all how fickle the weather was, even in June.

From the corner of my eye, I saw the papers Mayor Britland had been holding slip from his hands. I stepped forward to try and catch what I could, but they were blowing in the opposite direction toward Sam.

And that's when it happened.

Pain ripped through my left shoulder, and I reeled backwards from the force of it. Disbelief clouded my mind as I tried to process what had happened. I reflexively clapped my right hand over my shoulder where the pain was climbing to an unbearable burn. It felt like I was on fire.

The mayor turned to look at me, shock written in every line of his face, his eyes wide.

In that same moment, I saw Sam lunge forward the few feet that separated him from the mayor, wrapping an arm around the man's waist and hauling them both to the ground.

The group of reporters in front of us collapsed into a heap on the tarmac, some screaming and others shouting.

I looked down at my shoulder, where my hand was now warm and wet.

Blood.

My hand was covered in blood.

I'd just been shot.

Chapter 30

Jason Hunter

HMP Belmarsh, London

Friday 10th June

Fuck. Fuck. Fuck.

My brain kicked into overdrive as it tried to work out just what the hell was going on.

Bullet to the shoulder. Mayor Britland on the ground.

I looked to the trees where the shot must have come from, but it was impossible to work out the gunman's location.

I could have sworn I saw a figure just to the left within the treeline, but by the time my eyes had tracked the movement, it was gone.

Bastard.

Something told me I'd recognise the face behind the rifle. A bland, easily forgettable face that had once sat in my living room waiting for me, just so that he could deliver a USB of the most damning evidence I had ever seen in my life.

I gritted my teeth as the burn continued in my shoulder, spreading down my arm and setting my fingers on fire.

"You fucker," I ground out and headed to the treeline.

"Jason!" Sam called, but I ignored him.

There was utter chaos behind me as I crossed the grassy verge and reached the trees.

I don't know what I was expecting to see, but there was no one there. The trees crowded close together, and behind them lay the road that led to HMP Isis. I knew he'd be long gone by now.

Emerging on the other side of the trees, there was a small outbuilding next to the path. It looked like an outbuilding for a generator, with blue steel doors that were locked when I tried the handle.

Looking up, I noticed that it had a flat roof, meaning it would have been easy to climb and remain hidden. I knew his style. He liked to scope out the place beforehand and position himself high up. I could just make out the commotion by the podium through the treeline, so it wasn't out of the realm of possibility.

I scanned the area around the outbuilding, looking for any hint that he might have been here.

And then something caught my eye.

The pain in my shoulder was causing darkness to creep in at the edge of my vision as the adrenaline started to wear off. I looked at my hands, wondering how the hell I was going to pick up what I'd spotted without contaminating it. Blood coated my right hand and was seeping into the sleeve of my blazer.

Shit.

I looked back towards the press conference to see that Mayor Britland and the prison governor were nowhere in sight, and Sam was racing towards me with a paramedic.

"Sam," I called and then nodded to the ground, clamping my right hand back over the wound in my shoulder.

"Mr Hunter, is it?" asked the medic who was carrying a first aid pack. He slung the pack onto the ground and began rummaging through his supplies.

"Gloves," I said.

The medic looked at me with a frown.

"Gloves," I repeated, wishing for the millionth time that my voice didn't sound the way it did.

"Uh, sure." The medic pulled out a pair of latex gloves and offered them to me.

"Sam," I said, nodding in his direction. Suddenly, I was starting to feel light-headed.

The medic pivoted and handed the gloves to Sam, who took them.

"I need you to sit down," the medic instructed, pointing to the grass.

I did as he said while Sam slipped the gloves on.

"Yes, boss?" he said.

I nodded to where I'd seen it. "In the grass," I rasped, my throat suddenly feeling dry.

"Slow, deep breaths," said the medic, opening a pack of gauze. "You're going into shock." He gently pulled my hand away from my shoulder, replacing it with gauze and applying enough pressure to make me groan.

"Got it," said Sam as he stood up and showed me the gold bullet case nestled in the palm of his hand. "Looks like someone cocked up," he added with a smile.

That's when I blacked out.

Chapter 31

JASON HUNTER

QUEEN ELIZABETH HOSPITAL, LONDON

Friday 10th June

I felt groggy.

Opening my eyes, I groaned. It was a horrible case of déjà vu, and my mind immediately flashed back to when I'd woken up after the warehouse explosion. Before I knew that the damage to my throat would likely be permanent.

I looked to the figure on my right, expecting to see Stacey, but instead... Hayley.

I let my head fall back against the pillow and looked up at the depressingly mundane, white-tiled ceiling. A pang of pain and longing washed over me. Where was she? What was Liam doing to her? The thought made me feel sick.

"Could you not have kept out of trouble for five minutes?" she asked.

I rolled my eyes.

Gingerly, I raised my left arm and felt a painful tightening in the skin of my shoulder.

"Keyhole surgery," she said. "They had to take the bullet out."

I nodded weakly.

"Drink?"

"Please," I whispered. She poured a cup of water from the jug on the bedside table and held a straw up to my lips. I drank greedily, each swallow feeling thick and heavy, but the liquid soothing the raw burn that had been building in my throat.

Before I could say anything else, the door to the ward opened and Mayor Britland walked in, closely followed by Sam.

"Fucking fuckity hell," I muttered, and Hayley suppressed a smile.

My bed was the furthest from the door, and Mayor Britland strode the length of the ward, nodding in greeting to the three other beds that were occupied, their inhabitants all staring at him in utter surprise.

"Ah good, you're awake," said the mayor, stopping by my bedside. "I wanted to check in to see how you were doing." Sam stood a few feet behind him, looking directly at me, concern etched into his forehead.

"Still alive," I said, looking back up at the ceiling.

"Good to hear."

There was an awkward pause.

"Any updates yet, Detective Inspector?" he asked, awkwardly turning his body so that he was facing Hayley.

"There are several teams working on it, sir. And I'll let you know as soon as I have an update. Thanks to Mr Hunter's quick thinking at the scene, we were able to preserve a key piece of evidence that's currently with the ballistics team. I'm hoping to know more in the morning."

Mayor Britland gave a decisive nod and didn't seem to know what to do with himself.

"Rest up, Jason. Let's book a meeting for when you're back on your feet."

"Sure. You're in good hands with Sam, Mr Mayor. He's my right hand and the best in the business."

The mayor looked over his shoulder at Sam as if he was seeing him for the first time before nodding again and marching back out of the room, Sam on his heels.

Once he was gone, Hayley turned to me.

"What the hell was that all about?" she asked.

"I think someone is feeling jittery after their recent brush with death," I said.

Chapter 32

JASON HUNTER

QUEEN ELIZABETH HOSPITAL, LONDON

Friday 10th June

"You think he was the target?" asked Hayley.

I nodded.

"Who else? The mayor had been reading the press release from the papers he was holding," I said, lowering my voice so the others in the ward wouldn't hear me. "They got blown out of his hands at the same moment that I stepped forward. So the shot missed him and hit me."

Hayley nodded thoughtfully. "That certainly matches the predicted trajectory we've got from the scene."

"First Alonso Torres, then Alek Gromov, and now Mayor Britland. What do all those names have in common, Detective Inspector?" I asked, feeling like we were inching closer to the truth.

"Alright, alright. I hear you. I'm not the SIO for Torres, though. And I'm not even in the loop for the Gromov investigation. I doubt I'll be able to pull any more strings for visibility on this one either," she said.

"I'm just saying. You're not going to have anyone from that fraud ring to prosecute at this rate. Somebody wants them dead. All of them."

She was silent for a moment.

"Different MOs, though," she said eventually.

She was right. Gromov was the odd one out. Torres had been killed by a sniper. I'd been shot in the shoulder, also by sniper. But Gromov, Gromov had been beaten to death in his prison cell. It wasn't exactly somewhere a sniper could get to him.

"I can see those wheels turning. Spit it out. What's your grand theory?"

"Well, until this morning, I would have said Mayor Britland was my number one suspect," I said. "But I think we can rule him out, considering how the press conference went."

"You ever think about joining the police?" asked Hayley with a smile.

I laughed. "No, thank you. Far too much red tape for my liking."

"Isn't that the truth?" she muttered and pulled her phone from a pocket.

I laughed again.

"Right, Mr Hunter." She glanced down at her phone screen and then repocketed it. "I need to go. Bad guys to catch and all that." She stood up and leaned over to kiss me on the cheek. "The doc has said you'll need to be off work for the next few weeks while that shoulder heals." She gestured to said shoulder.

I rolled my eyes. "Yes, thank you. I'm sure I can take care of myself."

"Because you were doing such a good job of that on your own," she mocked.

"Sorry, darling, I didn't know you'd have a visitor."

I looked in the direction of the voice to see a gorgeous redhead hovering at the end of my bed. She was dressed in a tight-fitting midi dress in the brightest post box red, with killer high heels.

"Hi, Cameron," I said with a smile.

"Why hello, darling," she said, her own red lips curving up into a soft smile.

Hayley raised an eyebrow at me, a smirk on her face.

"Oh, erm, Hayley, this is Cameron. Cameron, this is Detective Inspector Hayley Irons, an old school friend of Stacey's," I said, gesturing between the two women.

Cameron's smoky eyes flicked to Hayley. "Ah yes, the infamous DI Irons. A pleasure," she said and held out a hand. Hayley shook it.

"Cameron...?"

"Just Cameron, darling. The ambiguity works to my advantage, you see."

"Cameron now runs Mickey's club," I said.

Hayley looked between us. "I see," she said. "Well, I best be off anyway. I'll leave you to it," she said and patted me on the arm before leaving.

"Did I interrupt something?" asked Cameron, as she sat in the chair by my bed, then carefully removed the handbag from the crook of her arm and placed it on the floor by the chair.

"No. She was just telling me to look after myself."

"Well, she'd be right."

I didn't know what to say to that, so I didn't say anything.

In the short time I'd been awake, I'd had far too many visitors, and I was feeling exhausted. My shoulder was aching, and I wanted my next lot of painkillers. Maybe there was a button somewhere that I needed to press. Or maybe I was just expected to wait for the nurse to do her rounds.

"How are you?" asked Cameron.

She always seemed to drop the 'darling' when she was being serious. It was like the 'darling' was part of her outfit, a part of the persona she presented to the world. She was always so chic and glamorous, and a smart businesswoman too. But there was something about her that made me wonder just how far she'd cross the legal line if she needed to. And was that how she'd built her success in the first place?

After Mickey's death, our paths had crossed and we had formed a reluctant alliance. I thought I'd been looking for a bloke. A deliberate misdirection she used to her advantage. She did run an elite club for the superrich, after all. But through it all, we'd become friends. Sort of. And I knew Stacey liked her. A lot. She'd even approached Cameron with a business proposal. And suddenly my heart ached for my missing woman. The woman with the passion and the vision. The woman who wanted to create a space for females in Formula One, who wanted to dominate the world, one race at a time, with a team of powerful women behind her.

"Surviving," I said, my voice raspy.

And for once, I didn't feel self-conscious about how I sounded. Cameron knew what I'd been through. And likewise, I knew what Mickey's death had cost her. Emotionally as well as financially.

"Jason, just what the hell is going on?"

I frowned at her tone. Clearly done with the niceties, this was the real reason why she was here.

"What are you talking about?" I asked, wincing as I tried to prop myself up into a more comfortable position.

She got up from the chair to help me, moving the pillows so my head and shoulders were more upright.

"You know the mayor's dirty, right?" she whispered.

"I had my suspicions."

"Then what the hell are you doing protecting the bastard? Come on, Jason. The man is as dodgy as Alfonso Torres, and look what happened to him," she said as she sat down.

"I know, Cameron. But I can hardly turn down the Mayor of London when he rocks up at my office and demands I offer him protection. Especially when I don't have a bloody good reason to refuse him."

"Jesus Christ, Jason. You make one up!" she whisper-shouted at me.

I glanced around the ward to see if anyone was likely to overhear our conversation. One of the other occupants had their own visitor while the other two were watching the football.

"Look," I said, keeping my voice low and my tone even. "I know enough about dodgy clients to last me a lifetime. Are you forgetting I worked for Alek Gromov?"

"Are you proud of that?" she asked with disgust.

"No, of course not. I'm trying to make a point. I'd love to refuse any and every client who I think has scrupulous morals, but that's not how the world works. And I can't afford for Mayor Britland to drag my name through the mud because I turned him down, okay? I figured I'd be able to keep a better eye on him this way, too," I said, straining to sit up more and wincing. It felt unnatural to have this argument lying down. But my shoulder was killing me. Where the hell was that nurse? I looked around the bed for any kind of call button.

"Is this what you're looking for?" asked Cameron. She leaned forward and picked up a curved white handle with a blue button attached to a wire and dangling over the side of the bed. It looked weirdly like a controller for a games console. I nodded, and she handed it to me. I pressed it, thinking it would call a nurse, but instant relief flooded through me instead. I closed my eyes and leaned back into the pillows, savouring the calm that had descended on my body.

"I'm sorry," she said after a minute or two.

"It's fine," I said, my voice sounding hoarse even to me.

"Any news on Stacey yet?" she asked.

I cracked an eye open and looked at her. Worry lines were etched onto her face.

"Nothing yet," I said.

Before I could say anything else, the doors to the ward swung open and a doctor walked in, heading straight for my bed.

"I believe that's my cue to leave," said Cameron, collecting her bag from the floor. "Take care of yourself, Jason. Stay away from Britland if you can; he's bad news." She leaned over and kissed me gently on the cheek. "And call me if there's any news about Stacey," she said and then left.

The doctor didn't tell me anything I didn't already know; the operation went well, I would be discharged in the next 12 hours if there were no issues, and I needed to sign myself off work for the next few weeks.

I couldn't remember the last time I'd been off work for more than a few days.

"And I mean it. No sitting at your desk doing paperwork, either. You need to be at home resting," he said, his eyebrows raised as if he was talking to a petulant child.

I resisted rolling my eyes.

After he left, my thoughts circled round to Stacey, as they always did these days.

What would I do with myself? Mope around the house?

It was already too painful being in the house without her. Everything reminded me of her, and I was stressed enough as it was.

So what was I going to do?

Moping really wasn't my style. I needed to do something. Anything to get Stacey back.

And Hayley would definitely want me to stay out of trouble.

Maybe it was time I took a holiday.

Chapter 33

STACEY JAMES

LOCATION UNKNOWN

Saturday 11th June

She was standing at the sink in the kitchen washing the dishes from the last few days. It had become a ritual of sorts. Liam would unlock her bedroom door and take her outside for 15 minutes of fresh air before bringing her into the kitchen, where she was chained to the ancient, immovable AGA cooker and then expected to complete menial housework.

The first time he'd brought her in here, she'd scoured every inch of the place looking for any kind of utensil that she could use as a weapon. But Liam was more than a step ahead of her; the place was stripped bare. And the crockery? Plastic. The kind that was given to young children. The faded patterns of well-known cartoon characters grinned up at her from the soapy dishwater, mocking her.

Pots and pans hung in neat rows on the wall behind her. Shelves lined the wall to her right, all of which were empty. She imagined the vintage bric-a-brac that once sat there. Or maybe some favourite crockery pieces and a spice rack. The middle of the room was filled with a huge farmhouse table that could seat at least ten people.

The AGA was positioned in the middle of the kitchen cabinets and her chain was long enough that she could get around almost all of the kitchen. She could reach the sink easily enough if she draped the iron chain over the top, but it kept her a few feet from the doors at both ends; one led to the lounge and the other led outside to freedom. Not that she would be able to get far. She'd already tried that and failed.

They were well and truly in the middle of nowhere.

An old, rundown barn sat a short distance from the farmhouse, and a single-track dirt road led away from the property. But in the other direction was rolling farmland as far as the eye could see. And although it wasn't her ticket out of there, it sure was a beautiful sight.

There could be worse places to die.

I won't die today. I won't die today.

She tore her eyes away from the scenery and looked down at her hands as she scrubbed food from the plates. Her arm screamed in protest from the movement, but she couldn't let him know how much he'd hurt her.

"Yesterday afternoon at a press conference outside HMP Belmarsh in southeast London, there was an attempt on Mayor Britland's life."

The voice floated in through the open door to the lounge, and Stacey listened as she began to dry the plates on the draining board next to the sink.

"While the mayor was unharmed. Managing Director of Hawk Security, Jason Hunter, suffered a bullet wound to the shoulder and is currently in hospital for treatment."

The world came to a standstill, and the plate she was holding slipped from her hands. It clattered to the floor. Had it been ceramic, it would have shattered.

She stood there, immobile. Jason had been shot. Jason had been shot in London, while working for the mayor.

She was equal parts heartbroken that he'd been injured and relieved that he was okay. But then the wider implications of this news started to set in.

Something moved in the corner of her eye, and she turned to see Liam standing in the doorway, a cruel smile on his face. He stalked towards her and she took a couple of steps back before the chain snagged on one of the chairs at the table.

Still smiling, Liam gently took hold of the hair draped over Stacey's right shoulder and wound it around his hand. Forcing her backwards, he slammed his hand against the wall, yanking her hair.

He grabbed her by the wrist, causing a whimper to escape her throat at the pain that shot up her arm. He knew. She was sure of it.

"Looks like lover boy isn't coming for you, Stacey. No one's coming to get you," he said, his voice low and menacing. "Which means you're mine."

He pulled her hair down, forcing her face up, and then kissed her, thrusting his tongue into her mouth.

Chapter 34

BILL COOPER

GENOA, ITALY

Tuesday 14ᵗʰ June

The sun was glorious as he drove the winding coastal road to Genoa. He had the windows down, his arm draped out the window of his rental car, and the sea breeze was just perfect. It made it almost hard to remember why he was there. Almost.

As the car sped along the quiet road, he caught glimpses of the sea between the trees. He rounded the next bend and the foliage fell away to reveal a crystal-clear ocean, dotted with boats and dominated by a container ship.

God, this place is beautiful.

Shame he was here under less than pleasant circumstances.

He'd spent the last two days following up on the information he'd managed to get out of the boat owner, Matteo. It hadn't been hard; the guy wasn't exactly a hard-as-nails army veteran. But there also wasn't much to go on.

Liam hadn't been forthcoming about his plans with Matteo, and Matteo hadn't exactly wanted to ask. After extracting every last re-membered detail about the words uttered on board his boat, Matteo was able to tell Cooper that he'd heard Liam mention a car. There wasn't one waiting at the marina when they arrived, but it made the most sense. Liam had planned the whole thing meticulously; he wouldn't risk public transport like trains or buses. And considering the time of night they'd arrived in port, it would have been too late anyway. But the perfect time to pick up a car.

He'd already checked with all the rental companies in the area to see if anyone matching Liam's description had picked a car up, or even if someone had asked for a car to be available within the vicinity of the marina.

The answer was no.

So his thoughts had turned to stolen cars.

Based on the average age of the cars in Varazze, it wouldn't have been hard to steal one.

The local police had been useless, as expected. So he'd taken to discreetly asking some of the locals. That, and eavesdropping on whatever local gossip he could. His Italian was rusty, but it was coming back to him. Having spent a considerable amount of time in Italy over the years doing dirty jobs for the Italian Mafia, he'd picked up enough to get by.

But with the majority of Italian businesses not opening until the evening, it was slow going.

And so now, he was on his way to the airport.

There was someone he had to meet.

Chapter 35

JASON HUNTER

GENOA AIRPORT, ITALY

Tuesday 14th June

I shook hands with Bill Cooper, and he gave me a brief nod.

We'd never seen eye to eye, and I definitely wouldn't class us as friends, but we could at least be civil. And as much as I hated to admit it, I needed his skills now more than ever. Plus, having his number in my burner phone had come in handy more than once over the last year or so.

"How's the shoulder?" Cooper asked.

I raised an eyebrow.

He shrugged. "I can make small talk," he said and gestured towards the short-stay car park.

"It's fine. Healing."

"Nasty business, really," he said, and I rolled my eyes.

"Go on, just say it."

He looked sideways at me. "Say what?"

"I don't know. Sounds like you have something you want to get off your chest."

He smiled. Not a friendly smile, more of a smug smile.

"How does it feel to be shot?" he asked.

"Not my first time," I muttered.

And this time, both his eyebrows went up. "When have you been shot before?"

"It's a long story," I said. "What's the latest?" I asked, hoping to change the topic.

"Not much. We're looking for a stolen car."

"Stolen?"

Cooper stopped by a new black Lancia and clicked the fob he was holding, the headlights blinking once. I opened the boot and dumped my holdall on top of the one that was already in there before climbing into the passenger seat of the car.

As he drove, Cooper updated me on his latest theory.

"Seems like searching for a needle in a haystack, if you ask me," I said with a frown. Casually eavesdropping in every local bar until we happened to come across something didn't seem like the best plan.

"I didn't ask," said Cooper, his eyes on the road. "But not as much of a blind search as you might think."

"How do you mean?" I asked. I looked out of the window, watching the stunning scenery pass. The moment we'd left the airport, I'd opened the window and currently had my right arm propped on the door, enjoying the feel of the warm sun on my skin.

"Think about it," he said. "Liam gets to port on an unfamiliar boat."

I turn to look at him, waiting for him to continue.

"I've already established that Matteo didn't know Liam outside of the couple of days it took him to get to Monaco and back. No prior relationship. Liam had never been on that boat before."

"Right."

My phone vibrated in my pocket. I pulled it out to see an update text from Sam:

All good. Britland team rotation smooth. No news.

Short and sweet. Exactly Sam's style. Although I guessed that no news was good news. I'd delegated the whole project to Sam. I knew he could take care of it while I was away.

"So, he's on an unfamiliar boat with an unwilling hostage," said Cooper, bringing me back to our conversation. "He gets to Varazze and needs to transport himself and Stacey to his next location. To do that, he needs a vehicle of some kind. And he can't risk Stacey making a run for it. So, she was either unconscious, meaning he would have had to carry her, and I doubt he could do that for very long. Or she would have been held at gunpoint, which also has its own risks. She probably also had her hands bound, which would draw unwanted attention. So, the transfer window needs to be small."

"Right. So, what are you thinking?" I asked. His logic was impeccable, but it still felt like an impossible task.

"He'll have stolen something locally. I'm thinking he would have left Stacey confined on the boat while he went and dealt with it and then came back for her."

"That feels risky. She could have escaped."

Cooper didn't reply.

I glanced over at him. "You think she was unconscious."

"I do," he gave a small nod.

I let his words sink in. I didn't like the bubble of panic that began to swell in my chest. The *how* of that was terrifying.

"Did you find something on the boat?" I asked.

When he didn't answer me, I glanced over to see that he was fixated on the road ahead. Then he glanced out of his driver's side window before replying, "There were some empty bottles that suggest he might have made his own chloroform."

"What?!"

He didn't reply.

"And you didn't think to mention this sooner?!" I asked, furious.

"What difference would it have made?"

"I–," I trailed off. What difference would it have made? I'd been an absolute wreck the last few weeks. It would have sent me over the edge, if anything. "Point made," I muttered.

We lapsed into silence.

"Do the police know?" I asked.

"They received an anonymous tip about some questionable items being loaded onto the boat, and I believe a team searched it after I was done questioning Matteo," he said.

We lapsed into another silence.

"Where are you with the stolen car idea, then?" I asked after a while.

"Starting with the bars closest to the marina. I'm assuming he's snatched something close by."

"I take it the local police haven't been very useful?"

"No."

Part of me felt like it was important to pass this information on to Hayley, but I knew she'd be obligated to alert Italian authorities, and the last thing we needed was to get caught up in all of that. I knew how Cooper worked, and he wouldn't thank me for the holdup. Stacey had already been missing for 15 days. Time was definitely working against us.

Chapter 36

Jason Hunter

Boma Caffè, Varazze

Thursday 16th June

"Imagine my surprise earlier when I called the office and Lucy told me you were away on holiday," said Hayley on the other end of the phone.

I wasn't ashamed to say I'd been dodging Hayley's phone calls the last few days. I'd texted her on Monday to tell her I'd been discharged and that I was going to take some time off. I'd told her Sam was running things in my absence and that I'd call her at some point to check in.

Since then, she'd bombarded me with texts and unanswered calls, getting more annoyed when I didn't reply or answer. Her use of exclamation marks and capital letters was getting increasingly erratic the longer I left it.

Standing at a bar table outside Boma Caffè, I'd finally given in and answered my phone.

"You said to take some time off work."

I could feel her exasperation through the phone as she said, "Yeah, but leaving the country is a little extreme, don't you think?"

"I thought it was a good idea. I can't remember the last time I went away."

Leaning against the table opposite me, Cooper took a swig from his bottle of Messina beer, a smirk playing at his lips.

He might look the picture of casual arrogance, but I knew our lack of progress so far was grating on him.

Every evening we'd been visiting local bars for a couple of rounds of drinks, asking owners and locals about any unusual incidents in the last few weeks, anyone who might be missing a car, showing Liam and Stacey's photos to anyone who would spare us a few minutes, but nothing. On more than one occasion, we'd been asked to leave for disturbing the patrons, and we'd done so without a fuss, but I knew it was wearing Cooper down. Hell, I didn't exactly feel good about the whole thing, but it did feel good to at least be doing something proactive.

"Please, dear God, tell me you're not in Italy."

"Okay, I'm not in Italy."

"Jason!"

I shrugged, even though I knew she couldn't see me. "What do you want me to say?"

She groaned. "You're gonna get yourself killed."

"It's honestly not that exciting. No sign of Liam yet."

"I almost don't want to ask this."

"Then don't. Don't ask questions you don't want to know the answers to," I said, knowing exactly where this was going.

"Alright. I won't. But promise you'll call me the moment you have something?"

"Of course."

"Promise me, Jason!"

"I promise," I said.

"And tell Cooper he'd better bring both of you home safe," she said before hanging up on me. I looked at my phone with a smile, half in disbelief.

"You get a telling off?" Cooper asked.

"Big time," I said and picked up my own bottle of Messina.

Boma Caffè had become a favourite spot of ours. Not just because it seemed to be where the locals hung out after a day on the water, but it had a great vibe about the place. It mixed the feel of a sophisticated wine bar with casual dining for the perfect atmosphere. We often found ourselves at one of the standing tables right on the water with a good view of the comings and goings.

Every now and again, one of us would circulate with the photos of Liam and Stacey, asking if anyone had seen either of them. It always ended in a no, but as the owner didn't mind too much, we persevered. By now, we were being recognised by the regulars who would give us a friendly nod as they went by.

I took a swig of my beer and looked over the water to where the sun was beginning to set, casting the water in the most stunning pinks and oranges.

No sooner had I put the bottle down than my phone rang again. An unknown mobile number flashed on the screen and my stomach sank. I knew exactly who that was.

Cooper looked at the phone.

"You gonna get that?" he asked.

I swiped the phone from the table, answered the call, and pressed it to my ear.

"Mayor Britland," I said as genially as I could.

Cooper's eyebrows shot up.

"Jason, where the hell are you?"

"I've been signed off work for a few weeks. I thought Sam had filled you in?"

"Even so, I was hoping to sit down and have a conversation."

"Sorry, but I'm unavailable for the foreseeable future. Any concerns you have about your protection, please speak directly with Sam and he'll be able to handle it."

"So where are you?" he asked again, his tone menacing. "Because you're not at home, are you?"

I paused. Britland was checking up on me.

"What do you want, Britland?"

"Oh, dropping the niceties, are you? I need to see you. Sooner rather than later," he added. "Otherwise, I can't be held responsible for the consequences."

He cut the call, and I was left stunned.

Pocketing my phone, I picked up my beer.

"Britland, eh?" asked Cooper casually.

"Don't start," I said. "I've already had it in the neck."

Cooper shrugged and downed the rest of his beer.

My mind still whirring, I didn't notice the young woman who looked to be in her early thirties walk past and join a table inside.

I looked out at the water, processing what Britland had said. I needed to speak to Sam, tell him that Britland was on edge and that the bastard had visited my house. Or at least one of his goons had. I'd need Sam to swing by and check the place. Maybe even ask him to stay there for a night or two just to be on the safe side.

As my thoughts raced, I watched an older couple with a sausage dog amble past. Followed by an older guy in waterproof trousers and a thick waterproof coat who'd clearly spent the day on the water.

There was an endless trickle of people, and it was nice to see the town still so alive, considering its size.

"Another?" asked Cooper, nodding to my half-finished beer.

"Sure," I said, knowing this would probably be our last before we moved on to another local spot. He had a list mapped out, and the plan was to keep circulating until one of us got a lead. Or at least until one of us came up with a better idea about what to do next. The longer this went on, the higher the likelihood that we would need to speak to the police, and I really wanted to avoid that at all costs. Mostly because Cooper would likely be arrested as soon as they knew who he was, and I didn't want to spook Liam if he was nearby.

I watched Cooper head inside. The owner saw him coming and opened two new bottles before he even reached the bar. He grabbed them by the necks and stood there making small talk for a few more minutes.

I had to hand it to him, for someone who made a living out of killing people, he could sure be charming when he needed to be.

Looking back over the water, I watched as a middle-aged man tied his boat up for the night and then stepped onto the pontoon that would bring him back to land.

Glancing back inside, I saw Cooper was no longer at the bar, but at a table of women. He was holding the photos of Liam and Stacey and was deep in conversation with the same woman who'd walked past us just five minutes ago.

Chapter 37

Jason Hunter

Boma Caffè, Varazze

Thursday 16th June

The woman was frowning at him as she spoke, and my gut tightened. Was this a lead?

I was trying to read Cooper's body language but failing miserably. You would have thought that I'd know his tells more now that I'd been in his company for three days straight, but he was a master at keeping himself to himself. Kind of came with the territory, I guessed.

Cooper looked up at me, and we locked eyes. He inclined his head towards the woman and I understood; this was important.

Leaving the table, I joined Cooper under the marquee-style covering that shaded the tables out front. It was cooler here than in the sunshine, although the breeze coming off the harbour was always a welcome reprieve. The woman watched as I approached while Cooper said something in Italian. She nodded but eyed me warily.

The bar sat inside the building, in a narrow room just wide enough for a few patrons to lean against it and gossip. Outside was where the customers dined and drank at tables. It was a common setup I'd come across during my time here.

Cooper gestured at me as he continued to speak in Italian. Other than a few courtesy words here and there, I didn't speak the language. I certainly didn't understand a single thing that rolled easily off Cooper's tongue.

The woman nodded again, and then Cooper turned to me, switching to English.

"This is Giulia. She works at a late-night pharmacy on the outskirts of town. She recognises the photo of Liam. Says he came in about a week or so ago and bought supplies. His Italian was pretty rubbish, that's why she remembers him. They don't get many English speakers around here."

I glanced at the woman who was watching Cooper relay the information to me.

"*Sì, sì,*" she said, nodding. "He... er," she flapped her hands around in the air, looking for the right words. "Buy—" She let out a frustrated sigh and switched back to Italian, speaking quickly and getting more animated.

"He wanted a first aid kit. Bought several. And then asked about painkillers. Specifically, any that might knock someone unconscious. She remembers the conversation because it was late, almost closing time, he was on edge, and she didn't trust him."

Specifically, any that might knock someone unconscious.

Unconscious.

What the hell was he doing to Stacey?

My thoughts immediately began to run away with themselves.

It was clear that he was drugging her. But to what end?

To keep her compliant?

To abuse her?

I felt sick.

All I could think of was Stacey locked up in some dingy room somewhere and that sick bastard...

"Jason." I heard my name echo somewhere far away. "Jason." This time it was more insistent.

I felt myself snap back to the present. Cooper was looking at me, a frown on his forehead. "Mate, this is good news."

"Good news?! How can you say—"

"It means he's nearby," interrupted Cooper. "It means he was here in the last week, and we've got a solid lead to follow."

I nodded numbly but couldn't shift the image of an unconscious Stacey from my mind. Her emaciated body strewn across a dishevelled bed.

Chapter 38

JASON HUNTER

BOMA CAFFè, VARAZZE

Thursday 16th June

Cooper thanked the woman and wrote her mobile number down on a napkin which he tucked into the inside pocket of his jacket.

"You never know," he said. "We might need to speak to her again."

I nodded, wondering why he wouldn't just save the number in his phone, but didn't ask.

Glancing down at my watch, it was still early. Not even 8pm.

"How late did she say the pharmacy was open?" I asked.

"Closes at 10pm," he answered, and then drained half his bottle of beer before putting it on the counter and walking out.

"I pay," I said to the owner, who gave me a small smile and nodded his head. He pressed a few keys on the card machine and then held it out for me. I tapped my phone against it, thanked him, and then hurried outside to catch up with Cooper.

I found him leaning against a lamp post a short walk from the bar, typing on his phone.

"Know where we're going?" I asked.

He nodded without glancing up. I watched as he used his index finger and thumb to manipulate a street view map before zooming out.

Satisfied with whatever he'd worked out, he pushed off the lamp post and we made our way back towards his apartment and to the rental car that was parked a few streets away.

As Cooper drove the Lancia away from the town centre, I wondered if this really was the lead we'd been looking for.

It took about half an hour of navigating the tiny roads of Varazze, including a couple of wrong turns, before we arrived.

"There," I said, leaning forward and pointing through the windscreen to the pharmacy sign that stuck out from the wall.

Cooper cruised past. It was definitely still open; the lights were on, a lone attendant stood behind the desk, and the big green *Farmacia* letters above the doorway were lit up. He parked the Lancia halfway down the street and we both climbed out.

"Let me do the talking," he said.

"Of course." I rolled my eyes. He shot me a look. "I don't speak Italian," I said.

Glancing down the street, I suddenly realised how this area of town seemed less than desirable. Rubbish littered the pavement, and further along the street, unturned bins rocked in the breeze, their rubbish spewing out onto the road. All the houses I could see had bars on their ground-floor windows, as did the doors.

The hairs on the back of my neck prickled. This was not a good neighbourhood.

"Even so." He paused. "Don't go getting a conscience on me now, Hunter. You might not like what's about to happen, okay?"

"The bastard is drugging her, Cooper. I'm not playing nice anymore."

He threw me a smirk as we approached the pharmacy.

"Good. Just keep out of my way."

I nodded.

He was right, I knew he was. I was a liability. And if I tried to intervene with whatever he was about to do, things could get a whole lot worse. Like the police showing up and arresting us kind of worse. Which we really didn't need.

But I was done playing games.

Stacey was in serious trouble, and if the police couldn't get to her, then it was down to me. And Cooper. I'd had no issue using his unconventional methods in the past. Out of sight, out of mind, right? If I wanted to be here, if I wanted to find her, then I needed to get a grip and do what needed to be done.

We reached the door of the pharmacy, and Cooper gestured for me to go in.

"After you," he said.

I pushed the door open, a distant beeping sound announcing our arrival.

The lone attendant looked up from where he was going through an inventory list and gave a welcoming smile.

"*Buonasera,*" he said.

"*Buonasera,*" I echoed, and I watched the smile fall from his face.

I turned to see Cooper had closed the door behind him and flipped the sign on the door from 'Open' to 'Closed'.

Chapter 39

JASON HUNTER

VARAZZE, ITALY

Thursday 16th June

The attendant started speaking in rapid Italian. He sounded panicked, and I couldn't blame him. This wasn't exactly what I'd had in mind when Cooper had said we were coming to talk to him, but he had warned me.

And it took every ounce of self-control to hold back the instinct to jump in.

Cooper had told me not to get involved.

I was purely here as a courtesy.

Leaning against the counter, Cooper started talking in Italian. He mentioned Guilia's name, the woman we'd spoken to at the bar, and then pulled out the photos of Liam and Stacey from his inside jacket pocket.

The attendant shook his head, babbling away in Italian and nervously glancing from Cooper to me. Not that I was much of a threat. My arm was still in a sling, and although I had my jacket slung over my injured shoulder, I was very clearly not likely to be in a fist fight anytime soon.

Cooper nodded as the man talked. His voice turned high, and he spoke even quicker. Where *had* Cooper learned to understand Italian like this?

After a minute or so, the attendant trailed off, his words all spent. Cooper continued nodding as if he was weighing up an important decision and then straightened. The attendant flinched.

"You speak English?" he asked.

The attendant glanced from Cooper to me again and then nodded.

"You see, we have a problem," said Cooper, turning to me. "Our friend here doesn't want to give us access to the CCTV footage."

I frowned and looked back at the attendant who visibly paled.

"That is a problem," I said.

"I—I—I can't," he stammered. "I don't—"

Cooper waved a hand in the air.

He turned to look at me. "What do you think?" he asked.

I raised an eyebrow. Hadn't he explicitly told me not to say anything?

"You're right, you're right," he said and then switched back to Italian. As he talked, Cooper stepped around the counter and slowly approached the attendant. His size dwarfed the other guy, and I had a sinking sensation that this was about to go very badly, very quickly.

"No—no—no—no," stammered the attendant, his eyes wide in panic, his hands held up in surrender. With every step Cooper took forward, the attendant retreated until he was pressed up against the medicine shelves at the far end. "*Aspetti!*" he shouted.

"*Sì?*" asked Cooper, a smirk on his face.

The attendant said something and then held out his hand. Cooper gave him the two photos, and the attendant looked at them closely. He said something else and then carefully edged around Cooper to reach the mobile on the counter. Scooping it up, he tapped at the screen a few times and then put it to his ear.

"He's just calling our mutual friend," said Cooper, nodding at the attendant.

I was starting to get a good idea of how Cooper got things done. Pure intimidation. I slowly let out a long breath, relieved it didn't look like we'd be leaving blood on the floor.

Whatever Giulia said to him on the phone seemed to work because five minutes later, we were in the back room looking at CCTV footage from the previous week.

Based on what Giulia had told Cooper, we only had a rough time-frame and not an exact date, which meant we needed to go through hours of footage to pinpoint the exact moment that Liam visited. The good news was that we knew it happened shortly before closing, which really narrowed it down.

Starting from Sunday, Tommaso, our attendant friend, loaded the half hour before closing and played it on triple speed, slowing the playback every time someone entered the store, which wasn't often.

Tommaso sat in front of the grainy CCTV screen while Cooper leaned over him, an intimidating hand on his shoulder. I leaned over Tommaso's other shoulder, attempting to keep as much distance between myself and the attendant as possible. I didn't think he needed any more persuasion. Besides, Cooper was doing a good enough job on his own.

And so we worked backward, looking at the footage from Sunday, Saturday and Friday with no luck.

Thursday saw a few people come and go, but no Liam.

But on Wednesday, we saw him.

And it was unmistakably him.

Chapter 40

Jason Hunter

Varazze, Italy

Thursday 16th June

"That's him," I said as I felt a familiar fury begin to bubble in my gut.

Tommaso rewound the footage a little, and we watched as Liam entered the pharmacy. He sauntered over to the far wall of cough and cold medicines. He glanced over a couple of times at Guilia, who was behind the counter and dealing with another customer. The woman must have been a regular because it felt like they were talking for ages before she finally left.

With one last glance around the pharmacy, Liam approached the counter. The footage was too grainy to see Guilia's expression. As they spoke, she pointed to the wall adjacent to where he'd been looking just moments ago. He glanced and then nodded before saying something else. Guilia shook her head, but Liam was persistent. She shook her head again before crossing her arms and taking a small step away from the counter. Her body language was clear; she didn't like him.

Liam approached the wall she'd pointed to, found what he was looking for, and scooped the whole shelf into his arms. He crossed the small pharmacy and dumped the boxes of medication onto the counter.

"What's he got?" I asked, pointing to the screen.

Tommaso glanced at me before Cooper translated.

He rattled off more Italian, but Cooper's blank expression told me he wasn't quite as fluent as I'd first believed.

With a heavy sigh, Tommaso got up from the chair and beckoned for us to follow back out onto the shop floor. He walked over to the shelving Giulia had pointed to in the footage, and I glanced up at the camera mounted in the corner of the room before looking back at the shelves.

It was all typical stuff you'd find in a first aid box. Mostly bandages, gauze pads, and pain killers.

Glancing around, I noticed ready-made first aid boxes in the corner.

"Wouldn't he have been better off grabbing one of those?" I asked, pointing at the boxes.

Tommaso must have understood what I was trying to say because he replied before Cooper could translate, "Not enough. Man, er—"

"Liam," I offered.

"*Sì*, Liam. He want lots."

"Lots?" I frowned. Why would he need lots? *Because he's hurt Stacey,* a small voice in my head said. *And he couldn't risk taking her to a hospital.*

I looked at Cooper who was also frowning. I guessed his train of thought mimicked mine.

Whatever the reason, it didn't bode well.

We returned to the back room where Tommaso played the rest of the footage. Liam grabbed a few more items from around the shop and then paid for everything he'd dumped on the counter.

He left approximately 15 minutes after he entered.

"Is that it?" I asked.

"*Sì*," said Tommaso.

Right.

So now what?

Cooper spoke in Italian again and Tommaso shook his head.

"No cameras on the street," he said.

"That doesn't give us much to go on," I said.

"We have confirmation he was here. We have a time and date of exactly *when* he was here. We can work out the rest."

"Since when were you Mr Sunshine and Rainbows?" I muttered.

"Got to think positive, mate. Or the rage might eat me alive."

There was a glimmer of something in his eyes, and I knew exactly what it was. It was the same ugly beast I could feel writhing around in my chest.

Chapter 41

Jason Hunter

Varazze, Italy

Thursday 16ᵗʰ June

I thanked Tommaso before following Cooper out of the pharmacy and onto the street. Before we'd left, he'd video recorded the CCTV footage of Liam should we need it. For what, I wasn't sure. Maybe just evidence that he was here in case things went south.

Back on the street, I looked around. There wasn't much to go on.

Glancing at my watch, I realised it was gone 9pm.

I turned around so I was facing the pharmacy and then took a step back until I was on the edge of the narrow pavement. Looking up at the building, I noticed it was fairly well-kept compared to its neighbours.

Then I checked to make sure the road was clear before stepping out. I only had to take a few steps backwards until I was in the middle of the road and had a good view of the windows above the pharmacy as well as the ones on either side.

"What are you doing?" asked Cooper.

"Just give me a sec," I said.

There were three floors above the pharmacy, each with two sets of shuttered windows and two small wrought-iron balconies, most of which were decorated with potted plants. One or two were bare, and one had neglected the plants that were now brown and shrivelled in their pots.

The building to the right was five floors, with a long balcony spanning the entire front of the first and second floors. The top floors just had shuttered windows.

The building to the left looked to be a long-out-of-business convenience store with a flat roof.

I spun around to face the other side of the road and found myself confronted with graffiti-covered garages. They, too, had a flat roof.

A padlocked gate was to the right, except one side of it was mangled and barely hanging onto its hinges, making it easy to jump if someone wanted to get in.

"You gonna tell me what you're doing yet?" asked Cooper, interrupting my thoughts.

"There," I said, pointing to the garage on the far left. "And there," I said, spinning to face him and seeing that he was leaning against the little Peugeot parked outside the pharmacy. I pointed to the entrance of the closed convenience store. "And there." I pointed to the corner of the long balcony on the building next to the pharmacy. "At least three cameras on this street."

Cooper raised an eyebrow at me, and I got the impression he was impressed.

"I doubt the one above the convenience store is in use. That place doesn't look like it's been visited in months. The one above the garage," I waved a hand over my shoulder, "is right next to a security alarm, so we can assume it's working. The one underneath the balcony is pretty tucked away, which tells me the owner didn't want it to be noticed, so we can assume that one might still be working, too."

"Which one do we go after first?"

I glanced over my shoulder. "The one above the garage would have the best view of Liam coming and going. It depends on whether it has a wide-angle lens or not. Let's hope so."

Cooper nodded and pushed off the car.

"Garage camera it is."

It didn't take us long to find the camera's owner. The garage was clearly marked as belonging to number 31. And it just so happened that Flat 31 was on the second floor of the building next door.

The door was answered by a balding middle-aged man. He was very polite and explained that there had been a couple of break-ins to his garage a few years ago which had prompted him to install the security camera. While he drove a battered old Ford to work every day and parked it on the street outside, the garage housed his vintage Fiat, his pride and joy.

He welcomed us into his home and offered us a nightcap, which we both politely declined, before showing us the footage from the camera. There was nothing of note. Turned out, the camera solely covered the entrance to the garage. Plus, it only stored footage from the last three days.

We thanked him and left.

The camera on the balcony was a little harder to track down. We tried speaking to the owner of the flat that the balcony belonged to, who was less than happy at the interruption so late at night, especially when we heard the cry of a baby inside.

She was just the tenant and didn't know anything about a camera anywhere.

We tried a few other apartments, but everyone gave the same story; they didn't know anything about a camera and told us to speak to the building's owner.

By then, it was gone 10pm and too late to call the business number in Genoa that the first tenant had given us.

"Best head back then. We can call the landlord tomorrow. Pay him a visit if we need to," said Cooper.

I nodded, mute.

I'm not sure what I'd expected, but this felt too much like a dead end, too much like we were putting a pause on the whole thing, and I'm not sure I could cope with a whole night of waiting. I knew I wasn't going to be able to sleep.

We headed back to the rented Lancia and Cooper drove us back to the apartment, making sure to park a few streets away as a precaution.

"We've made good progress today," he said, clapping me on my wounded shoulder.

I winced and bit back the yelp that wanted to escape.

"Ah, sorry mate," he said.

Outside of the apartment, he paused. Then turned to look at me.

"Fancy going for a beer?" he asked.

"Absolutely," I said. Perhaps drowning the images of a beaten and bloody Stacey from my mind with alcohol was the only answer.

Chapter 42

Jason Hunter

Varazze, Italy

Friday 17th June

What is that noise?

I cracked open an eye and squinted around the room.

It was the same room I'd been sleeping in for the last week. The same room Bill Cooper had been sleeping in for the last two weeks.

The noise, though.

That was new.

And my God, it was crippling.

A relentless pounding that felt like it was hammering the inside of my skull.

My mouth was dry. Parched even. Like I'd eaten a bucket of sawdust.

Vague memories came back to me.

The pharmacy.

A balding, middle-aged man.

A woman and a baby.

Stacey.

The fact that she hadn't been my first thought made my guts twist, and I instantly sat up.

But I really shouldn't have.

I just about made it to the bathroom down the hall before vomiting into the toilet.

And that's when I remembered the beers.

I groaned.

Rinsing my mouth with water from the sink, I brushed my teeth and then headed back to the room.

Cooper was sitting up on the other rickety metal-framed bed and grinning at me.

"You are far too happy for someone who drank that much," I croaked, my raspy voice sounding even worse after being dehydrated by alcohol.

"I actually didn't drink that much," he said with a smirk. "At least not as much as someone."

"Will you stop grinning at me," I groaned, and dropped onto my bed, my face scrunched up against the bright sunlight streaming in through the windows. I let out another groan and covered my face with my hand, hoping the room would stop spinning and the nausea would subside.

"Nope."

I could hear the smile in his voice.

"You're enjoying this way too much," I muttered.

"Yep."

There was a silence. I dropped my hand and glanced at Cooper, his grin growing impossibly wider.

I rolled my eyes.

"Where's the best spot for a hangover cure?" I asked.

"I know just the place," he said, still grinning.

We stopped at a quaint little hole-in-the-wall espresso bar that was just up the coast on the way to Genoa. The kind of place you'd never know was there unless you were a local dog walker or maybe one of the runners jogging along the coastal path.

A couple of tables were set up out front, but they were mostly empty. It was still early, especially for a Saturday. It was a miracle the place was open really, considering most places didn't open until noon on the weekend.

Just as we sat down, my phone rang. Pulling it from my pocket, I let out a groan when I saw Hayley's name on the screen.

"I distinctly remember saying I'd phone you when I had an update," I said as I answered.

"I thought you'd like to know the investigating team has officially confirmed the weapon that shot you is the same one that killed Alfonso Torres."

That got my attention.

I sat up straight.

"Fuck."

"Exactly," she agreed.

"And what about Gromov?" I asked.

I glanced across the table to see Cooper watching me closely. *Shit.* How much could I say in front of him? Hayley would get into trouble just for telling me. How much damage could he do with this information?

"No news on the Gromov murder yet. It's looking unlikely that we'll be able to prove anything unless we can find out who bankrolled the hits. If we can find them, we might have a chance of linking Gromov."

I took a moment to look out to sea, processing exactly what this meant. Someone was killing off the rich and powerful to cover their tracks.

"Is there a money trail?" I asked. Cooper cocked an eyebrow at that.

"I need a suspect first. Can't follow the money if I don't have a start point. Besides, I'm not the SIO, remember? I'm just getting updates as a courtesy and giving advice when they need it. They're checking ballistics against Gemma and Mickey's murders, so I might get roped in if that comes back as a match. But that's relying on the killer having the same weapon as last year. Unlikely, if you ask me."

I nodded.

"Well, thanks for letting me know."

"Of course. Any update on your end?"

"We've found CCTV footage of Liam visiting a pharmacy. We're just tracking down the owner of a private camera that might have caught the number plate of his car."

"Sounds promising," she said, a glimmer of hope in her voice.

"I'll call if we find him," I said and then ended the call.

"Well, that was an interesting conversation," said Cooper expectantly.

I ignored him and instantly called Sam. He answered on the second ring.

"Boss."

"Looks like Britland's a higher-profile target than we initially thought. Hayley's confirmed it was the same weapon that shot me and killed Torres, which means—"

"They might target him again," Sam finished my sentence for me.

"Exactly," I said. This was really, really bad news. If someone was going round with a celebrity hitlist, we were right in the firing line. "Have you put yourself on rotation, or are you just running operations?" I asked.

"I'm on rotation," he answered. Good lad. Sam was like me and couldn't help but be in the trenches. It's one of the many reasons why my teams trusted him; he wasn't afraid to do the job with them.

"Perfect. I need you to keep your eyes and ears open. I don't want you caught off guard."

"Yes, boss," said Sam.

"Oh, and Sam," I said. "Do me a favour and swing by my place. I had a call from Britland yesterday. He's pissed, and I don't like what he insinuated."

"What—?"

"I'll fill you in later," I said, cutting him off as I glanced across the table at Cooper, who was trying very hard to look disinterested in my conversation.

"Sure thing, boss," he said and hung up.

Cooper reached into the back pocket of his jeans and pulled out the business card the woman with the baby had given us last night. I watched as he typed the number into his phone and then put it to his ear.

Putting my phone away, I thanked the waitress who brought two espressos to our table.

Cooper then said something in Italian and hung up.

"No luck?" I asked.

"Voicemail." He picked up his espresso, downed it in one, and reached into his other back pocket for a wallet. Pulling a few notes from it, he dumped them on the table and then stood. I downed my own espresso, relishing the burn in my throat, and followed suit.

"I think we should go pay the landlord a visit," he said. "And on the way, you can tell me what the fuck is going on."

Chapter 43

STACEY JAMES

LOCATION UNKNOWN

Friday 17th June

She felt weak and groggy. Again.

The cloud slowly lifted from her brain after what felt like hours of lying motionless in her bed, but it could have been minutes for all she could tell.

She opened her eyes, and the room slowly came into focus.

She felt *awful*.

Worse than that.

She felt like she was going to be sick.

She shifted on the bed and then froze.

There was a body next to her.

A big, warm body that was snoring softly.

And then she felt the soreness between her thighs.

Tears pricked at her eyes as she realised once again how Liam had violated her in the most heinous way possible.

She rolled onto her side, knowing she'd be too weak to stand and make it to the bathroom, and then wretched over the side of the bed. There'd be hell to pay for it later, but it would be her cleaning it up anyway. Except, there was nothing in her stomach to throw up.

Instead, the acid taste of bile filled her throat as it dribbled from the corner of her mouth and onto the dirty sheets.

She heard Liam's breathing change and froze, hoping he'd sleep at least a little longer. He rolled onto his side away from her, and she shakily wiped her mouth on the back of her hand. Nausea twisted her gut and she focused on taking a few deep breaths before carefully rolling onto her back and glancing at Liam.

His top half was naked and he was facing away from her. She was still fully clothed though. Carefully moving her hand over her body, she could feel the scanty vest and shorts set that she wore as pyjamas. Which meant he'd been rough with her last night.

Having been conscious for far too many of his episodes, she knew that his insatiable need would have taken over, and he would have simply yanked her clothes out of the way for access.

Carefully, she sat up and slid from the bed, trying her best not to jostle him. It was a painfully slow process; move too quickly and she'd be sure to wake him, but if she took much longer, he'd wake up anyway.

As the bedroom was the only room he didn't keep her chained up like an animal, she was able to quietly slip into the en-suite and close the door behind her with a soft click. No lock, of course.

She turned the tap on and greedily scooped the water into her hand, slurping it as quietly as she could. Satisfied, she scooped a final handful of water and splashed it on her face. Looking into the mirror above the sink, she didn't recognise the woman staring back.

Gone was the strong-willed woman. Gone was the glint of determination. Instead, the woman looking back at her was haggard, thin, and sickly. She looked like she would keel over at the slightest breeze. It was a shock, but it wasn't unexpected. She didn't feel strong. She didn't feel determined. She wasn't even sure how many days had passed since

Liam had brought her here, but during that time he had utterly and thoroughly broken her spirit.

How much more could she really take?

I won't die today. I won't die today.

She repeated the mantra to herself, just as she had done since the day Liam took her.

She thought of Jason as the tears began to fall, and wondered whether he would still love her if he could see her like this.

She thought of his beautiful kids; 8-year-old Max who loved racing and playing on the PlayStation, and 6-year-old Lily, the kindest, sweetest soul Stacey knew, who loved to colour and draw pictures.

She thought of how she adored them both and how, as a family, they'd welcomed her with open arms.

The tears were falling freely down her cheeks, and she just couldn't stop them.

"Stace?" came Liam's voice from the bedroom.

Her heart instantly lurched into her throat and her tears dried up. Frantically wiping her hands down her face, Stacey wiped away all trace of weakness.

Now, when she looked in the mirror, she saw someone who wanted to live to see her loved ones. She saw someone who would fight until the very end.

She splashed more water on her face and took a final deep breath.

"In here," she called back. "I'll just be a minute."

Moving to the toilet, she closed the seat and stepped up so she was standing on the lid. Leaning forward so one foot was on the sink, she reached a hand up to where the cistern was mounted on the wall and felt around for the tea towel she'd carefully placed there a few days before.

Now wasn't the time, but at some point soon, that tea towel would be her ticket out of there.

Chapter 44

Jason Hunter

Genoa, Italy

Friday 17th June

I'd tried the landlord's number a few times while Cooper had driven us to the address on the back of the business card. But each time it had gone straight to voicemail. I'd hung up without bothering to leave a message.

"Sounds sloppy to me," he said.

"What do you mean?"

"The Alfonso Torres murder was at least two weeks ago, right? So why hasn't he disposed of the weapon? Why has he used the same rifle on two different jobs?"

"Good point," I muttered. I didn't have an answer, but it did make me realise that Cooper would know this guy's mindset a hell of a lot better than me.

We pulled up outside a nondescript office block.

I made a mental note to ask him more about the shooter and see if he'd be willing to share any other trade insights.

I looked up at the building where the landlord supposedly worked. The façade was bleak at best. While Varazze was quaint and charming with typical Italian architecture, Genoa was a mix of heritage and modernisation, with a large number of buildings lacking character completely.

I knew Genoa was a medieval hub. I'd seen as such on my first journey here when Cooper had collected me from the airport. But looking up at the address the sat nav had brought us to, it was hard to imagine this city was anything but drab.

Cooper killed the engine, and we both climbed from the car.

"Certainly doesn't look like much," I said.

Cooper didn't reply, just squinted up at the office block.

The whole thing stuck out like a sore thumb. On either side, the buildings were a typical yellow and peach with the classic little Italian balconies and white shutters. However, this building was made of grey concrete.

The ground floor was occupied by a row of shops, a veterinarian, and a café, all of which looked closed.

We entered the lobby of the building and found it was deserted. On the wall next to the lifts was a directory of businesses. Scanning through the names, we found the one we were looking for.

Up on the third floor, we found the right door. The plaque on it said *Casa Bellissima*, but the door itself had seen better days.

"*Casa Bellissima*, my ass," muttered Cooper.

I smiled. The guy had a point.

Cooper gave a sharp knock on the door and then opened it.

Inside was a sparsely furnished reception with a dehydrated fern plant in the corner. A woman sat behind the single desk in the room, typing at a computer. The phone on her desk began ringing and she ignored it, continuing her typing. Eventually the phone rang out.

Cooper cleared his throat and the woman said something in Italian, not even bothering to look at us.

He looked at me and the smirk on his face was unmistakable.

Cooper walked past the receptionist's desk, and I quickly followed. We headed down a basic corridor with just two doors. The first one was open and led into a boardroom. The table had seen better days and most of the chairs were missing. At the end of the short corridor was another door, this one was closed.

The receptionist had scrambled to her feet and was shouting at us in Italian. Cooper ignored her and the door at the end of the corridor opened before we even reached it, revealing a middle-aged man with slick-backed hair wearing a poorly fitting suit. He was scowling at the commotion and his eyes widened in surprise when he saw us coming towards him.

Without breaking his stride, Cooper grabbed he guy by the collar and shoved him into the room and up against the wall. I swiftly closed the door behind us, giving a brief nod to the receptionist who watched, dumbstruck.

The man was speaking rapid Italian, a look of panic on his face. His hands were up, fingers splayed and palms facing Cooper in a gesture of surrender.

"Stay by the door," Cooper said to me.

"Sure thing."

"*Inglese?*" said the man.

Now that I did understand.

"Do you speak it?"

"*Sí, sí,*" he said, nodding enthusiastically. "I do business with English," he said, his accent thick.

"What kind of business?" I asked.

He paused at that, clearly not expecting us to question him.

"Holiday rentals," he said, suddenly regaining his composure. He looked from me to Cooper, who still had him pinned to the wall.

Whatever he'd thought when we'd first walked in, he was reassessing the situation.

"You're not *Ndrangheta*?" he asked.

It wasn't a term I was familiar with.

Cooper barked out a laugh. "Do we look like the mafia?" he asked.

My eyebrows shot up. Mafia? Just who the hell was this guy?

He seemed to regain his composure before shouting, "What are doing?" Followed by some angry Italian. I guessed he was swearing at us.

"No need for that," said Cooper.

The guy kept speaking in Italian, and Cooper's face darkened.

"We just need—"

"*Vaffanculo!*" the landlord spat. Cooper slammed the man into the wall, let go of his suit jacket, and punched him square in the face. I heard the crunch of bone and winced as the man's face exploded, and a stream of red gushed from his nose. He screamed and shouted at us some more.

Cooper took a step back and flexed his hand.

"Good receptionist," he said, nodding towards the door. "She hears you scream and doesn't even come running. Do you get beaten often?" he asked with a smirk.

I couldn't help my own ghost of a smile at the comment. Cooper had a point.

"Do you think she'll call the police?" he asked, turning to me.

"I could always go and check," I suggested with a shrug.

"*No, no,* no police. She not call police."

"Look, we just need you to show us the footage from your apartment block and then we'll be out of your hair." Cooper said it in the friendliest tone I'd ever heard, as if he hadn't just broken this guy's nose.

Cradling his nose in an attempt to staunch the bleeding, the landlord stumbled over to his desk. He fumbled around in a drawer and pulled out a packet of tissues. I stayed by the door, not wanting to give him a clear run to the exit. I noticed that Cooper didn't move either.

We watched the landlord clumsily try to clean himself up, not that it made much of a difference. Blood stained the front of his suit and shirt. It covered his hand and was already starting to dry on his face from where he'd wiped at it.

Pinching his nose and leaning forward slightly, he let out a long, exasperated sigh.

"What you want?" he asked.

"You own a block of flats on Via Gio Batta Camogli. Wednesday last week, this man—" Cooper pulled the photo of Liam from his pocket and showed it to the landlord, "—visited the pharmacy. We need to see the CCTV footage you have of the street."

"Last week?" he asked nervously.

"Yes, Wednesday 8th April," I clarified.

He glanced between us and wetted his lips. "I-I don't know if I have footage from last week. I-I think it deletes every seven days."

"You better hope, for your sake, that you're wrong," said Cooper, his tone menacing.

The man nodded and opened the laptop sitting on his desk. He glanced at us a few times over the screen as he clicked buttons and then typed on the keyboard.

Cooper wandered over to the window where a grimy set of yellowing blinds had been pulled down.

"Nice view," he said, using his fingers to widen the gap between the blinds.

The landlord's eyes darted from the computer screen to Cooper and back again, clearly agitated and torn between logging into the

CCTV footage and keeping an eye on Cooper. I had to admit, I'd probably be doing the same in his shoes. Cooper was clearly unpredictable. Even I didn't know what he was going to do next, and I bloody knew the guy. Well, kind of. The more time I spent with him, the more I realised I didn't really know him at all.

"Here, here," said the landlord, pointing to the screen. "It deletes every two weeks."

"Excellent," said Cooper. And that's when I realised why he'd gone to the window. It put him so much closer to the desk. He turned and took the two steps he needed so he could peer over the landlord's shoulder and see the screen. "Show me."

Glancing at the office door, I joined Cooper behind the landlord as he loaded the footage from last Wednesday.

"You can skip to 9.30 pm. The guy arrived not long before closing."

The landlord did as instructed and we watched a very quiet, very empty street. The guy jumped forward a few minutes at a time until we saw Liam walk into view.

"Where's his car?" I asked.

"Must have parked it up the street," replied Cooper with a frown.

"You don't think he walked?"

Cooper shook his head. "Unlikely. Too risky."

The landlord kept jumping forward until we saw Liam reappear from the pharmacy carrying the bag of items we'd seen him buy on the pharmacy's footage. He walked back in the direction he'd come, and I let out a frustrated growl.

"Now what?" I half-shouted.

Cooper stood up straight and crossed his arms over his chest. "I'm not sure," he said. I could see he was thinking, weighing up options.

"We'll have to see if there are any other cameras nearby. Either on this street or on others nearby. There might be some traffic cameras or community-owned ones for crime prevention." I knew I was talking to myself at this point as Cooper was still frowning at the laptop screen.

"*No, no,*" said the landlord, waving a hand at me. He beckoned for me to come back over. "Road is one way only." He pointed at the screen, and we watched a car drive past.

Cooper laughed. "Fucker tried to park out of sight but forgot the road is one way. Rewind," he said to the landlord, who did as he was told. "Pause."

Grabbing a pen from the desk and pulling the landlord's business card from his pocket, Cooper wrote down the license plate of the car on the screen and then took a photo. Zooming into the photo on his phone, he said, "Impossible to confirm it's Liam driving the car, but we can say it's a strong likelihood."

He handed the phone to me, and I saw what he meant. It wasn't a clear shot. The CCTV was cheap, so the image was grainy, but from what we could see, it was reasonable to assume it was Liam.

Cooper clapped me on the shoulder as he took his phone back.

"Let's go get this bastard," he said.

said and took a sip of my Coke. It was still early, and after the previous night's rowdy drinking, I didn't fancy getting wasted again.

We looked out over the water and watched a couple of skippers tidy up the vessels they were on before leaving the marina. There was a whole row of boats close to the edge of the marina that had their own crews. We'd seen the same skippers take them out each day, and then occasionally they'd be joined by a man, usually in his mid to late fifties, who was clearly the owner, and that's when the boat would disappear for a day or so. Sometimes the owner would be accompanied by a pretty young thing who laughed and giggled and wore scandalously revealing clothes.

But there was none of that today as the afternoon slowly morphed into the evening and the sun took on that warm hue that happens just before it begins to set.

"Is she even still alive?" I asked. I didn't need to elaborate. I didn't need to clarify exactly who I was talking about. Cooper knew.

"Our girl is alive and kicking," he said.

I nodded morosely, not quite believing him.

"She's a fighter. And she's out there fighting. We've just got to go give her a hand."

Chapter 47

Jason Hunter

Boma Caffè, Varazze

Friday 17th June

Cooper's phone lay on the table between us, and the screen lit up with the name Sh4rkByte!

"Who the hell—"

Before I could finish my question, or even work out how to say the name, Cooper had swiped it from the table and answered the call, pressing the phone to his ear.

"You got something?" he asked.

And I realised this was his hacker.

God, if she did have something, she was fast. We'd only left Genoa a couple of hours ago.

"That's great. Text it to this number."

He hung up and drained his bottle of beer.

"She's tracked the car," he said, slapping a few notes down on the table.

Adrenaline coursing through my system, I followed him as we practically ran back to the apartment.

"She's tracked the car out of town," he explained as we both chucked our things into our respective holdalls. "Down the SP542, and then she picks him up a bit later on the SP334. She loses him at a little village called Giovo Ligure. He could have gone one of two ways but she can't be sure which. The village has a garage, but it's old school. Their cameras aren't connected to the cloud, so she can't access them remotely. We'll start there."

I nodded, zipped up my bag, and followed Cooper down the stairs, silently hoping we wouldn't be coming back. Because I was praying with everything I had that we were on our way to get Stacey.

Back outside, we headed to the car, chucked our bags in the boot and climbed in. Cooper didn't waste any time in turning on the ignition and getting us onto one of the main roads out of town.

SP542 was one of only two roads that led inland - the others trailed along the coast. This meant there were fewer people and not many stops along the way. Less stops meant less cameras and far too many rural tracks for my liking. There was a high possibility we might lose Liam's trail. It was already a week old which didn't bode well.

Despite being a main road, it was still treacherous. Winding through the hilly terrain that surrounded Varazze, it narrowed dangerously in some areas where overgrown trees made it impossible for more than one car to pass at a time. Thankfully, we didn't meet many other cars on the road, but when we did, Cooper slammed the brakes on, jarring my shoulder painfully as I was pitched forward and then slammed back into my seat.

On the other side of San Martino, the SP542 merged with the SP334 and continued further into the countryside. It only took about half an hour to reach the small village of Giovo Ligure. And it really was just a village. The SP334 passed through the middle and then forked.

Small houses lined either side of the road, but there wasn't much else. Not even a convenience store. Cooper went right at the fork and pulled up at the garage. After a few moments, a man in his sixties wearing dirty overalls appeared from the garage building. He ambled over to us and then leaned down to speak to Cooper through the window.

"*Inglese?*" Cooper asked.

The man shook his head and said something in Italian, so Cooper instantly switched languages to explain why we were there.

The man stooped lower to squint at me and then nodded his head, gesturing for us to follow him. We both climbed out of the car, and I could feel the adrenaline pumping through me, drumming a relentless beat in my ears. We were so close. I could *feel* it.

Cooper threw me a sideways glance as we approached the garage shop.

"What?" I asked.

He ignored me.

Opening the door, we walked past the boxes of groceries that were propped up outside and entered the dimly lit garage. While the outside was coated in peeling paint and looked set to collapse at any second, the interior was spotless. Clean black and white tiles checkered across the floor, while neat lines of shelves dominated the space, filled with carefully organised groceries.

This was a man who took pride in his work. He shuffled behind the counter and gestured to the old TV mounted on the wall. It showed a live feed of the forecourt and the familiar black Lancia parked there.

Cooper pulled the dog-eared photo of Stacey from his pocket and showed it the garage attendant. He shook his head, so Cooper showed him the photo of Liam. This one just as dog-eared from the number of times I'd seen him take it out of his pocket to show someone.

The garage attendant paused and then nodded. My heart rate sped up, and I inched forward, unable to stop myself.

Cooper offered him a small smile and pocketed the two photos. Then he pulled out his phone and showed the images he'd taken from the CCTV at the pharmacy, and the photo of the car we'd acquired from the landlord in Genoa.

Again, the garage attendant paused, looking thoughtful. He nodded and spoke, but I could feel frustration begin to creep along my skin. It wasn't anything new. During my time here, I'd felt like a useless third wheel, and my inability to speak the language only exacerbated the issue.

"*Sì, mercoledì,*" said Cooper.

And a torrent of Italian spewed from the garage attendant's mouth.

"*Più lentamente, per favore,*" Cooper chuckled.

Suddenly, the man started speaking more slowly, and there was more back and forth as Cooper clarified information. I was completely excluded, and I shuffled restlessly from foot to foot just for something to do.

Cooper held out a hand and the man shook it, giving him a big smile.

"*Ci vediamo,*" said Cooper,

"*Ciao,*" the garage attendant replied with a smile. There was that Cooper charm in action once again.

We left the small shop and Cooper let out a long sigh.

"Right," he said. "Good news and bad news."

Chapter 48

JASON HUNTER

GIOVO LIGURE, ITALY

Friday 17th June

"What's the bad news?" I asked.

"The bad news is the garage doesn't record its CCTV. They just use it as a live feed of the forecourt," said Cooper.

We climbed back into the car.

"So, what's the good news?" I asked, glancing at my watch. It was getting pretty late, and I wasn't sure how much more we could achieve before everything would be closed. I looked up and down the road, seeing nothing. Not that there was anything to be open.

"The good news," said Cooper, starting the engine, "is this little hamlet has a B&B, and as it's not hiking season, it's likely they'll have some rooms for us. Oh, and there's a restaurant next door," he added.

Ah, that answered that question then. We'd be here until we could find the next lead.

Turned out the B&B was just up the road. The old guy at the garage had given Cooper directions and had warned him that it wasn't at all fancy, to which Cooper had reassured him that we'd be fine.

As he drove, Cooper filled me in on the rest of the conversation he'd had with the attendant. The man hadn't recognised Stacey's photo, but he had recognised Liam's and had told Cooper he'd seen the car at least twice, which told me Liam couldn't be that far away.

A quarter of a mile up the road, Cooper took a left, and we pulled into the large front courtyard of a three-storey building with the large letters *Albergo Ligure* painted across the brickwork on either side of two recessed balconies that belonged to the upper floors.

Pretty hanging baskets hung from the balcony railings, with flowers in full bloom and thick ivy climbing up the old copper drainpipe on one side. All the windows were covered with dark wooden shutters, and if it weren't for the people occupying the white plastic chairs out front, it would have looked abandoned. Seated at white plastic tables, each with their own white parasol, the restaurant-goers all looked up from their food and halted their conversations as we pulled up and then climbed out of the car.

"Don't expect a warm welcome," muttered Cooper, slamming his car door shut.

"Why not?"

"Small town life. We're clearly not hikers or holidaymakers, so they're going to be wary."

"We could be," I grumbled as Cooper shot me a smirk.

"*Buonasera*," said Cooper with a wave and a smile I'm sure was meant to be charming.

No one replied, they just watched us approach.

Cooper said something in Italian, but still no one replied. We halted a few feet away, and I watched as the locals exchanged glances.

A woman appeared in the main doorway and waved to us.

"*Buonasera*," she said with a friendly smile and ran forward to greet us, wiping her hands on the apron tied around her waist as she did.

She waved at the locals over her shoulder, who all went back to their food as she spoke.

"Ignore them," she said, switching to English and offering me a warm smile, her eyes glancing down to the sling around my left arm.

She must have been in her mid-sixties, with grey hair that was braided and wrapped around her head like a crown. Her plump face was weathered, and her eyes crinkled when she smiled.

"I'm Maddalena, but call me Lena. Me and my husband own the B&B," she gestured at the building behind her. "My husband cooks in the kitchen. Please, come. Edoardo telephoned to say you would be coming."

"Edoardo?" asked Cooper.

"He owns the garage."

Blimey, how long did it take us to drive the 250 metres up the road, if Edoardo had time to call ahead?

Cooper nodded as if it were the most natural thing in the world.

Lena led us into the empty downstairs restaurant, past the bar and through to a small reception room where an old wooden counter was mounted into the wall. She disappeared through a door to the left and then reappeared on the other side, pulling an old, heavy-looking book from underneath the counter. Behind her were several rows of hooks, each with a key dangling from it.

"Two rooms, yes?" she said and glanced up at us.

"Yes, two rooms," said Cooper.

"We don't know how long we'll need to stay," I added.

Lena glanced at me and offered her cherubic smile again. "No problem," she said. "Two-night minimum stay, and then you pay per night."

"Perfect," I nodded. Cooper agreed.

She scribbled something in the heavy book before turning and reaching for two sets of keys. She placed them on the counter between us.

"Breakfast is at 6am. We serve dinner from 7pm. You can join us once you have seen your rooms," she said with another smile and gestured through to the restaurant.

"That would be great, thanks," I said, admiring how good her English was.

Taking our keys, we headed back out to the car. Cooper opened the boot and I took out my holdall, hoisting it up over my good shoulder.

"I don't know about you," said Cooper. "But I'm famished. I'm gonna grab a shower. Dinner in 30?"

"Sounds good to me." And it really did. The wash facilities at the apartment in Varazze had been sparse at best. And it was made even more difficult with the limited movement in my arm. But it was starting to loosen up a little. It certainly didn't feel as tight.

Following the instructions that Lena had given us, we found our rooms next to each other on the first floor, with a connected balcony that overlooked the front. And blissfully, a decent shower in the en-suite bathroom.

I dumped my holdall on the bed, stripped off my clothes and carefully extracted my arm from the sling. I rotated my shoulder, still wincing slightly when I pulled my arm back, but it felt almost normal. I examined the stitches in my shoulder, noticing how a couple had already begun to fall out, and the skin underneath was healing nicely.

I carefully washed the wound in the shower as I'd been instructed at the hospital, and after my shower, I did my daily exercises to help keep the muscle moving.

Dressed in a pair of worn jeans, I was interrupted by a knock at my door. I opened it to see Cooper looking clean and fresh.

"Not quite ready?" he asked as he took in my shirtless state and then glanced at my unbandaged shoulder.

"Obviously not," I said and rolled my eyes. I headed over to the vanity table where I'd dumped my bag of medical supplies. Mostly pain killers and a few new bandages. Rummaging through the bag, I pulled out a packet that contained a square gauze pad with an adhesive border.

I ripped open the packet and then peeled back the first corner.

"Want a hand?" offered Cooper.

"Sure," I said. With expert ease, he peeled the adhesive backing and then placed the island dressing over my stitches. "You clearly do this far too often," I muttered.

"Not your first bullet wound, eh?" he asked, too casually. He was clearly digging.

"Afghanistan. Medical discharge," I said.

I watched as Cooper's eyebrows shot up.

"What? Your background check didn't tell you that I was in the army?"

"Can't say it went into that much detail."

"Liar," I said with a half-smile.

"I knew you were medically discharged. I didn't know why."

"Well, now you do. Happy?"

He didn't say anything, just gave me a single nod. And then we left for dinner.

Chapter 49

JASON HUNTER

GIOVO LIGURE, ITALY

Friday 17ᵗʰ June

We sat down at one of the tables near to the bar. A couple of old-time locals were propping the bar up, while the restaurant goers who'd been sat outside when we'd arrived had gone and the place was pretty quiet.

"Ah, there you are," said Lena when she spotted us. "Tonight's special is stockfish stew. And I would recommend our *chinotto* sorbet afterwards."

"Sounds great," said Cooper. "And some *farinata* on the side."

Lena beamed and then bustled off into the kitchen to give the order to her husband.

"Farinata?" I asked.

"It's a flatbread made from chickpeas."

"Of course it is," I said.

"So what's the plan, big man?"

"You're asking me?" I said, surprised. This was Cooper's gig. I was just here to help. Well, here to stick my nose in because sitting back and twiddling my thumbs while my shoulder healed was a big fat no.

"I've made all the plans so far, I want to hear your thoughts."

It felt like a test.

"Well..." I thought for a moment. "We could ask at all the houses and businesses along the main road to see if any of them have any CCTV, but that would be really time-consuming. We could keep showing Liam's photo around and see if anyone else recognises him."

Cooper nodded his agreement just as Lena arrived with our food. She placed two bowls of stockfish stew on the table, one in front of each of us, and a wrought iron dish on the chunk of wood in the middle of the table. In the dish was the thin flatbread-like farinata, embellished with thinly sliced onion and black pepper.

I thanked Lena and took a tentative bite of the stew. It was delicious. A little salty, slightly fishy, and whatever she'd added to the stew created a complex taste I didn't think I'd ever be able to replicate. It's like the flavours exploded onto my tongue.

"Good?" she asked, still hovering at our table.

"Amazing," I said, and she rewarded me with the biggest smile.

"*Buon appetite*," she said and then left.

Cooper helped himself to a slice of the farinata. "You were saying?" he prompted.

It took me a moment to regain my train of thought. "Er, yeah. So, we could show Liam's photo around, like we did in Varazze, but that relies on potluck and might take a while. And that makes me nervous."

Cooper nodded and took a bite of his stew.

"If he hasn't exited the village by one of the two main roads, then unless he's here, he's likely taken a lesser-known road. Did your hacker mention where the next camera is on the road? That would give us a perimeter to work with. I suggest that we show Liam's face to as many people as we can; it doesn't hurt to have people on the lookout for him. And at the same time, we map out all possible routes and explore them in the car in the morning."

"Solid plan," said Cooper, who was now more than halfway through his stew.

After Lena had cleared away the plates, we both enjoyed two scoops of her chinotto sorbet, which was the perfect bittersweet palate cleanser.

A couple of tables had come and gone in the time it had taken us to eat our food and discuss our next move. Now, our bellies full and table cleared, we sat with a beer each. The restaurant had closed, and only the bar remained open. The locals still sat at the bar, chatting.

We were close enough that I could hear everything that was being said. Just a damn shame I didn't speak Italian. Occasionally, Lena would chime in.

"I think—" I said.

"Sssh," hissed Cooper. And that's when I noticed he was covertly eavesdropping on whatever conversation was happening at the bar.

Lena served them two new drinks, and then she was embroiled in whatever it was they were discussing.

A smile curved Cooper's lips.

"I think I know where we're gonna start looking tomorrow," he said.

Chapter 50

WESLEY GRAY

AURORA'S, LONDON

Friday 17th June

Wesley Gray was a very rich man. And that made him very happy.

He'd spent the first 20 years of his life grafting hard, right up until he found himself in the world of financial banking. Specifically, as a hedge fund manager. From there, it was a cutthroat rise to the top. And he wasn't ashamed to say he'd screwed a fair few people along the way.

But that was the beauty of being so filthy rich. He didn't need to worry about shit like that anymore.

He could do what he wanted, when he wanted. And on Fridays, he wanted to be sitting at his regular table at Aurora's, Soho's chicest restaurant. Known for its flamboyant history as a former brothel, Aurora's was an exclusive club for the mega-rich.

Which is exactly where he was.

It wasn't a big place, but it was still decadent in every way imaginable, with tables spaced far enough apart that multi-million-pound business deals could be discussed without the risk of being overheard. It was famed for its extensive drinks list with wines from all around the world, some of which were almost a hundred years old. And the best part? The Michelin-star, world-renowned chef in the kitchen delivering a fresh menu every week.

The room was accented with deep red walls, plush leather chairs, and artwork from the latest talent London had to offer. It was full, as it always was. It took months to get a table at Aurora's.

But Wesley Gray had a permanent reservation.

Second table along, at the front. Far enough away from the door that he wouldn't be disturbed, but close enough that he didn't feel like he was at the back of the room.

The waiters all knew him.

He tipped generously, so they knew to anticipate his every whim.

Now in his fifties, Wesley Gray had long since retired. If retired was even the right word. Sure, he owned London's largest investment firm that spanned multiple continents and had huge offices in all the major worldwide cities; New York, Singapore, Hong Kong, and San Francisco to name a few. They were just his favourites, and he visited them all regularly, mostly for pleasure, not business.

Turns out when you're not chained to a desk from 6am to 9pm, there's a lot of pleasure out there in the world. A lot of women who would happily throw themselves at him. And he didn't even need to treat them well.

Opposite him sat his latest conquest. She was tall, long-legged, and had black chin-length hair. He'd surprised himself really, because normally he was into big-boobed blondes, but this one had practically fallen into his lap at the fundraiser gala on Tuesday, and she was deliciously submissive in the bedroom.

The waiter approached the table to take their order.

"Good evening, Mr Gray," he said.

"My usual wine," said Wesley Gray. "And we'll both have the chef's special."

The menu didn't offer a chef's special. But it had become a tradition of sorts. It normally resulted in a hand-picked dish from the menu with an added flourish.

The waiter nodded, jotted the order down onto his little pad and then disappeared from the table, taking the menus with him. Another thing he liked about this place – it was old school.

No mobile phones allowed inside. Which meant no cameras. Making it the perfect place to meet with people you didn't want to be seen with by the paparazzi. It didn't stop them camping outside almost 24/7, but it did offer a modicum of privacy that was impossible to get anywhere else.

Less than five minutes later, another waiter appeared at the table carrying the already uncorked wine. He showed Wesley Gray the bottle and poured it into the wine glasses on the table. Normally, Wesley Gray would be offered the courtesy of tasting the wine before being poured an entire glass.

He glanced up at the waiter and realised that it wasn't a face he recognised. In fact, it was a perfectly neutral face, the kind you forgot almost instantly after seeing it. The waiter didn't smile or acknowledge him in any way. He simply finished pouring and paused as Wesley Gray brought the wine to his lips and took a sip. Then the waiter gave a small nod of his head and left.

Frowning, Wesley Gray took another sip of the wine, wondering at the strange behaviour. It tasted perfectly fine. Not that he was a wine connoisseur by any means, he just liked the feeling of power that came from buying expensive things.

Glancing across the table, his date looked bored. Her eyes were flitting around the room, clocking the different faces sitting at the tables, and he immediately regretted bringing her. But there was nothing he could do about it now.

He opened his mouth to speak, but a wave of dizziness overcame him and he gripped the arm of his chair. His breath came in frantic pants and the glass of wine slipped from his fingers, spilling on the plush cream carpet as he gasped for air.

Desperately, he pushed his chair away from the table in an attempt to stand up, but he couldn't breathe. By now, restaurant-goers were turning to stare at the commotion, and several waiters rushed forward to assist as he fell to the floor.

"Someone call an ambulance!" shouted his date, horror written all over her face.

But it was too late.

Wesley Gray was dead.

Chapter 51

STACEY JAMES

LOCATION UNKNOWN

Saturday 18th June

This was it.

It had to be.

She wasn't sure how much more of it she could take.

Wrapped in a tea towel and hidden in her en-suite toilet was her salvation. Her escape. She just needed to time it right.

There was a deep cut on her cheek, and her right eye was swollen shut from last night. Liam had backhanded her so hard she'd seen stars. Collapsed on the floor, he'd completely lost it, kicking her with all the force he had. At least two of her ribs were broken.

She had no idea what had triggered the outburst.

When they'd first arrived, she'd been able to anticipate his moods more easily. She'd been able to see what his triggers were and avoid them as much as possible. But as the days had trickled past, his volatility had become so much worse. He was aggressive and violent with no warning.

He rarely left the house now. At first, he'd pop out for supplies and would be gone for hours at a time. It was a sweet reprieve. But these days, he barely left her alone in a room for more than five minutes.

Being cooped up was putting him on edge and it was making her nervous.

Any hope of life outside of this living hell was slowly fading away. There was a tiny glimmer deep down. She knew Jason would be looking for her. She knew he'd be doing everything he could to find her. But it wasn't enough. She didn't know how much more of this she could take.

She was in the kitchen, again. This time, cooking breakfast. Liam had brought some eggs in from outside. Where he'd got them from, she had no idea. But here she was, cooking his eggs.

Liam was nearby, moving between the kitchen and the living room where he had the news on. She was watching him from the corner of her eye.

Today was the day. No more of this shit.

She'd managed to swipe some of whatever it was he kept drugging her with a couple of days ago. He'd been distracted. Not as sneaky as he usually was. And now she was just waiting for the opportune moment.

She stirred the scrambled eggs in the pan.

Liam wandered into the kitchen to check on her and then wandered back out again.

And this was her chance.

She pulled the harmless-looking pills from her pocket and crushed them, tipping the powdery contents into the eggs and stirred. Then she scooped up the pill casings and threw them into her mouth. Less risk of being found out that way. She tried to swallow, but her throat was so dry. Too dry to swallow. They lodged at the back of her throat, and she could feel herself beginning to choke.

As calmly as she could, she reached for a glass and filled it with water from the tap, knowing the noise would bring Liam back into the kitchen. Whether it would bring his wrath, she didn't know. It was a risk that she would have to take.

And there he appeared, in the doorway. A frown on his face as he watched her drink from the glass. She swallowed several gulps of water, and the pill casings eventually moved down her throat. She tried not to wince as she felt them make the long journey down into her stomach.

They sat at the large farmhouse kitchen table. Liam on one side, Stacey on the other. Her ankle still chained like she was some kind of dog.

She watched Liam as he ate his eggs with gusto while she self-consciously pushed hers around on her plate. She took one or two bites of her toast to keep up appearances, but mostly she just watched him.

She'd deliberately served him a larger portion, praying there was enough sedative in them to do the job. Because if there wasn't, she knew he'd kill her.

Chapter 52

STACEY JAMES

LOCATION UNKNOWN

Saturday 18th June

The sedative wasn't instant. But it was working. Liam was groggy and disoriented.

He stood from the table, muttering something about having a lie down, and then walked into the living room, taking the key with him.

She really hadn't thought this through.

How the hell was she going to get out of this nightmare now?

The key to her shackles was most definitely in Liam's pocket.

She'd thought he'd fall asleep at the kitchen table, or at the very least, collapse on his way out of the room. Or the sedative would have enough of a delay that he would have unchained her and moved her to the living room with him. At least then she'd have been able to get the damn key.

"Fuck," she muttered.

Sitting down in the middle of the kitchen floor, she examined the manacle around her ankle more closely. It looked like the bastard had modified a pair of handcuffs. Instead of two manacles, one for each wrist, there was one manacle attached to a chain that was tied and padlocked around the leg of the kitchen table.

She had three choices. One, try and pick the padlock holding the chain in place. That seemed impractical and she'd have to take the chain with her into the woods if she escaped. *When, not if.* Two, she could cut the chain. It didn't look that thick, but glancing around the kitchen, she wasn't sure exactly how she'd manage that. Or three, she could try to break the handcuff around her ankle. The third option seemed the most plausible.

She'd heard of characters in movies breaking a limb to escape handcuffs, but that wasn't even an option. She'd need both her feet, ankles, and legs in good working order to be able to run as far as she could from this hellhole.

The lock on the manacle seemed superficial. If she could find something small enough to get into the gap, she might be able to jimmy it open somehow. She didn't have any hair grips. That would have been her first and most obvious choice. So, what could she use?

And then she spotted it.

She glanced towards the living room where she could see Liam's arm draped over the sofa, and turned back to the kitchen sink, half-filled with soapy dishwater.

On the side, where she picked it up at least half a dozen times a day, was a wired dish scrubber. It had a wooden handle and steel bristles, perfect for getting grease off cast iron pots and pans.

She picked it up. All she had to do was extract some of the wire bristles and form her own makeshift key. How hard could it be?

Chapter 53

Jason Hunter

Giovo Ligure, Italy

Saturday 18th June

We'd woken up fairly early. Having decided exploring an unfamiliar road in the dark wouldn't have worked in our favour, we'd decided to hold off until morning.

Last night, Cooper overhead the two locals at the bar talking about their friend Giovanni, and how they hadn't seen him for at least two weeks. The friends had been over to his farmhouse, but the place had looked deserted. His truck was out front, but there was no sign of Giovanni.

"It's just so unlike him," one friend had said.

"Maybe he's gone on holiday," suggested Lena.

"What? Without telling any of us?" the other friend had asked, gesturing at the two of them at the bar.

Lena had shrugged. "You know what he's like. A liability at the best of times."

Cooper's ears had pricked, and he'd smoothly inserted himself into the conversation, asking about this Giovanni and where his farmhouse was.

And that's exactly where we were heading today.

The farmhouse was about 2 km up the road, near Sansobbia Creek.

We'd just finished breakfast when my phone rang. It was Sam.

Before I could say anything, Sam cut to the chase.

"Boss, have you seen the news?"

I frowned.

"No. What's happened?"

"There's been another murder."

My phone beeped to say I had another incoming call. Glancing at the screen, it was asking me if I wanted to put Sam on hold to answer Hayley.

"Hang on, Sam. Hayley's calling me. All good though?"

"All good," he said and hung up.

I switched to Hayley's call.

"I think you were right," she said.

"That's a very bold statement. About what exactly?" I asked.

"Last night, Wesley Gray was murdered."

Everything stopped for a moment as I processed what Hayley had just said. Wesley Gray was a big name in the finance business. And one of the names at the very top of the list of people involved in the NFT fraud ring.

This wasn't good at all.

"Sniper?" I asked.

"Actually, no."

"Oh. Then why did you think it's connected?"

"You're gonna like this," she said.

"Hang on."

Cooper appeared at the entrance to the restaurant, having popped back to his room for his car keys. He was looking at me and pointing to his watch, a look of irritation flashing across his face.

I held up a finger and mouthed 'Hayley' to him, which instantly changed his attitude. He strode over to the bar and leaned across it, looking for Lena.

"Go on," I said.

"Wesley Gray was at Aurora's last night," she said. One of the most exclusive and upmarket restaurants in London. I wasn't surprised. The guy was literally made of money. And he knew *everyone*. "He was poisoned."

"Poisoned? That doesn't match the MO of our guy."

"No, it doesn't. I think he's deliberately switching things up to get the job done and throw us off."

"Why?"

"Wesley Gray and his date were served by someone who wasn't on the payroll. The waiter who was meant to be serving their table had received an urgent family call that had distracted him. By the time he realised it was just a hoax and headed over to their table, someone had already served them their wine, and Wesley Gray was gasping on the floor. He died a few seconds later. Cyanide in the wine."

Cooper had found Lena, and now I realised why. She was turning on an old TV mounted in the corner above the bar and tuning into the international news. And there was Wesley Gray's face, plastered all over BBC Worldwide.

Finance mogul died in upscale London restaurant.

"Shit."

"Turns out, his date gave a very good description of the waiter who served the wine. They did a profile sketch. And guess what?"

"Come on, Hayley. Just spit it out, will you?"

"The sketch matched the one you did."

"Fuck. You're kidding me."

"Nope. So they've positively ID'd the guy as being the same one who gave you the memory stick and who rocked up at Mickey's funeral."

"Now what?" I asked.

"They've brought me in as a senior investigating officer. But it's not looking good. This guy is on a killing spree, and we need to stop him."

"So, you definitely think he's killing off our fraudsters?"

"I'm pretty confident."

"How many other names are on that list?" I asked, knowing I wouldn't like the answer.

"There's at least eight more names. Two of which are already in prison for corruption and bribery. But we know that won't keep them safe. Just look at what happened to Alek Gromov."

"So the question is, who of the eight left is taking them all out? Or is it someone else entirely?" I said, my brain whirring through the possibilities.

"There could be someone outside of the fraud ring list that's trying to clean house to prevent them from being dragged through the mud by association."

"Cutting all ties, so to speak."

"Exactly," said Hayley.

"Okay. I've got to go. We've got a strong lead on Stacey's location. If I think of anything else, I'll let you know."

"Good luck," she said before we both hung up.

I looked over to where Cooper was still watching BBC Worldwide, but the news story had moved on to the conflict in Iraq.

"I take it that was about Wesley Gray?" he asked without turning to look at me.

"Yeah, did they say anything of note?" I asked, gesturing to the screen.

"Not really. Didn't even mention where it happened or that he was murdered, just that it was suspicious."

"Aurora's."

"Shit. That's gonna be bad for business."

"How difficult would that be?" I asked, curious.

"What? Getting into somewhere like Aurora's? Bloody difficult. I certainly wouldn't do it that way." And just like that, I was reminded just how dangerous Cooper was. It was weird. I knew what he did for a living, but somehow my brain compartmentalised it so well. And then comments like that brought it all back.

And then something occurred to me. Cooper did run in the same professional circles as our killer, and since we'd developed a tentative friendship, perhaps there was a way he could help to put an end to the killings.

"Could your hacker friend find out who put the job out?" I asked.

Cooper looked at me, and I didn't like the expression on his face; it was cold and hard. A stark reminder that he was still a gun-for-hire.

"I wouldn't want to do that. And you shouldn't be asking me."

"Why?"

"Do you know how fucking dangerous that is? You'd be putting all our lives on the line. Not to mention my job. That's not how we do things. Clients are entitled to their anonymity. If we go breaking that, we're fucked."

I frowned. Not the response I was wanting to hear, but not entirely unexpected either.

"I get that, but a lot of people are gonna die."

"Yeah, rich pricks who probably deserve it. Mate, I'm not gonna put my neck on the line so you can be a hero."

Ouch. That comment stung. But I knew he had a point.

"You said you probably knew who it was. Is it the same guy you thought?"

Cooper held his hands up in surrender. "I'm not getting involved," he said.

I felt the frustration bubble up, but I knew what he'd said was right. My hero complex was going to get in the way. Besides, I was meant to be looking for Stacey, not chasing a highly trained hitman-for-hire across the streets of London. That was Hayley's job.

"Come on, then," I said, annoyed but changing the subject. "We're meant to be looking for Stacey."

Chapter 54

STACEY JAMES

LOCATION UNKNOWN

Saturday 18th June

Her fingers were bleeding, and she was sobbing silently, the tears streaming down her face, occasionally blurring her vision.

Each minute that ticked by felt like an hour, and at any moment, Liam was going to wake up and it would all be over.

She'd painstakingly pulled at the bristles over and over again until she'd collected enough to twist them together. But the makeshift key wasn't strong enough. Whenever she slipped it into the lock on the handcuff, the bristles bent the wrong way. She needed more of them.

Her fingers were sore, and the blood made it difficult to grip them.

She wiped her hands on her trousers and pulled a teaspoon from the drawer. Wrapping a few of the bristles around the spoon, she twisted and pulled with all her might. A whole clump of them slipped free, and she sobbed with relief.

There was a grunt from the living room, and she looked up to see Liam shifting on the sofa.

Shit. He's waking up.

She really didn't have much time left.

Adding the new bristles to her makeshift key, she twisted them until they were tight and inserted the key into the lock. Turning it one way and then another, she fiddled until she felt the tension from the lock press down on the wire bristles. Now she just needed them to be strong enough to hold. To lift the locking mechanism enough that she could slip her foot out.

And with a whoosh of relief, she was free.

Instead of rushing for the door, she ran through the living room, up the stairs and into the en-suite just as she heard a thud from the living room.

Fuck. Fuck. Fuck.

She slammed the toilet lid down and stepped up onto the toilet to retrieve her secret weapon from the tea towel that was wedged between the ceiling and the cistern. Pulling it out carefully, she gently unwrapped the large kitchen knife she'd managed to swipe during one of Liam's careless moments. She'd seen her opportunity and taken it, knowing that it was just a matter of time before she'd be rid of him for good.

Dropping the tea towel on the floor, she gripped the handle of the knife in her fist, raising it above her shoulder as she heard the heavy thuds coming up the stairs.

Liam roared.

She was ready.

Chapter 55

STACEY JAMES

LOCATION UNKNOWN

Saturday 18th June

Not giving herself time to hesitate, she rushed from the en-suite and out of the bedroom to find Liam dragging his still drugged body up the stairs.

But that wasn't what made her stop dead in her tracks.

He had a gun.

The kind that was used for hunting. The kind farmers owned. The kind that would blow her to pieces in this small space.

She didn't want to die. Not now. Not when freedom was so close.

I won't die today. I won't die today.

The stairs were clearly out of the question. She couldn't get past him. Couldn't risk the gun going off. He was sure to hit her at such close proximity, and she didn't want to risk throwing the knife and missing. Instead, she ran across the landing and into the other bedroom. The window was shuttered, but she would just have to risk it. It would be a sheer drop to the ground. With what she knew about the layout of the house, she guessed she was above the kitchen.

She grabbed the handle for the single-paned window rusted shut with age. She glanced around the room for something she could use to smash the glass.

Thud. Thud.

Liam was steadily moving up the stairs.

"Stacey!" he screamed. "What the fuck have you done?!"

Panic quickly bubbled up her throat.

She grabbed a pillow from the bed, ripped off the pillowcase and tied it around her hand before firmly holding the knife as close to the blade as she could. Raising her hand, she smashed the butt of the knife into the window, and the glass shattered. She tapped the butt on all the remaining shards that clung to the window frame before shoving open the shutters.

Sweet relief flooded through her when she saw the sloping kitchen roof only a few feet below the window ledge.

Thud. Thud.

It was going to be a tight squeeze.

The gap wasn't very wide. The window was split into two narrow rectangular frames that sat on hinges, designed to open inward. But with the hinges rusted into place, she was going to have to squeeze out through the frame.

Thud. Thud.

She climbed up onto the windowsill and stepped over onto the ledge, slipping her right shoulder through and trying her best to avoid the glass still embedded in the window frame. Still clutching the knife in her right hand, her left clung to the lintel above the window as she ducked her head out.

All she needed to do was get her leg through and then step down.

She twisted, pulled her left arm through so she was clinging to the outside lintel, and was just about to pull her left leg through when a hand wrapped around her ankle and tugged, causing her to lose her balance.

She fell backwards. And for a terrifying second, she thought she'd die.

I won't die today. I won't die today.

"You fucking bitch," snarled Liam, his face appearing in window, his arm reaching out and holding on to her.

He was either going to follow her, or pull the gun out and shoot her there.

She kicked out with her right foot, enough to make Liam loosen his hold. She scrambled to her feet, wobbling slightly as she got her footing on the uneven, sloping roof. She could see Liam raising his other hand, the one that must still have the gun. And before she could question what she was doing, she lunged forwards and buried the knife in Liam's chest.

Liam stilled. He looked down at where half of the knife and the handle still protruded from where his heart was trying to pump blood around his body.

He looked up at her, surprise written across his face.

She watched him stagger a step, but she could still see him trying to raise his left arm. She turned and ran.

Chapter 56

STACEY JAMES

LOCATION UNKNOWN

Saturday 18th June

She stumbled down the tiles of the roof, desperate to be out of sight if Liam did manage to raise that gun through the window.

Without hesitating, the adrenaline pumping hard through her system, she reached the edge of the roof, lay down on her stomach and rolled over the edge while gripping the verge. She dangled in the air for half a second before she let go and landed in a crouch, facing the kitchen window.

The dirt track that led up to the farmhouse was at the front, so she skirted around the building until she came to the front door.

She had no idea whether Liam was still at the bedroom window. Whether she'd injured him enough to stop him from coming after her or not. She took a deep breath and then took off as fast as she could, heading for the dirt track and the cover of the trees as it curved away from the house. It wouldn't take her that long to find someone, surely?

There was a vehicle of some kind nearby, she was sure of it. How else had Liam been getting supplies? He sure as hell hadn't been walking for miles. She'd always heard the low grumble of the engine when he started it up, but she'd never actually seen it. And as she sprinted across the open ground, she caught sight of it, parked up behind an outhouse. But something in her screamed to keep running. She didn't have the key, wouldn't know how to hotwire it, and all she wanted to do was get away.

I won't die today. I won't die today.

She pumped her arms and legs as hard as she could, feeling twinges in her ribs, her shoulder, and her ankle. But she shoved all thoughts of pain from her mind as best she could as she focused on the freedom that was so close.

I won't die today. I won't die today.

She made it to the trees and risked a glance over her shoulder just before the house disappeared from view. It was eerily quiet. As if the weeks of abuse that had taken place inside were just in her imagination.

With each step, she could feel her pace slowing.

No. No. No.

She didn't want to stop. She needed to keep going. But her lungs were on fire, and she was gasping for air.

A few more steps and she was clutching a stitch in her side.

A few more, and the pain in her ribs was starting to take over. It felt like a slow burn that was spreading over her middle.

She slowed to a walk, risking a glance over her shoulder again, but the trees obscured her view. She'd cleared a few hundred metres but it was nowhere near enough.

Swallowing the thick mucus-like saliva that was coating the back of her throat, she broke into a steady jog, hoping to put as much distance between herself and the house as possible.

If Liam did make it to the front, she was sure he had a key to the old off-roader parked by the outbuilding.

Up ahead, a black car came into view, and she didn't dare let herself hope that this might all be over.

The car slowed.

Nervous, hopeful, scared, she slowed to a walk as the car doors opened.

Two men climbed out of the car and her heart sank.

They were tall, well-built, and rushing towards her.

That's when she realised that she knew them.

The one on the left was calling her name. He sounded frantic. And he was coming to her much faster than she was going to him. It was like she was wading through treacle. Thick gloopy treacle that sucked at her feet, threatening to pull her down.

The man on the left was running now. He was reaching out for her. And she wasn't sure if that was a good thing or not.

But she remembered him.

Remembered his kindness, his love.

He came. He came.

And then she was in his arms, except the trees were gone, and she was somehow looking up at the sky.

His face came into view. It hovered over hers, concern and worry etched into every crease.

She tried to reach up to touch the face she'd dreamed of so often recently, but her arms wouldn't move, so instead she whispered, "You came."

And everything went black.

Chapter 57

Jason Hunter

International Evangelical Hospital (Voltri), Genoa

Sunday 19th June

I watched as Stacey's chest slowly moved up and down with each breath.

It felt unreal.

I held her hand. Couldn't bring myself to let go in case she slipped away from me again.

She was gaunt and pale. Her hair lank and knotty. I smoothed it back from her face as I watched her sleep.

Tubes were fed up her nose, and more were hooked into the back of her hands. The drip bag hanging beside her bed slowly fed her the nutrients she needed.

She'd passed out in my arms on that dirt track and had yet to regain consciousness. The malnutrition, the abuse, and the drugs that Liam had been feeding into her system had played havoc with her body. Self-preservation had taken over, and the only thing anyone could suggest was that her body had shut down when she'd seen me, when she'd finally known she was safe.

The thought brought a lump to my throat as I fought to hold the tears at bay.

I'd wanted to get her straight to the hospital right there, but Cooper had checked her over and then said we needed to finish whatever she'd started.

It seemed ludicrous at the time, but I'm grateful. We needed to make sure Liam wasn't likely to get away. Again.

Turned out, Stacey had done enough damage.

Between the two of us, we'd managed to get her into the back of the Lancia, where I sat cradling her head in my lap and whispering words of encouragement while Cooper went to see what had happened.

He'd found Liam in a pool of his own blood, dragging himself towards the door, a knife protruding from his chest. Cooper had unceremoniously pulled the knife from his chest and stabbed him a few more times just for personal satisfaction and had then left his corpse on the floor of the farmhouse.

We'd arrived at the hospital in Genoa to a flurry of activity. Cooper had managed to call the emergency services while he drove like a maniac, so they were expecting us.

They'd rushed her through the double doors and performed all the scans and tests and checks they could, before a kind-natured doctor told me her body was just resting. He didn't think she was in a coma as her brain activity was too high, but if she didn't wake up, or the brain activity dipped, we may have a problem.

And so here I sat, almost 24 hours later. Holding her hand like her life depended on it and wishing with all my being that she'd open her eyes.

Chapter 58

JASON HUNTER

INTERNATIONAL EVANGELICAL HOSPITAL (VOLTRI), GENOA

Sunday 19th April

I must have drifted off, my head resting on my folded arms. I still had hold of Stacey's hand, and I swore I'd never let go.

I jolted awake and noticed the sun was starting to set. The room was filled with a warm glow at odds with the sterile surroundings.

It wasn't a private room. I'd asked for one, but I'd been ignored, the staff too busy dealing with all the other requests that were constantly pouring in.

Cooper had disappeared the moment Stacey had passed through the doors. He didn't follow. I'd turned to look for him, but he was gone. I was sure he'd reappear before too long. The nurse had warned me that Stacey was only allowed one visitor a day, so it was unlikely he'd materialise in the ward, but stranger things had happened. Besides, Cooper had his way of defying the rules and getting away with it.

I knew where he was, though.

Liam might be dead, but the farmhouse was a crime scene. One that needed to be dealt with. And the missing farmer. Where was he?

Cooper was likely tidying up the mess.

I hoped his 'tidying up' included tipping off the police. Within hours of arriving at the hospital, the police were breathing down my neck. I pleaded ignorance, hoping it would give Cooper the time he needed to do whatever he was doing.

The ward was quiet, the patients in the other beds mostly sleeping. But something had woken me up. Why else had I jolted awake so hard?

I looked around the room, but everything was calm. No unwelcome visitors. No emergencies.

And that's when I felt it.

A squeeze on my hand.

I looked down to where Stacey's hand rested in mine, and there it was again.

A squeeze.

She was squeezing my hand.

I looked up to see her eyes were open and she was looking down at me with a clarity I didn't expect.

"Stacey," I breathed.

Chapter 59

JASON HUNTER

INTERNATIONAL EVANGELICAL HOSPITAL (VOLTRI), GENOA

Monday 20th June

Stacey was being discharged from the hospital.

They'd kept her in overnight as a precaution and had spent that time getting fluids into her system and doing more checks and tests. This morning, the doctor had visited and told her she was to be discharged by the end of the day.

I was desperate to get her home. To get her back on British soil and as far away from this nightmare as possible. But she was tired. Exhausted, in fact. And I wasn't confident she'd be up for the journey.

So, instead, I had booked us a room at Hotel Cenobio dei Dogi for a few nights. It was on the other side of the city, almost an hour's drive away, but it would be worth it. The place had sea views and a gorgeous pool. I hoped the water would, at least, bring Stacey some peace.

"I heard they're letting you leave," said a voice behind me. I turned to see Cooper standing a few feet away, carrying a holdall.

She looked up from where she sat on the edge of the bed. Her face was pale and her eyes sunken. There wasn't a flicker of emotion across her face as she looked at Cooper.

"Yes," she said simply, her voice hoarse.

Cooper glanced at me, a small frown creasing his face.

"I brought you some things," he said, placing the holdall on the bed beside her.

"Thanks," she said, and her gaze dropped to the floor.

We stood there for a moment, no one saying anything.

"I'm just going to see where the doctor is," I said and squeezed her hand.

She nodded, turning to the holdall and unzipping it.

Cooper followed me into the corridor. It wasn't too busy. A nurse passed by with a patient. Another nurse headed in the other direction, pushing a trolley laden with medical supplies. Family members lingered further down, talking in hushed whispers.

"How is she?" he asked.

"How do you think?" I replied, gesturing back to the ward.

"Mate, she's just been through hell and back. She's awake and she's talking, for a start. That's a good thing. I've seen lesser people go catatonic."

I nodded and folded my arms across my chest, looking back at the doors we'd just come through.

"I just don't know what to do or say," I said.

"If you did, I'd be worried," he said, and clapped me on the shoulder. My bad shoulder. I winced. "You'll get there. The important thing is, she's safe. Everything else can be fixed. Just get through the next few days and get her home. She'll do better once she's home."

I nodded, not convinced. I didn't know what else to say to Cooper, but I knew I needed a moment.

A man in his sixties sat in a wheelchair, being pushed by a younger woman I could only guess was his daughter. The wheelchair squeaked on the linoleum floor as they passed. The woman pushing was chattering away in Italian, and the old man looked like he was trying hard to ignore her.

"Have the police visited yet?" he asked.

I nodded again.

"They took a statement from me and Stacey. I kept your name out of it."

"Appreciate it," he said and looked down the hall. "Though it won't take much for them to find out you were with me. They'll start asking the locals, and that will take them to the B&B."

I studied Cooper's side profile, trying to determine if he was worried.

He turned back to me.

"Don't worry. Lena was very hospitable. I even left her a generous tip. I doubt she'll be saying anything."

"What about the others?"

Cooper shrugged, not bothered.

"It's a risk. Always is. But by the time they catch up to me, I'll be long gone."

"When are you leaving?" I asked.

"In a few hours. I'll take you and Stace to the hotel and then I'll be off."

"Thanks," I said. And I knew he understood what I meant. I wasn't just saying thanks for the offered ride; it was for everything. His help in finding her. Who knows how things would have panned out if I hadn't enlisted Cooper's help. I tried not to think about it. Just like I tried very hard not to think about the statement she'd given the police.

It had come out in fits and bursts. Most of it came out in half sentences, like she was reciting a shopping list. The police had asked to speak to her alone, but she'd gripped my hand in a panic and insisted I stay.

"He raped her," I said in a low voice, unable to look Cooper in the eye. But I saw his jaw tick as he clenched it. And in the pit of my stomach, I felt it. The raw bubbling anger that felt like acid trying to claw its way out. I clenched my fists. "He abused the absolute shit out of her," I said, and I could feel the hysteria rising. I put my fist in my mouth and bit down. Hard. As hard as I could. The pain felt like a strange kind of release in my system and allowed me to momentarily tame the beast.

Cooper looked at me, and I could see my rage mirrored there. Good. I was glad I wasn't the only one affected by this. At least there was someone I could share my anger with, because there was no way in hell I could burden Stacey with it. She seemed so brittle, so broken.

"He died a slow and painful death," said Cooper. "It's just a shame I couldn't make it last longer."

Chapter 60

Jason Hunter

Hotel Cenobio dei Dogi, Genoa

Thursday 23rd June

It was warm and the sun was shining. Stacey sat on the terrace in her bathrobe.

I'd been on the phone with Sam, discussing business and contracts and all the usual stuff that normally occupied my day-to-day, but had been temporarily forgotten about in my hunt for Stacey.

He was managing things just fine, not that I'd doubted him. But I'd been away from the business long enough, and I needed to get back.

As I hung up and pocketed my mobile, I watched Stacey for a moment.

She looked almost regal. Sitting in the mid-morning sun, her eyes closed and face tilted towards the warm rays.

She even looked peaceful. But I knew it was fleeting. Her waking moments were filled with anxiety and paranoia, and when she was asleep, she was consumed by nightmares she couldn't escape. She'd jolt awake in the middle of the night, tears streaming down her face, her body clammy.

Despite sleeping on the sofa, I was instantly alert every time it happened. And I was there to soothe her, to hold her, to tell her she was safe and that Liam was dead. It helped a little. But it would take hours before she finally drifted off to sleep again, only to be plagued by more restlessness.

She was still exhausted. We both were. The deep purple bruises under her eyes gave it away.

"Hey," I said gently as I stepped onto the terrace.

"Hey," she said, opening her eyes and looking up at me.

"How you doing?"

She gave a small nod of her head and then looked out to sea, squinting against the glare of the sun.

"Flight is booked for tomorrow morning. Fancy going home?"

She nodded again, and this time I saw a tear escape.

I knelt down next to her and gently brushed it away with the pad of my thumb, the palm of my hand cupping her cheek.

"Hey now," I said. She leaned her face into my hand and closed her eyes again, another tear appearing. "Look at me." She opened her eyes. "You've got this," I said with conviction. "You're Stacey. Fucking. James."

And for the first time since I'd found her, she gave me a small smile.

Chapter 61

Jason Hunter

London office

Wednesday 29th June

It was the first time I'd stepped foot in the office in nearly three weeks. It felt like a lifetime, and in some ways it was. The last time I was here, Britland had summoned me for the damn press conference that had landed me in hospital with a bullet in my shoulder.

I rotated my shoulder, testing for any pain or tension, but it felt good. Still tight, but that would loosen up over time.

The lift dinged as it reached the office floor, and I stepped out. As I walked through the office, people started to stand. It wasn't a huge place, with just 12 desks arranged in three squares of four. And yet, it suddenly felt like the place was crowded with a hundred people as they all began to applaud.

Confused, I looked around, wondering if I'd missed an important event, and that's when I caught sight of Sam standing at the other end of the room, smirking at me. He lifted his coffee mug in greeting and nodded his head. I smiled.

Lucy emerged from behind her desk, still clapping with the others, a wide grin on her face and tears in her eyes. She threw her arms around my neck and squeezed me tight.

"You brought her home," she whispered before she let go. And that's when I realised this was my welcome back committee. This was their way of showing their support for everything that had transpired over the last three weeks. Everything I'd been through to get Stacey back.

Too choked up for words, I waved a hand at my team and smiled before heading into my office.

Lucy followed me in, and Sam appeared a moment later, closing the door behind him.

"Ready to get back to business?" asked Lucy.

"Probably not, but I'll give it my best shot," I said with a half-smile.

"Good answer."

She immediately launched into everything I'd missed while I'd been away. The new client meetings in my diary and the contracts that had been set up, and the internal politics between Roman and Richard, my Operations Manager who generally annoyed everyone. When she was finished, she handed me a two-page printout.

"It's all here."

"You're a star," I said.

"I'll let Sam catch you up on everything else. But you know where I am if you need me."

"Thanks, Luce," I said.

She paused with her hand on the door handle.

"It's good to have you back," she said and left.

A silence descended in her absence, and I slumped in my seat, taking a moment to stare out of the window and recalibrate my thoughts.

Stacey was at home on her own, and I was damn terrified by that. I hadn't left her on her own for more than half an hour since we'd found her, but a whole damn day felt like too much. She'd insisted that she'd be fine. Of course, she had. I could see the constant inner struggle that was happening, but I could also see the Stacey James I knew fighting to come back. She was still in there; she just needed time. And so, I'd left for work, but not before I'd made her promise to call me if it all felt too much.

I turned to look at Sam.

"What's the latest?"

"The Asia leg of Iris McCleary's World Tour starts next week and we've kept the same all-female team as before. They're happy with the assignment, especially as it comes with a boost in pay for all the travel. And Iris is happy, which means Vance is happy. So, it's a win-win."

I smiled. I liked Iris McCleary. I also liked her manager, Vance Cherry. Even if he was blunt. She was a dream client, and with a bit of luck, word of mouth would help us bag a few new high-paying clients in the right circles and help us reclaim some of our reputation.

"Good news. Thanks for picking that up."

"No problem," said Sam. "Royce Gill is happy with everything so far. We have a schedule of public appearances over the next 6 weeks in relation to his *The Last Lap* movie. But he may have us on a regular basis afterwards. TBC."

I nodded, this was good news.

"And the meetings in your diary are actually referrals from Cameron," he said.

My eyebrows shot up.

"She called last week and said there were a couple of her clientele that were looking for personal protection so she gave them Lucy's number."

"Amazing, what do we know about them?" I asked.

"Not much at the moment, Lucy's working on it."

"Good work."

"And Richard is spec'ing out three more proposals, which means we'll likely need to hire another team, but we can cross that bridge if and when they give the go ahead. However, I've given Divya a heads up, just so she knows it's coming as the recruitment window might be tight. She has a list of potential candidates already so I don't think it will take long."

I nodded. Divya, our Head of HR, was a miracle worker when it came to finding the right people. Like last year, when I'd asked her to source some all-female teams for the Iris McCleary job and she'd gone above and beyond.

"Ah, that's great," I said, feeling optimistic. It was nice to have some good news for once, and not just be running on adrenaline.

"And that's about it. I'll email you an official handover so you have it in writing."

"Thanks," I said. Thankfully, the regular updates Sam had been sending my way meant that I wasn't completely out of the loop with everything. Just the last few days where I'd been preoccupied with getting Stacey settled.

"Oh, and I've been helping Savannah with a data integrity issue," added Sam.

I raised an eyebrow. Savannah was our IT contractor. She did a lot of the maintenance around keeping our data and files secure, and generally helped out with anything else we might need. She was an old friend of Sam's, and before he worked for me, Savannah would occasionally hire him when she was busy. Nothing too time-consuming, but he'd done IT administration before, and it helped pay his bills.

"I didn't realise you still did work for her," I said.

"I don't. Not really. Haven't done in years, but she needed an extra pair of hands on this one."

"Right," I said, wondering where this was going.

"There was a whole batch of data erasure instructions. I wouldn't have noticed except the names are pretty current at the moment. Alfonso Torres, Alek Gromov, Wesley Gray. The same template was used for all three. Same urgency, too."

I frowned.

"That is weird," I said. "Can you get a copy of the instructions?"

"I'll try," he said with a nod.

"Should I mention it to Hayley?"

"Let me see what I can dig up first. I might have misunderstood."

"Sure," I nodded.

Sam stood up.

"It's good to have you back, boss," he said.

Chapter 62

Jason Hunter

Home

Wednesday 29th June

I'd left the office early. I glanced up at the camera above the front door as I fished my keys from my pocket and inserted the right one into the lock and turned it. The moment the door swung open, I heard laughter coming from the kitchen.

Shocked, I dropped my bag on the floor by the door and kicked the door closed.

It wasn't Stacey laughing, but I recognised it all the same. It was a full, rich sound, the type of laughter that came from people who were full of life.

I moved through the living room and as the kitchen came into view, I saw Cameron sat at the kitchen island, her head thrown back as she laughed. Stacey sat opposite her, a small smile tugging at the corner of her lips.

Cameron, as usual, was dressed head to toe in post box red. Her red hair was draped over one shoulder, showing off her elegant neck and bare skin. She wore an off-the-shoulder top and a pair of the tightest red jeans that looked hard to move in. On her feet were her classic red stilettos. As she turned to look at me, the red droppers hanging from her ears caught the overhead light and glittered.

"Cameron, what a lovely surprise," I said, and I genuinely meant it. I was relieved to know that Stacey hadn't been completely on her own. A friend is exactly what she needed.

"Darling," said Cameron in her familiar drawl. She stood up from the kitchen island and came over to kiss me on both cheeks. "I was just saying to our darling Stacey how wonderful it is to have her home."

Stacey's eyes flicked to my face and then away again.

"It is," I said, still looking at Stacey. Something in my gut told me that wasn't what they had been talking about at all.

"Well, I best be off. It's been so good to see you," said Cameron, turning around and placing a hand on top of Stacey's. "You had us all worried for a moment." She squeezed Stacey's hand, and I could have sworn I saw Stacey's lips twitch up on one side, or maybe it was more of a grimace.

"You don't fancy staying for food?" I asked. "I was thinking take-out."

"Sorry darling, I need to be off. The club won't run itself."

She blew a kiss across the room to Stacey and then left. I followed her to the front door. On the front step, she paused and turned back to me.

"How are you doing, darling?" she asked.

"Yeah, I'm fine."

"How's that shoulder of yours?"

"Healing," I said as I lifted my arm to rotate my shoulder. It was becoming a reflex move anytime someone brought it up. As if I needed to test it and check it was, in fact, healed.

"And Britland? Have you heard from him?"

I sighed. I knew this was why she'd stopped to talk to me, why she wanted to be away from Stacey.

"No, I haven't. Sam's managing his protection at the moment, okay? I've had bigger things to deal with," I said, gesturing to the house. I knew I didn't need to spell it out, but I could also feel my patience wearing thin. "What's your deal with him anyway? What are you not telling me?"

Cameron straightened and looked down the street. I could see she was weighing up whether or not she should tell me whatever it was that was bothering her.

"Come on, Cameron. We've been through enough shit as it is. Don't hold out on me. If there's something I need to know, then just tell me."

She turned to look at me, her bottom lip caught between her teeth.

"He's dirty," she finally said.

"Tell me something I don't know," I muttered, resisting the urge to roll my eyes.

"No, you don't get it Jason." And now she sounded half-scared. "The bastard is *dirty*. He's visited my club more times than I care to remember and the only reason I let him in is because he owns me. He was blackmailing Mickey, and you know what, he's blackmailing me too."

"How?"

"It doesn't matter how. There are things I've done that I'm not proud of, I have a past I'm not proud of. And that slimy snake of a mayor will exploit any and every weakness he can find to get what he wants." She let out a shuddering breath as I tried to read between the lines of what she was saying. "Just be careful," she said. "And for the love of God, keep that girl safe," she added, jabbing a finger in the direction of the house behind me.

"What do you think I've been trying to do this last month?"

"I know, I know," she said, regaining some of her composure. She placed a hand on my arm and leaned in to kiss me on the cheek. "Take care of yourself," she said. And something deep in my gut told me this might be the last time I ever saw her.

Chapter 63

JASON HUNTER

HOME

Wednesday 29ᵗʰ June

I closed the front door and leaned against the wall for a moment, trying to process everything Cameron had said. I knew the mayor had been blackmailing Mickey. At least, I'd guessed as much. But whether this was connected to the fraud ring or not, the mayor clearly had something over Cameron and was using it to his full advantage. That didn't sit right with me. I had a sneaking suspicion that was his default play; deliberately compromise someone and then hold it against them.

What the hell had Cameron done?

I walked back into the living room to see Stacey had moved from the kitchen island to the sofa. She was dressed in a pair of my joggers and an oversized t-shirt. It was her go-to outfit these days. She said it gave her comfort, made her feel protected knowing that she was wrapped up in my clothes.

"How was today?" I asked, dropping on to the sofa next to her.

"It was okay," she said.

She leaned into me, and I put an arm around her, pulling her close. I was surprised she was so willing to be close to me considering everything she'd been through with Liam, but she'd told me she needed it.

She needed to know that she was safe. And I was the only person who could give her that. I wasn't complaining, because I hated being even a few feet away from her.

It hadn't been a magical reunion like you'd see in the movies. She hadn't run into my arms like a damsel in distress. She was Stacey James. She was no damsel in distress. But there was also no intimacy. At least not yet. I knew it would come. Eventually. And I'd be here no matter how long it took. I'd help her piece herself back together if it was the last thing I ever did.

I kissed the top of her head and breathed in her scent. She stiffened slightly but she didn't push me away.

"What do you fancy for dinner? I was thinking maybe pizza?"

"Sure," she said.

I didn't have the energy to cook anything this evening. And from the statement she'd made to the police, it was clear that Liam had expected her to play chef and scullery maid alongside her less savoury duties.

I ordered online from the local pizzeria round the corner, knowing it wouldn't take long to arrive, and we found something to watch on Netflix.

Despite having clocked off early to get home, there was still a shit-load I needed to do. As much as I tried to focus on the *Minions* movie Stacey had picked, I couldn't switch off from work stuff.

I pulled out my phone and scrolled through my calendar app, checking my meetings over the next week. Then I opened my mail app. In my inbox sat the handover emails from Lucy and Sam. Something niggled at the back of my mind, but I couldn't place it. Something I was meant to have done but had forgotten?

I thought back to the conversation I'd had with Sam about Savannah.

The list of data erasure instructions wasn't that weird. It was a standard request that Savannah dealt with on a regular basis. And they often came from the rich and famous who wanted to limit reputational damage. But what was it that he'd said?

The same template was used for all three. Same urgency too.

Now that was strange.

Alfonso Torres was Spanish. Alek Gromov was Russian. And Wesley Gray was British. What were the odds that they all used the same lawyer? I guessed it wasn't out of the realms of possibility. After all, the rich and famous ran in the same circles, so it made sense that their legal representatives did too. But Gromov would have been especially careful about stuff like this. Both the Met and the FSB had their eye on him. And for all three names to come up in the same log meant that the requests had come in within a certain time frame. And that also seemed unlikely.

I opened up my notes app and began to write a to-do list for the morning, including a note to speak to Sam about Savannah's data integrity job.

Chapter 64

JASON HUNTER

LONDON OFFICE

Thursday 30th June

"Ah, there you are," I said as I walked into the kitchen and spotted Sam by the kettle. "I thought you didn't drink that much coffee?"

He turned to look at me, almost startled by my intrusion.

"Sorry," I said with a half-laugh. "You okay?"

"Yes, fine," he said, a little flustered.

"You sure?" I asked, still smiling.

Sam didn't get chance to reply when Lucy walked in.

"Oh hey," she said, flashing both of us a smile. She rinsed her mug in the sink. Then opened the fridge, pulled out the milk and poured some into her mug. As we both watched her make a cup of tea, neither of us said anything.

She scooped her teabag from the freshly made tea and dumped it into the bin before dropping her spoon in the sink. Then, she turned to look at us.

"Everything okay?"

"Yes," we replied in unison.

Lucy's eyebrow shot up. "Okaaay," she said, dragging out the last syllable before leaving the kitchen.

"You want to tell me what that was all about?" I asked once I was confident that Lucy was out of earshot.

"No," said Sam, turning back to the kettle, his cheeks reddening.

I smiled. Not wanting to embarrass him any further, I changed the subject to the real reason I'd tracked him down.

"I was thinking about what you said yesterday. About that job you're doing for Savannah," I said.

Sam turned to face me and leaned against the kitchen counter, arms crossed over his chest. His usual scowl back in place.

"You said the same template was used for all three?"

He nodded.

"It was niggling at me last night. What's the likelihood that they used the same lawyer?"

Sam shrugged.

"When will you be able to re-check the logs?"

Sam glanced at his watch. "I can do it now," he said. "I've got time before my meeting with Richard."

"Excellent."

We headed out of the kitchen and turned right towards Sam's office in the far corner, the furthest away from everyone. It suited him far too much.

Sam dropped into his chair behind his desk as I closed the door behind us. I couldn't remember the last time I'd been in Sam's office. He was forever in my office, so I often forgot that this place was even here. He was a foot soldier, a man on the ground. He hated the paperwork that came with the job. The security reports and the red tape. He wanted to be heading up the teams and supervising the rotations.

The room was sparse. Nothing hung on the walls, and there wasn't even a potted plant in sight. But the floor-to-ceiling windows that lined one side gave the room an airy feel. It was professional and clean but lacked personality. Sam had always been a man of mystery, and his office certainly didn't allude to anything.

"So, here are the logs," Sam said after a few minutes.

Without any spare seats, I was forced to round the desk and lean over Sam's shoulder. He rotated his laptop slightly so I could see better. His personal laptop, I noted, which sat on top of the closed lid of his professional laptop.

Sam pointed to a cluster of records that he'd highlighted amidst the hundreds of rows of data.

"They're pretty aggressive data erasure requests," he said, opening the first one. He wasn't wrong. I scanned through the request. It seemed pretty textbook to me. Maybe a little forceful, but how unusual was that?

Same opened the second record and we both scanned through it. Then he opened the third one. We both read it, and that's when I noticed a pattern. All three requests specified emails, corporate communications, and offshore files to be targeted during the data erasure process.

"Look at this," I said, pointing to a specific phrase. "*All cloud-hosted backups and index references to be permanently erased*," I read aloud. "And this one: *Pseudonymised data must also be purged.* They're exactly the same."

Sam went back into the other records and opened them up, positioning them alongside each other on the screen so we could compare. And sure enough, the phrasing was identical.

"That's weird, right?"

Sam frowned. "Well, there are standardised ways of requesting this, so I wouldn't flag it as that unusual."

"But who submitted the requests? Three different people aren't going to use the exact same wording. So, someone's done this on their behalf. And that begs the question: who and why? Torres wasn't British, he didn't even live in this country, just visited. I know Gromov uses a Russian legal team based in London; it's the one that reviewed our contracts. So how have they all ended up with the same legal representative submitting the same data erasure requests?"

Sam was still frowning.

"That's a good point," he said.

"When were the requests submitted?" I asked.

"That's what made me notice them," he said, and pointed to the date on each of them.

The requests had all been submitted within a 48-hour window. Right before Alfonso Torres was murdered on the red carpet.

"Okay, now this seems really fishy. Can you see who submitted the requests?" I asked.

Sam nodded and opened up another file. He mapped the data erasure requests across and highlighted the submission record. The same name submitted all three; Halberd Group.

Chapter 65

Jason Hunter

London Office

Thursday 30ᵗʰ June

"Who the bloody hell is the Halberd Group?" I asked. The name didn't ring a bell.

Sam shrugged.

"Bloody awful name though," he said.

I laughed. "You're not wrong."

Opening up a Google search, Sam typed in 'Halberd Group', and although the search returned thousands of results, nothing on the front page seemed even remotely relevant. He tried modifying the search by adding the word 'legal' at the end, but still nothing.

"Let me give this to Hayley, maybe she'll be able to tell us a bit more about who the Halberd Group is. Maybe it's a shell company or something."

Sam nodded and then checked his watch. "I've got to go, boss."

"Sure." I clapped him on the shoulder and he closed the files, then turned his laptop off. We walked down the corridor in silence, both thinking through what we'd just found.

"Let me know what Hayley says," he said, and then headed towards Richard's office.

I slipped inside my own office and closed the door. Pulling my phone from my pocket, I video called Hayley.

She answered almost immediately. The camera switched on, and all I could see was a close-up of her chin. Her brown hair was swishing around her face as if she were rushing.

"Are you in a hurry?"

"Can I call you back?" she asked, sounding out of breath.

"Sure—" She'd already hung up before I could finish my sentence. Weird.

I busied myself in my office, still catching up on what I'd missed while I'd been in Italy. I didn't feel quite ready to throw myself into client meetings, but I was keeping a close eye on the Mayor Britland job. It all seemed to be going as well as it could be, but I felt it was only a matter of time before he came barging into my office again.

My phone buzzed on my desk.

Worried I'd summoned the devil himself, I let out a sigh of relief when I saw Hayley's name on the screen.

"Sorry about that," she said when I answered. She was in her office looking a lot more composed than earlier.

"All okay?"

"Yes, just dealing with something. What's up? How's Stacey doing?"

"She's getting there. It's early days, though."

"That's understandable. That woman has been through absolute hell and back," said Hayley, her eyes softening.

"I know." I swallowed away the lump in my throat.

"I was going to call you, actually," she said. "It's been mad, so I haven't had a chance. And I didn't know what the situation was with Stacey, so I didn't just want to turn up at your place."

"Oh, you should. I think Stacey would be glad for the company."

"Alright," she said, glancing toward the other side of the room.

"Were you going to call for a particular reason?" I prompted when she didn't say anything else. It was unusual to see Hayley so distracted.

"Oh yes, sorry. I told you they'd brought me into the investigation, right?" She frowned as if she couldn't remember the last time we'd spoken.

"Yes."

"So, the e-fits you and Adrianna did last year are being combined with the new e-fit we got from the girlfriend at the restaurant. My boss is pushing for a public announcement and circulating it through all the media outlets. I don't think it'll help. The guy's a professional; it's not likely he'll have left much of a trace. But my boss is insisting. He wants to put pressure on the gunman – although I guess we can't call him that anymore, considering how Gray died.

"Anyway, the ballistics from your shooting came back - I've already told you this, right?"

"You told me it was the same shooter but you didn't go into detail," I said.

"Right, so they matched discharge casings from HMP Belmarsh with the shoot site in Leicester Square. This confirms that it's the same guy who shot you and Torres."

"How did they match?" I asked, not sure I understood.

"What?"

"The casings? How did they match?"

"Ah. So, something about markings from the weapon. Each weapon leaves specific markings on the casings. This means that with a bit of reverse engineering we can identify which one was used. Obviously, it's only circumstantial if we find the guy and then the weapon."

I let out a breath as I processed what she was saying. It sounded like they were making progress, but things weren't moving quickly.

"What about the next names on the list?"

"There's too many to offer protection to all of them. And that's where you come in."

"I don't contract with the Met."

"No, I know you don't. But maybe I can refer them to you?"

"Of course," I said. This was great news. There were still eight names on that list, eight potential clients with big budgets. But then my optimism for new business revenue popped. I couldn't forget that the reason these people needed protecting in the first place was because they'd been laundering money. And lots of it.

For fuck's sake. Stupid morals.

"I'm not sure that's a good idea," I said.

Hayley frowned. "Why not? I thought you needed the business."

"I do." I glanced out the window and then back at my phone screen. "These people are dodgy, right? That's why they're being targeted in the first place. I don't think I could, in good faith, take them on as clients knowing they have a criminal record."

Hayley paused a moment. "Yeah, that's fair."

We were both silent for a moment.

"So why did you call me?" she asked.

"I need a favour," I said.

"Of course you do," she laughed.

Chapter 66

JASON HUNTER

LONDON OFFICE

Thursday 30th June

"What do you need?" she asked.

I walked her through what I'd found with Sam. The more I spoke, the more Hayley frowned. By the time I'd finished, she'd propped her phone up on her desk and was scribbling furiously on some paper.

She leaned back in her chair and twiddled her pen between her fingers, clearly thinking things through.

"That doesn't sound right," she agreed with me. "But I also don't know enough about these things to give you any guidance."

"Can you check up on the Halberd Group? See what they do and how they fit in?" I asked.

She paused and then nodded. "It feels relevant to the case, so yes. But I'm gonna need those files from Sam. And his IT contractor friend can't complete those erasure requests until I'm done with the investigation and have given her the all clear."

I inwardly winced. I had no idea how Savannah would take that, and I really hoped I hadn't just cost her business.

"I'll relay the message," I said.

"No need, I'll speak to her directly. This could be something," she said. "Thanks."

"No problem. Let me know if I can help."

"Will do. I've got to go. I'll try and swing by to see Stacey."

I gave a small smile and a wave before ending the video call.

The office felt weirdly quiet afterwards.

I didn't know when Sam would finish his meeting with Richard. And I definitely didn't want to go barging into that one. The more I could avoid Richard, the better.

Before I could decide what to do next, my phone vibrated in my hand. I swiped the answer button before registering who it was. The moment I realised it was an unknown number, my stomach sank. It could be anyone, really. But I knew who it was.

"Jason Hunter, Hawke Security."

"Ah, Jason."

Mayor Britland.

"I saw you were back in the country. Your arrival at Heathrow wasn't quite as covert as you would have liked, I'm sure."

I frowned. The bastard was right.

The plan had been to come back to the UK quietly. Stacey was keeping a low profile. She hardly looked like her old self, so it wasn't exactly difficult. But someone had tipped off the press, and a pack of paparazzi were waiting for us the moment we exited customs.

My security training had kicked in and I'd been able to escort Stacey through the crowd to where Sam waited in the short-stay parking. But it had been an unpleasant experience.

"Not quite," I said through gritted teeth, biting back the urge to snap at him. "What can I do for you, Mr Mayor?"

"I just wanted to check in and find out when you would be taking over the management of my protection?"

I frowned. "Is everything alright? You can raise any concerns with Sam, he's more than capable of handling them."

"I know. But it wasn't Sam I hired, was it? It was you. And I want you in charge."

"Okaaay," I said, trying to figure out what his angle was.

"Do it, Hunter. I'm *your* client." He hung up.

Chapter 67

Jason Hunter

Home

Friday 1ˢᵗ July

After my phone call with Mayor Britland, I'd done exactly as he'd asked; I'd taken over his protection job from Sam.

Sam was his usual man-of-little-words self, but I could tell he was as pissed as I was about the whole situation. It was ridiculous and frustrating.

Turns out that Britland had made a bunch more requests while I'd been away, which Sam had been dealing with and so the protection detail I'd put in place initially was completely different from what was in place now. I knew there had been some modifications, there always were with high-profile clients like him, but Sam hadn't been completely honest with me on just how much of a nightmare Britland was turning out to be.

He was demanding, high-maintenance, and a drain on our resources.

When I'd asked Sam about it, he'd simply stated that it was all under control and I needed to recover.

Well, that just made me more annoyed.

All of this meant the last 24 hours had been spent sorting out the handover and dealing with the latest change request; Britland wasn't happy with the protection officers he'd been given and was insisting he choose his own team.

I'd rolled my eyes at the request. Alek Gromov had pulled something similar, but that was for a single event, a party he was hosting at his home. He hadn't demanded full control of the rota. And Iris Mccleary, well, her situation had been very different. She'd needed an all-female team to feel secure, and due to past incidents, I'd encouraged her to be involved in the selection process. They would be travelling with her throughout her tour, so it was important she was comfortable with whoever it was.

But this. Mayor Britland was just pushing my buttons. On purpose.

And then when I hadn't been dealing with Mr High-and-Mighty Mayor Britland, I'd been reconnecting with Iris Mccleary and Vance Cherry. Sam had enough on his plate that I'd already said I'd take the Iris McCleary job off his hands. Admittedly, that was before Britland had called me yesterday.

I was exhausted, and it was late.

I'd called Stacey just after lunch and apologised, telling her I would be home late. I had a call with Iris Mccleary's promo team at 5pm to check the setup for the upcoming final US locations. It was important because there were some serious gaps in the security reports I'd read for the different venues.

I opened the door to my house and for the second time that week, I heard voices in the kitchen. It wasn't Cameron who was visiting this time, but Hayley.

"Oh, hey," I said with a smile as I walked in. I walked around the kitchen island to where Stacey sat and kissed her lightly on the cheek. She gave me a small smile. I could already see the improvements in her.

She'd been home a week, and in that time, I could see her slowly starting to put the pieces of herself back together again. Next week, she was scheduled to start seeing Professor Lindberg, her therapist, again. Not that she ever technically stopped, but her international travel schedule often got in the way. So did being kidnapped by a maniac.

"To what do we owe the pleasure, DI Irons?" I asked.

On the kitchen island between the two women sat a collection of mismatched plates. They'd been loaded up with a random selection of snacks. Everything from pizza slices and chicken nuggets to sausage rolls and nachos.

"Are we hosting a kids' party?" I asked. It was all from the stash I kept in the garage freezer for when the kids came over and I didn't have anything decent in the main fridge. Or when I couldn't be bothered to cook for them.

Hayley laughed. "Nothing beats party food," she said, helping herself to a sausage roll and dipping it into a pot of ketchup.

Stacey reached for a breadstick sticking out of a cup and began to nibble on one end.

"What have you two been up to?"

"Not much," said Stacey. She looped an arm around my waist and pulled me closer as I helped myself to the beige buffet. "How was work?"

"Absolute hell," I said. "Mayor Britland is being a deliberate pain in my ass."

"There might be a reason for that," said Hayley.

"Oh, there's a reason, alright. The guy's a prick."

Hayley laughed. "No, I mean an actual reason."

"Yeah?"

"I managed to look into the Halberd Group for you."

"That was fast," I said, turning around to open the fridge and grab a beer. "Anyone want one?" I asked, holding the beer up. Both Stacey and Hayley shook their heads. I closed the fridge and turned back to the kitchen island, using the undercounter bottle opener to take the lid off.

"A guy in tech owed me a favour," Hayley shrugged. "Anyway, they're a legal firm in Mayfair that specialises in reputation management."

"As in the reputation of the rich and famous?" asked Stacey, frowning. I felt a rush of warmth in my chest at seeing her join the conversation. It was almost like old times. My mind flipped back to when she'd travelled with me to Budapest and I'd found her on the floor of our hotel room trying to piece together the evidence from Gemma's murder.

"Yep. And get this. The guy who runs the place, Miles Cummings, used to be part of Britland's mayoral ethics committee."

"Ethics committee?" I asked.

"Used to?" asked Stacey.

Hayley nodded.

"That's weird, right?" I said.

"It feels like more than a coincidence, that's for sure," said Hayley.

"What's your next move?"

"The offices are closed over the weekend. I've already tried calling, but the number on his Companies House listing was a dud, so I'll just have to show up on Monday."

"That's assuming the address he's listed is legit as well, though," said Stacey.

"True. But I've got to start somewhere."

"So, what are we thinking?" I asked.

"I'm not sure," said Hayley. "Britland is clearly one of the targets. That's how you got shot."

"As if I could ever forget," I muttered and took a swig of beer.

Stacey's head whipped round to look at me, shock in her eyes.

"I totally forgot," she said, lifting a hand to her mouth. "How did I forget?"

"There's been a lot going on," I said, keen not to have this conversation in front of Hayley. But Stacey clearly didn't care.

"I heard about it."

"You heard about it?" asked Hayley. "How?"

"I overheard the news. Liam had it on in the other room while I was in the kitchen. I was doing the dishes. I heard them say you got shot." I could see tears welling in her eyes as she spoke.

"Hey, hey," I said, placing my beer on the island and cupping her face in both my hands. "I'm fine. See. I'm here. Right as rain."

"He went in for surgery, they removed the bullet, and there were no complications," said Hayley.

Stacey turned shocked eyes to Hayley and I glared at her.

"Sorry," she winced. "I thought it would help."

"Show me," said Stacey.

"I think I'll be off," said Hayley.

"I'll see you out," I said and gave Stacey a brief kiss on the lips. "I'm fine, I promise."

She didn't look convinced.

I followed Hayley to the front door.

"Sorry," she said, her voice quiet. "I didn't mean to drop you in it."

"Don't worry about it. Was only a matter of time anyway. Not like I can hide the scar or anything."

"True," she said and paused, as if she had something else to say. "What do you think about all this?"

"What do you mean?" I asked and frowned.

"Britland? Halberd Group?" she said.

I let out a long breath and looked past Hayley to the quiet residential street behind her.

"The guy's a target. He's paranoid as hell. Maybe he's doing the dirty work of whoever's pulling the strings? Maybe the shooting was a warning? If Britland has pissed off the wrong person, then we're all in trouble. Whoever it is behind these killings, they're bloody dangerous and they've got shitloads of cash to fund it," I said.

"Which means we're all at risk."

I grimaced. She wasn't wrong.

Chapter 68

HAYLEY IRONS

MAYFAIR, LONDON

Monday 4th July

Hayley stood outside the registered address for the Halberd Group, and she immediately knew she was in the wrong place.

The bottom floor of the building on Albermarle Street was a high-end boutique shop, and above it were flats. She looked at the list of residences on the building registry by the door again and noted that the only business in the building was a virtual office company.

"Fuck's sake," she muttered.

She rang the intercom buzzer anyway, knowing this would be a waste of her time.

A few minutes later, she was welcomed inside by a young twenty-something receptionist with a warm smile.

"Hi, welcome to VirtualOffices4You. How can I help?"

Hayley held up her identification badge and watched the confident smile on the young woman's face falter.

"I was looking for a business, and they have this registered as their office address."

"A lot of businesses do, I'm afraid. That's kind of what we do."

"I gathered," muttered Hayley, looking around. It was tastefully decorated, albeit a bit boring. Potted plants in almost every corner, and all the furniture was either black or white. "Are you the only person here?" she asked.

The woman nodded. "I manage the location, take in mail, forward it on to the relevant business and manage any meeting room bookings."

"Can you give me the registered address for the Halberd Group?" she asked, wondering if this woman would be bold enough to cite data protection laws.

"I...I don't know. I...I don't think so," she stammered, thrown by the request.

Hayley held back the eyeroll. This was going to be harder than she'd thought.

She flashed the woman a reassuring smile. "No worries. Can I have the contact number for your boss? I'll put the request directly to them."

"Um, sure."

The woman retreated to her desk that was strategically positioned on the other side of the room so she could see the main entrance as well as the door to what she guessed was the meeting room she'd mentioned.

The woman pulled a business card from the top drawer and handed it to Hayley.

"Thanks," said Hayley, taking the card. Feeling frustrated, she said her goodbyes and headed back out onto Albermarle Street.

No sooner had she stepped outside than she pulled her phone from her pocket and dialled the one person she hoped could help.

Chapter 69

JASON HUNTER

LONDON OFFICE

Monday 4th July

"Hey, how's it going?" I said as I answered the call.

"Not great. The address was a dud, too," said Hayley.

"For the Halberd Group?"

"Yep. It's just a virtual office."

"What the heck's a virtual office?"

"A PO Box with a meeting room."

I laughed. "That's pretty clever," I said, glancing through the glass wall of my office and into the open plan space where Lucy sat.

"I guess, but it makes things pretty difficult for me," griped Hayley.

"What are you going to do?"

"I'm going to try and get hold of the real address through the proper channels, but meanwhile, I'm wondering if you can cheat the system?"

"What did you have in mind?" I asked warily. There was a knock at my door, and Sam poked his head around the door. I waved him in and he sat down in one of the empty chairs opposite me.

"Do you think Stace—"

"No," I cut her off. "I'm not dragging her into this," I said.

"That's fair. I'm sorry I even asked," she said, and I could hear the regret in her tone. "The bloody woman manning the desk gave me the classic data privacy line, which is ironic really, considering why I need to speak to Miles Cummings in the first place."

I laughed. "That is ironic."

"Okay, well, I'll speak to you later," she said and hung up.

I looked down at my phone, surprised by the quick cut off. I felt weirdly used. Although the number of times the situation had been reversed, I guess I couldn't complain.

"Everything okay?" asked Sam, a frown creasing his brow.

I relayed the conversation with Hayley.

"Good call," he said.

"I know she's thinking of when we tracked down Cameron, but I'm not putting Stacey at risk like that, especially not now."

Sam nodded.

"What about Cameron?" he asked.

"What about her?"

"Well, I assume Hayley wanted Stacey to enquire as a legitimate client to get more details. What if Cameron did it instead? She's practically an underground celeb."

"That's true," I said. And then smiled.

"You ready?" he asked. I nodded and swiped the top folder from the stack on my desk as I stood up.

"Born ready," I said.

Sam snorted. And then stood up.

"If you say so," he said.

I quickly pulled my phone from my pocket and sent a text to Cameron before following Sam out of my office and to the board room where we had a conference call scheduled with Iris McCleary and Vance Cherry.

Chapter 70

Jason Hunter

London Office

Monday 4th July

I'd spent the majority of the conference call distracted by my back-and-forth over text with Cameron.

Me: Have you heard of the Halberd Group?

Cameron: Yes. Reputation management, right?

Me: Yes. I need you to book a consultation meeting with them. An in-person one. And then text me the address.

Cameron: Do I even want to know why?

Me: I'm helping a friend. Their registered address is a fake.

Cameron: And by friend, you mean your detective friend?

Me: Yes. Is that a problem?

She hadn't texted me back yet. And I couldn't stop myself from checking my phone screen every few minutes for an update.

We were still sitting in the conference room, debriefing after the latest update. Iris Mccleary's world tour was going well. We'd had the finalised info from the last of the US venues, and the security knowledge gaps had been filled. The Asia leg was looking to be a lot more straightforward. As far as I was concerned, it was all plain sailing from here on out.

"Boss?"

I looked up from my phone to where Sam sat next to me at the long conference table. It was just the two of us now, Richard and the others having already left.

"You can't keep juggling like this," he said.

"What do you mean?"

"You're all over the place."

My phone buzzed on the table, and I glanced down at it to see Cameron's name on the screen.

"Both Iris and Vance noticed you were distracted," he said.

I looked back up at Sam. "I know, I know. Sorry. I think I'm still recovering from the whole Stacey thing. My head just isn't in it."

Sam nodded and looked up at the blank conference call screen mounted on the wall.

"I know you've been picking up my slack, and I truly appreciate it," I said, twisting in my seat so I could face him. "It's not gone unnoticed, trust me."

"I worry, that's all," he said and stood up to leave.

I opened the text from Cameron to see a Mayfair address, this one different from the one Hayley had visited earlier. I smiled.

"Hey, Sam," I said, looking up to see him pause halfway through the door. "Fancy an off-the-books job?" I asked.

Sam smiled. "Always."

Chapter 71

JASON HUNTER

MAYFAIR, LONDON

Monday 4th July

Sam and I loitered on the corner of Berkley Square, waiting for Cameron's car to pull up outside the office block where Halberd Group actually operated.

Initially, I'd wanted to go in after closing time so we could have a proper snoop around; nothing like the pressure of someone walking in at any second to get the adrenaline going, but Sam had convinced me it was too risky and we'd need to somehow bypass the security system. And that would be breaking the law. Not something I wanted to explain to Hayley, should we get caught.

Instead, Sam had suggested we go in at the same time as Cameron and simply use her as a decoy. I'd then video-called Cameron, who seemed more than delighted at the idea. And so here we were.

We'd both changed out of our usual suits and had borrowed some workmen's gear from the maintenance team in our own building before hightailing it over here as fast as we could. Cameron's meeting was this afternoon, which hadn't left us much time to plan.

Besides, Cameron had said she had a reputation to maintain, and if she delayed or rescheduled, it could cause suspicion.

Sam pulled a pack of cigarettes from his pocket and held it out to me.

"I didn't know you smoked," I said, surprised at the proffered packet.

"I don't," he grumbled. "But being out here on a smoke break is a lot less suspicious than us just standing here."

"Ah," I said and took out a cigarette. Sam pulled out his own cigarette and then tucked the packet back into his pocket, swapping it for a lighter. He lit his own and then handed the lighter to me. "Who knew you'd be so prepared?" I joked.

He didn't reply, just took a long drag on the cigarette.

"You ever smoke?" I asked, curious.

"When I was a kid," he answered. "You?"

"In the army," I nodded.

He nodded in understanding, and we stood in silence for a few minutes, watching the traffic come and go.

Cameron's car appeared around the far corner of the square, and we watched its slow approach. Unsurprisingly, it was a monstrosity. It was an old Hummer Jeep in her signature post box red, and *everyone* stopped to look. I rolled my eyes. Could this woman not do anything without drawing attention to herself?

The car stopped outside of the Halberd Group's office and I watched as Cameron climbed out. She was wearing her signature red jumpsuit with sky-high stiletto heels. Her red hair tumbled around her face in thick curls, and there was a red bag in the crook of her arm.

Sam let out a low whistle next to me.

I couldn't help but laugh.

He was right, though. Almost every pedestrian on the street had stopped to stare, and many were gawking. Her driver closed the door behind her and drove off, leaving Cameron to enter the building alone.

That was our cue.

Chapter 72

Jason Hunter

Mayfair, London

Monday 4th July

Stubbing out our cigarettes on the nearest bin, we scooped up the box and the manila envelope tucked behind the bush next to us and headed towards the building.

By the time we pushed through the revolving front door, the doors to one of the lifts closed, and I caught a flash of red that could only be Cameron.

It was a huge space, with high ceilings and glass everywhere.

"Fancy," I muttered to Sam.

We headed towards the lifts, and I caught the eye of the guy behind the sleek black reception desk. I held up the manila envelope and pointed to the lifts.

"Halberd Group on floor three. Just taking this up."

The guy looked at me, wide-eyed, as if he wasn't quite sure what to do. We reached the lifts, and Sam jabbed the call button. I prayed we didn't have to wait long. I didn't fancy being quizzed, or worse, blocked.

"Needs a signature," I said to the receptionist still watching us. He picked up the receiver for the telephone that was hidden behind the raised front panel.

"Shit," I muttered.

The lift arrived with a ding, and we stepped in. A businessman came rushing through the front doors to the building and slipped inside just as the doors closed.

Bugger.

I exchanged glances with Sam, who was smirking.

The three of us stood in an uncomfortable silence. Sam and I looking scruffy and out of place compared to the other guy's pristine suit. It didn't help that we were both about a foot taller than him too.

The floors ticked by slowly, and the businessman stepped out on the second floor.

I let out a breath of relief and Sam chuckled.

"We're gonna get a welcome committee," I said.

Sam nodded. "We sure are."

The lift came to a stop and the doors opened on the third floor.

A short man wearing glasses was waiting for us. His grey suit trousers and stiff white shirt looked at least two sizes too big. His hair was a curly mop on top of his head, and he was frowning.

"You're meant to see reception and call ahead when there's a delivery," he said, folding his arms across his chest.

I shrugged. "We're under strict instructions to ensure—" I glanced down at the envelope as if I'm checking the name. "—Mr Cummings signs for it himself."

Our curly-haired friend let out an exasperated sigh. "You'll have to wait here," he said, pointing to two sofas off to one side.

"Sure thing," I said and sat down on the first one. Sam sat down next to me and gingerly placed the box he was carrying onto the low-lying coffee table in front of us.

Curly looked at us one last time before giving me an eyeroll and then turning on his heels.

It wasn't a very big office, and I was surprised. A part of me had expected to see a hundred or so people working in here. The office floor plans had certainly implied there'd be that many in here. But Halberd Group clearly had a very discreet operation going on.

Other than the guy who'd 'welcomed' us, there was only one other employee, a petite brunette woman who hadn't even bothered to look our way since we arrived.

Sam and I sat in silence, watching our friend at his desk. Now and again, he would glance our way, and I'd give him a friendly smile. Curly would frown and then go back to whatever it was he was doing.

Chapter 73

CAMERON

HALBERD GROUP, LONDON

Monday 4th July

Miles Cummings was a slimy little thing in a well-tailored suit. He clearly had money, but the man obviously didn't know how to spend it.

The suit was a pinstriped number, and his tie was an awful, washed-out orange that made his complexion waxy and pale. He looked like he'd spent the last 24 hours vomiting in the employee bathrooms. The slight sheen to his forehead and greasy comb-over did nothing to help the look.

Cameron towered over him in her 4-inch heels. Even barefoot, she doubted the man came up to her nose.

Right now, they were sat in Miles Cummings' office. She was trying to come off as suave and sophisticated; her usual demeanour when dealing with her own clients, but she felt on edge. Somewhere outside these four tiny walls – walls that somehow felt like they were closing in – Jason and Sam were trying to find an opportune moment to snoop around.

Cameron had been only too happy to help. She loved a bit of drama. Except now, she was questioning her decision.

Miles Cummings was droning on about previous clients they'd successfully helped with crisis management. He wasn't naming names, but the slimy twat was dropping enough hints that it was easy enough to guess.

So much for client confidentiality.

"That sounds excellent, darling," she drawled in her usual manner.

Was that a blush she saw creep up his neck?

She had adopted the term 'darling' very early on in her illustrious career. She found that it did an awful lot when it came to getting what she wanted, especially from men. It made them feel special. And she was not above using her sexuality to get what she needed. If anything, that was what she was good at. Forget the fact that she had more business smarts than anyone else she'd ever come across. Although Mickey had been the exception; he'd never fallen for her charms. Not that way, at least. No. He'd seen her for the smart, sassy woman she is.

She felt a small pang in her chest at the thought of her old friend and business partner.

Mickey had saved her in more ways than she cared to admit. He'd pulled her from the gutter when she'd really needed it and given her the chance to stand on her own two feet. He was, and always had been, her biggest champion, and she missed him fiercely.

She'd warned him, though.

She'd warned the stupid oaf not to go and do anything stupid.

And that's exactly what he'd done.

And that's what had gotten him killed.

"I do believe you managed Alfonso Torres' reputation, is that right? While he was alive, of course, bless his soul," she looked up at the ceiling and made a vague sign of respect.

She didn't believe it was possible, but Miles Cummings paled and suddenly his attempt at being charming dried up.

"Where did you hear that?" he practically spat at her.

She wasn't surprised at his change in attitude. Dirty little bottom-feeders were always the first to turn nasty.

"He was a client at my club, darling," she said. "One of my best, if you know what I mean." She offered him one of her most charming smiles.

"Ah, I see," he said, and leaned back in his chair, clearly gathering his thoughts. "I obviously can't confirm or deny current or past clients," he finally said.

"Oh, of course not, darling. I totally understand," she said, and casually slid one leg over the other. "Do you mind if I smoke in here, darling?" she asked, leaning down to where she'd tactically placed her clutch bag on the floor.

Flustered by the change in topic and the perfect view of her cleavage, he said, "We—er—we have a no-smoking policy, I'm afraid."

She sat upright again, feigning disappointment. "I'll just have to wait until I'm back in my car then," she said, and gave a small tinkling laugh.

Miles Cummings seemed to relax at the sound, so she needed to move this along.

"Do you have a standard contract I can review, darling? You see, I'd like to make sure there are a few additions," she said, and began to rattle off a bunch of requests that got progressively more complicated as she went.

"I want all images of me removed from any website where I haven't personally approved the photographer." She held up a finger to indicate she was counting. "I will need you to send takedown notices for Instagram posts I appear in, even if I'm just in the background." She held up a second finger. "And I'll need monthly audit reports on what's been erased and who resisted, darling." She held up a third finger.

She could see Miles Cummings trying very hard to remain composed.

"Oh, and I need to see a physical copy of your standard draft take-down letter so I can assess for tone," she added, just for good measure.

"One second," he said and picked up the phone on his desk.

Bingo.

She'd counted at least two members of staff when she'd walked in. Hopefully, this little stunt would occupy at least one of them while Jason and Sam dealt with the other.

Chapter 74

JASON HUNTER

HALBERD GROUP, LONDON

Monday 4th July

We'd been sitting on the sofa for about 10 minutes when the petite blonde's phone rang on her desk. She picked up the receiver and listened intently to whoever was on the other end. I glanced at Sam.

"Of course," she said and hung up. She then got up from her desk and headed over to the bank of filing cabinets that lined one wall, rifled through a specific drawer, and took out a file. Checking through the file once, she closed the drawer and headed down the corridor to where I assumed Miles Cummings had his office.

This was it.

Sam cleared his throat, and the guy looked up from his desk. "Could I trouble you for a glass of water?" he asked.

Curly frowned.

Sam coughed again. "A bit dry, you see," he said and pointed to his throat.

Clearly unhappy about the interruption, Curly stood up from his desk and headed down the same hallway where his colleague had just disappeared.

Sam didn't hesitate as he stood up from the sofa and followed our friend.

"I can get it—" I heard Curly say. Followed by Sam's low grumble of a reply.

I didn't have long.

I jumped up from the sofa and sprinted to Curly's desk, shuffling papers for anything that might be of interest. I had no idea what the hell I was looking for.

Everything was filled with boring legal jargon. I skimmed the top few pages and then shuffled through to see if there was anything else that stood out. There wasn't.

I switched to the other side of the desk where another pile of papers was stacked. Still nothing. Draft press releases, draft contracts with notes scribbled on them, but nothing that told me anything about Alfonso Torres, Alek Gromov, or Wesley Gray.

I didn't have much time.

I looked around, thinking. Where would they keep stuff like that? Under lock and key, I guessed.

Then I remembered the petite blonde. She had been the one to go over to the filing cabinet. I didn't have time to rifle through every file they had, but I might get lucky with her desk.

Like the guy's desk, hers was covered in stacks of papers. I started on the right and began skimming documents again.

Underneath a few sheets of paper was a file.

Third-Party Erasure Authorisations – Q1 Archive

I frowned.

Opening the file, I read the first sheet of paper and my mouth dropped open. It was the draft data erasure letter for Alfonso Torres. I flicked the paper up. Underneath was one for Alek Gromov. And under that was one for Wesley Gray.

Shit. This was it.

Putting the file back down on the desk, I took a photo of each page on my phone.

Underneath the erasure request for Wesley Gray were several more, all for recognisable names. The same names in the fraud ring.

I looked up as I heard Sam's deep voice moving closer.

Shit. Shit.

I went to close the file and saw two sticky notes stuck to the inside cover.

Use Evergreen shell only. Don't CC Halberd

Cummings wants final sign-off on Evergreen drafts – no assistant approvals

I took a photo of the sticky notes before I closed the file and shoved it back into the pile, just as Sam reappeared on the other side of the office.

Chapter 75

JASON HUNTER

HALBERD GROUP, LONDON

Monday 4th July

Without warning, Sam doubled over and started coughing.

They were loud, gasping-for-air type coughs, and our Halberd Group friend behind him stopped in his tracks, his eyes going wide as Sam panted for air.

I gave the desk a final cursory glance to make sure everything was as it should be and then dashed across the office and threw myself down onto the sofa.

Sam's coughing subsided and he waved away the offers of help from the nervous employee.

"Do you know how long Mr Cummings will be?" I asked just as the petite brunette reappeared in the main office.

"What's going on?" she asked with a frown.

"Went down the wrong hole," Sam whispered, pointing to his throat.

She nodded slowly and then edged around him to return to her desk.

"Do you know how long Mr Cummings will be?" I asked again.

"No, I don't," said Curly, turning to look at me and adopting his haughty attitude once again. I made a show of looking down at my watch.

"Well, I think we're going to have to come back later, then. Do you know what time he'll be free?"

Curly was clearly pissed off. He so desperately wanted to take control of the delivery, and it secretly pleased me that he wouldn't. Besides, even if he did, the envelope was filled with a few blank pieces of paper. And the box? That was just shredded paper.

"I'm not at liberty to give out details about Mr Cummings' diary."

"Understandable," I said, holding up my hands in surrender. "Let me just check what to do with my boss," I said, standing up and pulling my phone out from my pocket.

A brief look of panic flickered across Curly's face.

Interesting, I thought. *What would Curly be panicking about? Who does he think I'm gonna call?*

I inclined my head toward Sam and he subtly moved over to where I stood, scooping the parcel from the table.

"I'll just be a minute," I said.

Sam pressed the call button on the lift as I pretended to dial a number on my keypad. As I pressed the phone to my ear, the lift doors opened, and we stepped inside.

The last thing I saw was the torn look of panic and annoyance on Curly's face before the lift doors closed.

Chapter 76

JASON HUNTER

CLUB DIONYSUS, SOHO

Monday 4th July

Less than an hour later, and Damarae, Cameron's preferred body-guard, was pouring drinks from behind the upstairs bar at Club Dionysus.

The place was empty, not due to open for another few hours, and it felt like we needed to regroup and compare notes.

I took a moment to send the photos I'd taken to Hayley via What-sApp, with a message saying, 'You're welcome'.

"You get anything?" asked Cameron.

"Oh, yeah," I said with a grin and slid my phone across the table with my camera gallery open.

She read the first data erasure letter and then swiped onto the second. Realising what she was looking at, she quickly swiped through the rest of the photos.

"Shit," she muttered under her breath.

"Halberd is clearly some kind of intermediary. Everything has Ever-green Consulting on it, whoever the hell they are. I've done a quick search, but it's coming up blank," I said, looking from Cameron to

Sam and back again. Sam had already seen the photos. I'd handed him my phone the moment we'd climbed into my old BMW.

"You have a bigger problem," said Cameron, pointing to the screen of my phone.

Hayley's name filled the screen as an incoming call.

I swiped my phone up from the table and answered it.

"What the fuck are these?!" she shouted down the line.

I winced. It was times like these when I wished my voice didn't always sound as raspy as it did. It made it hard to argue with conviction.

"Don't ask questions you don't want to know the answers to," I said, knowing full well it would piss her off.

"How am I meant to explain these appearing in evidence, then?!" she continued to shout. "Where the fuck did you get them, Jason?"

"Me and Sam paid Halberd Group a visit," I said, trying to go for nonchalance, but I was wound tight and my words came out defensive.

I stood up from the table, not liking the way Cameron and Sam were both trying to awkwardly look away while Hayley gave me a bollocking.

"And how the hell did you manage that when even I couldn't get hold of their address?"

"Hayley, do you really want me to give you all the details? You were the one who called me asking for a favour, remember?"

She let out a heavy sigh and I could almost see her pinching the bridge of her nose in frustration.

"I literally just wanted you to get an address. Nothing else. I wish you'd stop pulling this shit," she said, resigned. "Or at least tell me what it is you're doing. Before you do it," she clarified.

"I know, I know. But then you'd stop me. So, I won't. Look, I found some documents directly tied to our dead fraudsters and the guy running the show has history with Mayor Britland."

"I hear you. But this is all circumstantial at best. It doesn't prove anything."

"I know that, but it's one more piece of the puzzle."

"I'll see what I can find out about this Evergreen Consulting."

"Thanks, Hayley. This could be the break you need."

"Maybe," she said, but she sounded defeated.

I ended the call.

"What was that all about?"

I spun around to see Stacey hovering by the table, her eyes glued to me.

Ah, shit.

Chapter 77

JASON HUNTER

CLUB DIONYSUS, SOHO

Monday 4th July

I had no choice but to tell her everything. Not that I was planning to keep anything from her as such, I just hadn't had chance to tell her about this particular scheme. Everything had happened so fast.

"And when were you going to tell me?" she asked once I'd finished.

"I hadn't got that far," I answered honestly. I would have told her, of course I would have. Probably the moment I came through the door. I just couldn't quite work out how much to burden her with. But the fiery look she shot me now told me I was so very wrong.

"Stop treating me like I'm made of glass," she snapped.

I thought I saw Sam visibly wince from the corner of my eye.

"I'm not," I said, struggling to come up with something – anything – to say.

"I've already had to suffer through one man thinking he knew what was best for me, don't think for one second that I'll suffer through it again."

It felt like a slap across the face.

The place was silent.

And I could have sworn that Cameron and Sam had stopped breathing.

Not only had she cut me down, but she'd compared me to Liam in the process. As if I were just like him. That I could behave in the same way he could. Did she not know me at all? After everything we'd been through, after all I had done to get her back, is that really how she saw me?

I opened my mouth as if to reply, but nothing came out.

Instead, I turned on my heels and left, trying hard to ignore the pain that sliced through my chest.

"That was uncalled for, Stace," said Sam quietly.

But it was too late.

The damage was done.

Chapter 78

STACEY JAMES

CLUB DIONYSUS, SOHO

Monday 4th July

Stacey was angry. Pissed.

She wasn't exactly sure why Jason had kept this from her. He'd deliberately excluded her because that's what he thought was best.

Deep down, she knew that he was trying to protect her. But it had hit a nerve. A really big fucking nerve. One that was brutally raw.

Sam watched Jason's retreating back and then said quietly, "That was uncalled for, Stace."

She turned to him, still standing by the end of the booth, and she could feel her rage crumbling. Just like that. A pit opened in the bottom of her stomach, and it felt like the anger just fell right through, leaving her cold and empty.

"But, he—"

"I know," Sam said, using the same quiet, gentle voice. "But you have no idea what hell he's been through while you've been gone."

Stacey opened her mouth to reply, but Sam held up a hand to stop her.

"I know it's nothing compared to what you went through," he continued. "But Jason fell apart not knowing where you were. It almost destroyed him. And he did everything he could to find you."

There was a long silence as a tear silently slid down Stacey's cheek.

"And he'll hate himself for not getting to you sooner."

Sam stood from the booth and headed over to the bar where Damarae was quietly cleaning glasses.

Disappointment. That's what this was. Sam's disapproval at her reaction felt like more of a sucker punch than anything else. They'd always been such a team. To hear the disappointment in his voice was just too much. She couldn't contain it, and the tears streamed freely down her face.

Spinning around, she ran to the edge of the mezzanine floor, where she glimpsed Jason as he exited the empty nightclub.

"Give him a minute, darling," said Cameron, getting up from the booth and coming over to the railing.

They stood in silence before Stacey finally said, "I just want it all to go away."

"Oh, I know, darling," said Cameron, turning to face her. She gently tucked a lock of Stacey's hair behind her ear. "It's going to take a while before you feel okay again. You'll have good days, and you'll have bad days. And some days, you'll feel like you're right back there, trapped in that nightmare. You'll be triggered by the most random things, and it will feel like a living hell. But you know what, darling?"

Stacey turned to look at her, wiping away at the tears still falling freely down her cheeks.

"What?" she asked.

"You'll use it to be better. You'll become stronger. You won't let that bastard win. And you'll use the pain to create something phenomenal. I just know you will."

The conviction on Cameron's face made Stacey pause. The way she was talking made her think Cameron had lived through something terrible. Something similar, even. Had she?

"Damarae, darling," Cameron called over her shoulder. "Four Macallan's on the rocks, please."

Damarae placed four tumblers onto the bar, filled them with ice, and then poured a generous amount of whiskey into each. He slid one across to Sam who perched on one of the barstools, and then placed the other three on a tray. He delivered them to the table.

"I'll go and get him. You stay here, darling." Cameron placed a gentle hand on Stacey's back and nudged her toward the table before striding off in the direction of the stairs.

Chapter 79

Jason Hunter

Soho, London

Monday 4ᵗʰ July

It was a hot July, and the bright sunlight dazzled me as I stepped out from the dark club. Lifting a hand to shield my eyes, I squinted down the street.

People were milling about at the two pubs that flanked the end of the street while others casually strolled about, shopping bags in hand.

My mind was reeling.

Liam. Liam had done this. Liam had abused her, had broken her, and this was where things were. But the one thing my mind kept circling back to; what was I going to do about it?

And that was the real question, wasn't it?

What *was* I going to do about it?

I had no idea. I felt helpless, and that was terrifying.

I felt my phone vibrate in my pocket and pulled it out to see a WhatsApp from an unknown number. Half-assuming it was Cooper, and momentarily forgetting he only ever contacted me on my burner phone, I opened the message and froze.

There was a photo of me and Sam in our work overalls entering the building of the Halberd Group.

Halberd Group isn't your concern. Stop snooping before someone gets hurt.

Before I could fully understand the implications, several more photos came through. I downloaded them to see that they were all CCTV snaps of us entering the building, in the lift, in the office. One even had me at the brunette's desk looking through the papers.

Shit. Shit. Shit.

The hurt I'd been feeling before from the fallout with Stacey was quickly morphing into anger. A cold fury that cut through my bones.

Whoever was behind the text wasn't messing around.

It was like being stuck in a maze with no way out. The walls were closing in, making it difficult to breathe, difficult to think straight. Had I just made a big fucking mistake?

I was frustrated. Angry and frustrated.

Balling my right hand into a fist, I turned and punched the brick wall next to me. Pain exploded through my hand and wrist, and I instantly regretted it.

Looking down at my hand, the knuckles were grazed, bleeding, and already swelling up. I winced and chided myself for my stupidity.

"Feel better?"

My head snapped up to see Cameron casually leaning against the entryway to her club.

"No," I grumbled.

She clicked her tongue as if she were scolding a small child.

"I'm fucking pissed, Cameron," I said.

"I can see that," she said, and I could hear the disapproval in her voice at my outburst.

I couldn't tell her about the text. Not right now. I couldn't risk Stacey hearing about it. Couldn't add that kind of stress to her plate right now. And so I defaulted to the conversation that had led me to be out here in the first place.

"The prick might be dead but look at the damage he's still doing. She's never going to be free of him. No matter how hard we try. And better yet, she thinks I'm just like him. I mean, where the fuck did that come from—?"

I was shouting now, and people were looking as they walked past.

Cameron held up a placating hand.

"I hear you, darling," she said simply.

I gritted my teeth as my hand throbbed and turned away from her.

After a minute, Cameron said, "So what are you going to do?"

It was the same question I'd been asking myself just before my anger had gotten the best of me.

What *was* I going to do?

Well, in reality, the answer was easy.

I was no quitter.

I'd be there for Stacey; I'd hold her up when she needed it, and I'd be her punching bag on the hard days. Not literally, of course, but I was under no illusion that this tongue-lashing would be the last. If I knew Stacey, and let's face it, we'd been through a lot together, I knew she'd be pushing back the moment she felt cornered.

With regard to the Halberd Group. Well, that was an entirely different problem. And I wasn't going to let a faceless bully push me around.

Without another word, I walked back into the club, Cameron following closely behind me.

I walked up to the mezzanine floor and slid into the booth next to Stacey. Cameron slid in opposite.

Wordlessly, Cameron slid a whiskey on the rocks across the table to me and then picked up the other. I noticed Stacey cradling her own, and when I glanced over at Sam at the bar, he was draining his glass.

I took the offered drink and downed it in one.

Chapter 80

Jason Hunter

Home

Monday 4th July

The drive home had been quiet. Neither one of us spoke.

As I reached the door and pulled out my keys, Stacey placed a hand on my arm.

"Hey," she said quietly.

I turned to face her. My anger was long gone. In its place was sadness. I could feel it burrowing into me, sinking its claws in. And with it came a sense of hopelessness.

"I'm sorry," she almost whispered. "I didn't—"

"I know," I said. And I did. It wasn't her, it was the trauma.

She looked so sad. Like the weight of the whole world was pressing down on her, and she'd never be able to smile again.

"I—"

Before she could say anything else, I kissed her.

She kissed me back, placing a hand on the day-old stubble on my cheek.

There was a cough, and we broke apart to see Hayley standing awkwardly on the path.

"I brought food," she said, and lifted the takeout bag in her right hand to prove her point.

I let out a small chuckle, suddenly feeling lighter.

Turning back to the house, I opened the front door.

Ten minutes later and the three of us were sitting around my kitchen island, boxes of Chinese takeout spread out. Stacey sat next to me, her hand casually resting on my knee. The physical contact grounded me.

"I wanted to apologise," said Hayley around a mouthful of noodles.

"For what?" I asked.

"Biting your head off," she said, avoiding eye contact with me.

I smiled. "Does that mean you found something?"

"It's not good," she said, glancing up.

I stopped eating.

"What is it?" asked Stacey.

"So, I looked into Evergreen Consulting, like I said I would. It's a shell company that was used for property deals. But it had been dormant for over ten years."

"Had been?" I asked.

"It reactivated three weeks before Mickey died."

I paused, a sweet and sour dumpling on the end of my fork hovering in mid-air.

"You're joking."

Hayley shook her head.

"Hang on a minute," said Stacey, frowning. "This Evergreen Consulting starts back up again, Mickey dies, and then they start sending out data removal requests for the people who just so happen to be on the USB that Mickey was using to blackmail his way out of a dodgy deal."

Hayley nodded.

"That is fishy."

"It gets worse," said Hayley. "Guess who Evergreen Consulting's only property client was back in the day?"

"You have got to be kidding me," I said, knowing immediately who she meant.

Hayley nodded.

"Britland?" I said, with my mouth full. "Really?"

She nodded again.

"Ah, shit."

"So what does this mean?" asked Stacey.

"I don't know," said Hayley.

"Why is Britland going around cleaning up messes, when his own head is on the chopping block?" I asked. "Who the hell is pulling the strings?"

"Maybe Britland wasn't the target," suggested Stacey.

We both turned to look at her.

"At the prison. Maybe the shooter wasn't targeting Britland. Maybe it was you," she said to me.

The room was silent.

"But he didn't kill me," I answered.

"Maybe he wasn't meant to," she countered.

Now she really had our attention.

"What if the whole thing was set up to look like it was a hit-gone-wrong to throw us off the idea that Britland is behind it all, but actually, it was a warning to you. A way of taking you out of the picture, even if only temporarily."

I thought for a moment, processing her words.

She made a good point, but it still didn't make sense.

"That's pretty far-fetched," said Hayley.

"Why not just kill me?" I asked.

She shrugged. "You're too useful. You know where the USB is, and maybe it was just a way to scare you into cooperating."

"But I haven't cooperated with anything," I pointed out.

"No, you disappeared off to Italy instead," said Hayley. I could see from the way she was looking at Stacey that she was seriously considering this line of thought.

"Hang on, hang on. So, you think I got shot on purpose, but it was made to look like an accident, while Britland was not shot on purpose, and the not shooting him was made to look like an accident."

Stacey nodded, a small smile tugging at her lips. "Well, when you put it like that," she said.

"It does kind of make sense. You disappeared to Italy, which no one expected. Perhaps Britland had plans for you, but he didn't predict that you would run off to go and find Stacey. He couldn't have known that's what you were going to do," said Hayley.

"I guess," I said. "It does explain why he's been so pushy about seeing me."

"What do you mean?" asked Hayley.

I stood up from the kitchen island and opened the fridge.

"Anyone want another?" I asked, grabbing a beer and holding it up.

"Please," said Hayley as Stacey nodded.

Pulling three beers from the fridge, I opened all of them and placed them on the island, then removed the empty bottles.

"When I was in Italy, Britland was pretty insistent on speaking to me and not Sam. He wanted to know when I'd be back. And he was pretty pissed when I did come back, but didn't tell him."

I let my words sink in.

"It all screams paranoia, if you ask me," I said.

"Which makes total sense," said Hayley.

"How so?"

"Think about it; Britland is in a compromising position. The moment the Met finish compiling evidence and bring charges against him, he'll be on remand, and that's goodbye to the luxury lifestyle we all know he lives. Not just that, but it's a huge smear campaign. Even if he got out of it scot-free, anyone on that fraud list has the power to bring him down," she said.

"He's cleaning house," I said.

"Control. The man clearly thrives off it," said Hayley, taking a swig from her beer.

We sat in silence for a while, slowly making our way through our food.

"It's not enough, though, is it?" said Stacey.

"No," said Hayley quietly. "It's not."

Hayley's phone, sat on the table alongside the half-eaten take-out containers, lit up. She glanced down at the notification that had popped up on the screen and grimaced.

"What is it?" I asked.

"The official line is to leave Halberd and Evergreen alone."

"Tell me you're joking," I said.

"'Not enough evidence to escalate. Apparently.'"

"But—" said Stacey.

"I know," interjected Hayley. "Someone's shutting it down from the top."

I stared at her. It was one thing to get a hold of evidence with my less-than-legal methods; it was another to have the whole thing dismissed based on... what? Nothing.

"So, we just wait for another body to drop?" I asked.

Chapter 81

STACEY JAMES

JASON'S HOUSE

Tuesday 5th July

Jason had left for work fairly early. He'd been calmer than last night, and a peaceful kind of truce had settled between them since the argument the day before. If it could even be called an argument. More of a Stacey bitch-slap.

Shame washed over her. The way she'd spoken to Jason, the way she'd compared him to Liam, was completely out of order and she knew it. She was just grateful Jason wasn't so much of a hothead that he'd exploded on impact. But she had seen the state of his knuckles when they'd gone up to bed last night. She'd cringed at being the cause. And then he'd gently comforted her, told her that this was Liam's fault, not hers. Well, not that he ever said Liam's name, at least not to her. He was always referred to in vague terms as *him* or something like it. But she knew who he was talking about.

She needed to make it up to him.

And the best way to start would be with a home-cooked meal.

She knew what Jason liked; anything pasta-based was normally a huge hit.

And she had a craving for lasagna.

After jumping in the shower and towel-drying her hair, she threw on some clothes and headed downstairs.

"Hey Sam," she said to the burly bodyguard sitting in the armchair by the window. Sam raised a hand in greeting but didn't pause reading his paperback.

"Is it a good one?" she asked, trying her best to hide her smile.

"Yes," said Sam, still not looking up.

She walked into the kitchen, where she rummaged through the cupboards looking for ingredients. With a sigh, she resigned herself to the fact that she was going to have to visit the shops.

Anxiety clutched at her chest for a brief moment. But after a few deep breaths, it eased. Besides, she'd have Sam with her.

"Fancy going shopping?" she asked, poking her head into the living room.

"What kind of shopping?" he asked, without looking up.

"Food shopping."

That got his attention as his head snapped up. "Yes," he smiled.

She grabbed her bag from the hook by the door, checked her purse was inside and headed out. They wouldn't be long, and the fresh air would do her good – isn't that what everyone always said?

Instead of heading towards the nearest convenience store, they turned left, in the direction of Shepherd's Bush Market.

"You gonna be okay?" asked Sam quietly.

"I'll be fine," she reassured him.

For some reason, today she needed the hustle and bustle. The anonymity of being in a crowded space. With Liam, she'd been isolated. And since coming home, she'd been lonely. Jason was needed at the office, and even though he was coming home earlier than usual, she was still left with hours to fill. Sure, she had a bodyguard to keep her company. But Sam was the only one she really felt comfortable around, and he was often needed elsewhere, which meant she usually ended up with someone she wasn't familiar with, and they weren't always the chattiest.

She needed to get back in the gym, really. Get back to her training. But she'd just been so tired. She ventured out here and there, but it always left her feeling exhausted.

Tomorrow was her first counselling session with Professor Lindberg since she'd been back. The sessions had been doing her good during her last race season. They'd been helping her handle the anxiety and lack of confidence from the first time Liam had exploded into her life. It would be interesting to see what her therapist thought of the person she was now. The shell of a person she'd become.

Pushing the thoughts from her mind, they crossed the road and entered the market.

The place was alive with shoppers and traders selling everything from clothes and jewellery to fresh produce and international spices. You could smell it in the air, and it made her mouth water. It was noisy too, with traders shouting above the noise to get the attention of passers-by. It kind of worked, but mostly just added to the cacophony of sounds.

It was overwhelmingly chaotic, immediately setting her nerves on edge. She knew Sam could feel her tension by the way he moved closer to her, almost touching. And his reassuring presence was all she needed.

Taking one deep breath after another, she slowly felt herself relax and marvel at the busyness around her.

They wandered up and down the market, stopping at stalls for Stacey to inspect goods. She was jostled and shoved a few times, but each person turned to apologise. The first time had left her feeling unsettled, but she soon relaxed into it, knowing it was just part of London life.

After nearly an hour, she had everything she needed, except the mince, so they stopped at a butcher selling cuts of beef.

"What can I get you, love?" asked the guy behind the counter, an apron tied around his waist.

"Half a kilo, please," she said, pointing to the mince at the front of the display. Sam stood a few paces away, his back to her and his arms crossed, scanning the crowd of people for anyone who might pose a threat.

As the butcher rang up her order, Stacey caught sight of someone out of the corner of her eye. A tall man with dark hair. He stood to one side, avoiding the throng of people hurrying in every direction. And that's what had made him stand out. He was so still in a sea of movement, and he was looking right at her.

"Sam," she said, turning to him, her voice uneasy.

He looked at her, immediately on high alert.

"There you are, love," said the butcher, handing her a plastic carrier bag containing the meat. She tapped her phone on the payment machine, gave her thanks, and pretended to rummage around in her bag as she surreptitiously glanced over her shoulder at the man.

"What?" asked Sam, coming closer.

The man was gone, and she let out a sigh of relief.

"Nothing," she said. "I thought I saw something." Maybe it was just her mind playing tricks on her.

Satisfied that she had everything she needed to make dinner, they headed home.

Chapter 82

JASON HUNTER

LONDON OFFICE

Tuesday 5ᵗʰ July

I was still reeling from the conversation with Hayley last night. Frustration was only part of what I was feeling, and it was making me snippy.

Lucy had already given me one of her 'looks'.

I dug around in the hidden compartment of my desk drawer and drew out my burner phone.

Switching it on, I had several notifications appear in my WhatsApp. All of them were urgent, and they all said the same thing.

Call me.

I felt sick.

"You're in deep shit, Hunter. You've rattled the wrong cage."

"What are you talking about?" I asked, my voice sharp.

"I don't know what the hell it is you've done, but your name is circulating in the wrong places. Keep your wits about you. And keep our girl safe. I can't get back to the UK for a while yet, so it's up to you."

I nodded, forgetting he couldn't see me, and cut the call.

If poking around Halberd Group and Evergreen Consulting was making someone nervous, then it meant we were looking in the right place. The only problem was, I still felt blind. We had no idea who was behind this, or how it was connected to the fraud ring.

Hayley's hands were tied, and there was only so much Sam and I could do.

If Cooper was on edge and warning me, then this was a serious problem.

A knock at my door had my head whipping up. I tucked my phone away in my pocket to see Lucy with a tight smile on her face.

"What's up?" I asked.

"Mayor Britland is here to see you," she said.

I was speechless.

Standing from my desk, I watched as Britland approached and pushed roughly past Lucy.

She gave a huff of disapproval before storming off, closing my office door behind her.

"Mr Mayor," I said, glad I was standing. "What can I do for you today? Is everything okay with your security?"

"I'm not happy," he said.

"I can see that," I said and gestured to the seat opposite my desk.

"I'll stand, thank you," he said. "This won't take a long."

I remained standing.

"Your conduct, Mr Hunter, has been questionable. What do you think you're playing at, impersonating a courier?"

Ah. Interesting.

"I'm not sure I know what you're talking about," I said with a frown.

"You know damn well what I'm talking about," he said, his face turning red. "You have no idea the people you're dealing with, Jason.

They are dangerous and ruthless and—" his voice dropped to a venomous whisper "—you're going to get me killed!"

My eyebrows shot up at that.

"Britland, what the hell are you talking about?"

"Stay away from the Halberd Group. And if I can't trust you to do that, I'm going to have to take matters into my own hands," he spat before storming from my office.

Chapter 83

STACEY JAMES

SHEPHERD'S BUSH MARKET, LONDON

Tuesday 5th July

They wove their way through the market, going back the way they'd come.

Yet another person bumped into Stacey's shoulder, but she was feeling jumpy after seeing the man staring at her. She glanced over her shoulder at the person who'd accidentally barged into her and was distracted by the same tall figure and dark hair that she'd seen before. She blinked, and he disappeared into the crowd again.

Her mind was definitely playing tricks on her. She was sure of it.

Finally free of the market, they headed up the street with Sam carrying her bags. Stacey couldn't help but glance over her shoulder every few paces.

"You okay?" asked Sam, a frown on his face.

"I thought—" She looked over her shoulder again, and there he was. The same man she'd seen watching her in the crowds.

Her breathing hitched in her throat as she tried not to panic.

"Sam," she said, and she could hear the strain in her voice.

Sam looked in the same direction, and she knew the moment he saw the man; his body stiffened and he was on high alert. It was a scary change to witness. Sam was always so calm and friendly, to see him in 'protector' mode was something else.

"Keep walking," he said quietly. "And in a minute, we're going to cross the street."

Stacey did as she was told, her heart rate increasing with every passing minute.

They walked in silence, and then Sam said, "Let's go into the newsagents."

She nodded and did as he instructed, both of them entering the small convenience store. The bell dinged as the door opened, and Stacey headed over to the rows of magazines.

Sam lingered by the door, watching out the window.

Whoever the man was, he wasn't being subtle. Even from where she stood, Stacey could see him lingering outside, looking at his phone as if he was waiting for someone.

Stacey went through the motions of buying a random gossip magazine and joined Sam by the door.

"We're going to head home. Don't look back. Keep a steady, even pace and pretend you haven't seen him," said Sam.

Stacey nodded and less than 10 minutes later, she was closing the front door to Jason's townhouse, feeling scared and out of breath.

Sam deposited the bags on the floor by the door and headed into the living room, where he looked through the window to the empty street outside.

"Has he gone?" she asked.

"Maybe," he said, and then called Jason.

Chapter 84

Jason Hunter

Home

Tuesday 5ᵗʰ July

"Are you okay?" I asked as I walked into the living room. I'd packed my laptop up and headed home the moment Sam had called me.

Stacey sat on the sofa watching something on TV. She sprang up the moment she saw me and threw her arms around my neck.

I quirked an eyebrow at Sam.

"The newsagent had CCTV," said Sam. "I'll go and ask if they caught him on camera. The guy was careful. Didn't come too close, so not sure if they'll have clocked him."

I nodded and Sam left. He would have been itching to follow up on whoever the mystery man was, but Stacey's safety was his priority, and he wouldn't risk leaving her on her own, even if it was for five minutes.

"Tell me what happened," I said, my arms still wrapped around Stacey's waist.

"We went to the market. And I saw this man in the crowd. I blinked and he was gone. I—I thought my mind was playing tricks on me. What with everything…"

She pulled away from me and took a deep breath, gathering herself.

"I saw him again. He followed us out of the market. I told Sam, and he said to go into the newsagents."

I nodded my head. It was a good tactic. He would be less likely to follow and more likely to be caught on CCTV.

"And then you came straight home?" I asked.

She nodded, glancing towards the window.

None of this was new information. It matched exactly what Sam had told me on the phone, but I'd wanted to hear it from her.

"What did you buy at the market?" I asked, hoping to distract her.

Her lips parted in a round 'o' and she dashed into the hallway where she picked up a bag that had been sitting by the door.

"I completely forgot," she said.

I laughed. "What's that?"

"Dinner!" she said and disappeared into the kitchen.

I blew out a steady breath and then followed her.

While she busied herself with cooking dinner, I made us both a cup of tea and patiently waited for Sam, hoping this didn't have anything to do with Evergreen Consulting. Because if it did, we were all fucked.

Chapter 85

Jason Hunter

Home

Tuesday 5th July

I didn't have to wait long.

By the time Sam returned, I'd pulled my laptop from my bag and was working through contract approvals as Stacey cooked. I was too on edge to do anything else, and I was trying so hard not to let her see how jittery I was. At least throwing myself into work acted as some kind of balm.

Without a word, he handed his phone to me.

It was a photo of a CCTV screen showing a grainy shot of a guy lingering on the corner.

Sam swiped.

The next photo showed the man in a better line of sight, but his face was tilted away from the camera.

"Is this the best they had?" I asked.

Stacey came and stood next to me, leaning over my shoulder to look at the photos. Using her fingers, she zoomed in on the photo, but it was too grainy to be of much use.

Sam swiped again and played me a short clip. The guy clearly knew what he was doing. He kept his face angled from the camera the whole time he was in view, which made it almost impossible to identify him. *Almost.*

I nodded and then turned back to my laptop.

Last year, I'd had my own security system installed at home as a precaution. Not that it had stopped the gunman from getting inside my house, but it had certainly offered Stacey an additional level of security. I doubt the place was as secure as her penthouse apartment in Belgravia, but she hardly stayed there these days. She much preferred being here.

Opening up the website that stored my security footage, I went back to the time that matched the timestamp on the CCTV and watched the recording.

Sure enough, Sam and Stacey arrived back home less than five minutes later.

Sam came around the island to sit on the stool next to me and watched the screen.

Less than a minute after getting through the front door, a man with dark hair passed by and glanced at the house.

"That's him," said Sam, nodding towards the screen.

Stacey nodded her agreement.

We all watched the screen for a few more minutes and saw the same guy appear, this time on the other side of the street. He paused, watching the house for a moment before walking by.

"Did you see him go past?" I asked.

Sam shook his head.

I rewound the footage and paused it when the guy came into view for the first time. He clearly hadn't seen the cameras mounted above my door and I had the perfect screenshot of his face. It was a little blurry, but clear enough that I could see who it was. And boy, was his face familiar.

"He's from Britland's security team," said Sam.

"Isn't he just," I said.

I'd seen the guy on more than one occasion: when Britland had first come to my office, and then later at the press conference at Belmarsh prison.

"Why is Britland following me?" asked Stacey.

"I don't know," I said, turning to face her and ignoring the sharp twist in my gut. I did know why, not that I could tell her. I looped an arm around her waist and pulled her in close.

"What do you want to do?" Sam asked me.

"For the moment, nothing." I felt Stacey stiffen at my side. "It's not worth it. I can let Hayley know, but that's more of a courtesy than anything else. But if the Met have dropped the case, it's not going to exactly work in our favour. Britland is clearly up to something; let's see what it is."

Chapter 86

Jason Hunter

Home

Wednesday 6th July

Stacey sat at the kitchen island eating a bowl of cereal.

I made myself a coffee to go and poured hers into her favourite mug. It was one Lily had painted for her for Christmas, covered in flowers and love hearts and what was meant to be a racing car.

It felt like an age since I'd seen the kids. With everything that had been going on, it just didn't feel right to bring them over. Adrianna understood. We'd reached a weird and comfortable truce since Mickey's death.

I placed the mug on the island next to Stacey and kissed her on the cheek as she chomped her way through another mouthful.

"I'll see you later," I said.

"Mmm-hmm," she mumbled.

I opened the door to find Sam standing there, fist raised to knock.

"Good timing," I chuckled.

He gave a single nod and stepped inside, a frown on his face.

"What is it?" I asked.

"Car outside," he said. "Parked on the other side of the road, a guy sat in the driver's seat."

I frowned and looked past him. He was right. Opposite the house was a black Ford with a guy sitting in the driver's seat on his phone. He glanced at the house and then back down to his phone, but he clearly had no intention of driving off anytime soon.

"Britland paid me a visit yesterday," I said, glancing over my shoulder to make sure Stacey was out of earshot.

"What? And you didn't think to mention this sooner?" asked Sam.

"It's complicated. He said we're going to get him killed."

Sam's eyebrows shot up.

"Want me to stay?" I asked.

"We'll be fine," he said.

"Call me if anything changes," I said.

Sam nodded and went to join Stacey in the kitchen.

Chapter 87

Jason Hunter

Home

Wednesday 6th July

When I got home from work, the car was still there.

"Hasn't moved all day," said Sam on his way out.

"Has the driver gotten out?" I asked.

"A couple of times. But he lingers by the car, doesn't go far and then just gets back in."

"Fuck's sake," I muttered. If this was Britland, then he'd made his point. I dug my phone from my pocket and dialled Britland's number.

"Alright, you've made your point," I said when he answered.

"About what?" he asked. He sounded distracted.

"The car. Outside my house. Move it," I said through gritted teeth.

"That has nothing to do with me."

"Well, who else would it be?"

"I told you, Mr Hunter," said Britland, his voice calm and lethal. "You've pissed off the wrong people. You shouldn't have gone snooping."

He hung up the phone.

Sam was frowning.

"Not Britland?"

I shook my head and felt my gut clench with worry.

I peeked out of the living room window at the car parked on the other side of the road.

"I'll send one of the guys over to keep an eye on the place," said Sam.

"Thanks," I said and clapped him on the back as he left.

I watched Sam climb into his Jeep and drive off, my eyes flitting to the black Ford still parked opposite.

If Britland wasn't responsible for the car outside, I dreaded to think who was. The harsh reality was that I'd made a fair few enemies over the last few years. This felt personal, though. They weren't just keeping tabs on me, they were keeping tabs on Stacey. No one followed me to the office today. Instead, they sat outside my house like some jailor.

Whoever it was, they were seriously pushing my buttons.

Dinner was leftover lasagna from the night before. And while the food was good, the company was... quiet. I glanced at Stacey across the kitchen island to see that she was just pushing the food around on her plate. I'd nearly finished, but she'd hardly touched hers.

"You okay?" I asked.

She looked up at me like I'd caught her doing something she shouldn't have been and nodded her head. Then her eyes flickered briefly towards the living room.

"Sam tell you?"

She looked back at me again and nodded.

"Is it Britland?"

I let out a sigh. "I actually don't know."

Her eyes flashed at that.

"Who else could it be?" she asked.

I bit the inside of my cheek. Normally, I wouldn't hesitate to tell her. But now... I didn't want to burden her. She had enough to deal with.

My mind flicked back to the argument at Cameron's club. As much as I didn't want to tell her, I couldn't keep this from her. She deserved to know.

"Britland told me we've pissed off the wrong people."

"Who?" she asked, her eyes narrowing.

"I honestly don't know. He was rattled. Told me I'd been an idiot for snooping around Halberd Group and that it was going to get him killed."

"Get him killed?" She frowned.

"Mmm-hmm," I said.

She nodded and returned to pushing her food around the plate. After a few more minutes of silence, she got up from the island.

"I think I'm going to go to bed," she said.

I nodded, unsure what to say. Instead, I watched as she walked into the living room. She hesitated by the door and then, as if she couldn't help herself, she went over to the window and peeked out between the curtains. Then she headed into the hallway. I heard her unlock and re-lock the door, followed by the sound of the door chain rattling and then her retreating footsteps as she disappeared upstairs.

This was getting ridiculous. It was just one thing after another. And Stacey really needed the world to cut her some slack. Somehow, this felt like my fault. It was my fault. And I'd had enough.

Getting up from the table, I decided there was only one thing I could do.

Chapter 88

JASON HUNTER

HOME

Wednesday 6th July

Opening the front door, I was halfway down the steps when I realised the driver of the parked car was no longer in it. Instead, he was leaning against the door, smoking a cigarette and watching a dog walker further down the street, oblivious to the fact that I was storming his way. Perfect.

I scanned the road for cars before stepping out. I was only a few paces away when I called out, "You lost, mate?"

The man's eyes snapped to me, and panic flickered across his face. He threw the half-smoked cigarette onto the ground and did the one thing I didn't expect. He ran.

There was no way I was letting him off the hook that easily. I ran after him.

He sprinted down the street and turned left at the end. I followed.

As I rounded the corner, I saw him just about avoid a collision with a young mum and a pushchair. She was shouting at him, but he didn't care. He looked over his shoulder to see I was closing in fast.

I was breathing hard as I pumped my arms and legs. I was still wearing my suit trousers and shirt from being in the office all day, but I'd be damned if that was going to slow me down.

Expecting him to run to the end of the street, I was surprised when he took a sharp right and disappeared down an alleyway between two houses. There was a high possibility that it would be a dead end and the guy would be trapped. But as I rounded the corner, I saw him vault over the fence at the other end. I followed, using a tipped-over bin to give me a step up.

On the other side of the fence was a well-tended garden. It wasn't big, and the guy had already barrelled through the side gate and back out onto another residential street.

The adrenaline was keeping me moving, but I could feel the burn in my lungs and the ache in my legs. I was getting too old for this shit.

I was so close to grabbing the guy. There were perhaps only a few feet between us, and it was making him nervous, I could tell. We rounded another corner and he yanked on a nearby bin, pulling it into my path. I stumbled as I jumped over it, and he gained a few extra feet.

He made a sudden sharp left turn, and I followed him into another narrow alleyway. This one was tighter than the last and featured a garden gate every few metres. He was almost at the other end when something hard and unforgiving hit me in the face.

Chapter 89

JASON HUNTER

SOMEWHERE IN SHEPHERD'S BUSH

Wednesday 6th July

I was on my back, blinking up at the darkening sky, and my face was wet.

The wetness was everywhere. It had spread down my face, over my chin and across my neck.

Dazed, I sat up.

"Oh my gosh! I'm so sorry!"

A woman easily in her sixties with grey hair cut into a short pixie cut hovered over me, her face stricken.

Raising my hand to the wetness on my face, I pulled it away to see my hand covered in blood.

Ah, shit.

My face felt swollen and my nose bloody hurt. The damn woman had most likely broken it.

"I told him he needed to fix the gate," the woman was rambling. "He wouldn't hire someone to do it, and the silly bastard put it on the wrong way. It's not meant to swing out, you see." She was still rambling, but she held out a hand to help me sit up. "Are you okay?

Here." She felt around in her pockets and then pulled out a small wad of tissue and handed it to me.

I took the offered tissues and pressed them to my face.

"What were you doing out here? You were running pretty fast."

The man.

Double shit.

I looked past the woman and down the alleyway, but the guy was long gone. I scrambled to my feet and reassured the woman before jogging to the end of the alleyway. He was nowhere in sight.

Feeling frustrated that I'd missed my chance, I turned and headed home.

Despite how fast we'd been running, we hadn't actually gotten that far from my house, and it only took me ten minutes to get back. And the car was gone.

Chapter 90

JASON HUNTER

HOME

Wednesday 6ᵗʰ July

I knew I couldn't face Stacey. Not in my current state. I was fuming.

Instead, I'd done the cowardly thing and texted her to say I was heading out, grabbed my keys, and left.

Jackson Yang sat in his car, right in front of the house. Looked like he'd pulled the short straw.

I tapped a knuckle on the window. Startled, he looked up at me and then wound the window down.

"I'm heading out for a bit. Don't know when I'll be back," I said.

"No worries. "Are you okay?" he asked, a frown appearing.

"Yes," I grunted.

"Okay, erm, I'll be here," he said and gave me a tentative smile but I wasn't in the mood to be friendly.

And so I'd headed to the one place I knew I'd be able to let off some steam, no questions asked.

"What the hell happened to you?" asked Cameron the moment she saw me.

Remembering the incident with the garden gate, I swiped at my face. My hand came away with congealing smears of blood on it. *Ah, crap.* Well, at least that explained why Jackson had looked so concerned.

"Sorry," I said, my voice thick over the usual raspiness.

Cameron glanced around at her patrons. It wasn't late, but the club was already starting to fill up.

"I can't have you out here looking like this," she hissed and grabbed me by the hand. She led me past the dancefloor and through to the VIP area. We passed booth after booth, all of which were empty, to the cleverly concealed door at the far end.

I'd been in here before. It was Cameron's private office and had a large bank of security screens where she could watch what was happening in every corner of her club.

Marching past the screens, Cameron opened a door I'd never noticed before and shoved me inside. It was a bathroom. A damn nice bathroom. With a marble countertop and an emerald green sink bowl set on top. Gold taps curved elegantly from the marble countertop. Every inch of wall space was taken up with floor-to-ceiling mirrors and two emerald green doors on the right led to what I could only assume were toilet cubicles.

"Sorry, I—" *What? What exactly was I going to say?* "I wasn't sure where else to go," I finished lamely.

Cameron tutted as she bent down underneath the sink and pulled out a first aid kit. Tonight, she was wearing a pair of post-box red jeans that hugged every inch of her with a pair of red stilettos and an off-the-shoulder top that left her collarbone and shoulders exposed.

"Do you have many injuries in here?" I quipped.

She shot me a look as she laid the first aid kit on the counter and opened it. Reaching under the counter again, she pulled out a pack of cotton wool balls. She turned the tap on, and I watched as she checked the temperature, pulled a cotton ball from the pack and ran it under the water before turning to me.

Without a word, she began to clean the blood from my face. And as hard as I tried not to, I couldn't help but wince when she pressed too hard around my nose.

"You might have broken it," she said.

Oh God, I hoped not. I'd broken my nose once before as a teen, and it was painful as hell. Not to mention the swelling and the two black eyes it gave me.

She continued working in silence, dropping the used and bloodied cotton balls on the countertop.

"You gonna tell me what happened?" she asked eventually.

And so I did.

I told her about Evergreen Consulting, about the photos sent to my phone, about the guy from the market, about the car outside my house, about the chase, and the garden gate to the face.

And as I talked, I could feel the tension easing in my shoulders.

"I'm pissed, Cameron," I said.

"I can see that," she replied wryly.

"After everything, she's not even free now. I've brought this to our door. Britland's angry and scared and that makes him unpredictable. I thought this whole nightmare was over with last year. But it won't. Just. Fucking. Go. Away." I punctuated each word with a thump on the countertop.

She stayed silent for a moment, inspecting my nose, before saying, "Men like Britland need to be in control. When that control starts slipping, that's when they start silencing people," she said. "They erase them. It's all about control and the image they portray to the world. If you ruffle that, then he's going to be a very angry man with a lot of power. He abuses the systems to get what he wants. And he's not afraid to play dirty."

"Ain't that the truth," I muttered.

Cameron pulled away slightly to look at me with her eyebrows raised.

"I hear you," I said.

"If Britland isn't behind the car camped outside your house, then who is?" she asked.

"I don't know," I sighed.

"Well, whoever it is, they know you well enough to know that following or threatening Stacey in any way will push your buttons."

"What are you saying?" I asked, not liking where she was going with this. Was I really that easy to aggravate?

"Just be careful about what happens next. Take back control and keep your cool."

Cameron had a point. Of course she did. And having her say it all out loud made me feel a lot less like a crazy person and a lot more grounded.

"There," she said, stepping away and dumping the last of the cotton balls on the countertop. I turned and looked in the mirror.

"Ouch," I said. The bridge of my nose had ballooned, and there was already one hell of a bruise forming around my right eye.

"Yeah, looks pretty nasty," said Cameron, turning to clear away the stuff on the side.

"Hey," I said, and grabbed her wrist. She turned her face to look at me. "Thanks," I said.

"Anytime."

Chapter 91

Jason Hunter

Home

Wednesday 6th July

As I climbed the steps to my front door, I felt guilty. Guilty for having left Stacey at home. Guilty that I'd dragged her into this mess. And guilty that I couldn't do anything about it.

Take back control. That's what Cameron had said. But how?

I definitely felt calmer after having talked to Cameron, but there was something bubbling away just under my skin. An itch I couldn't quite get to. No matter how you looked at it, Britland was a manipulative prick. And whatever was going on right now was far from over.

Glancing over my shoulder, I confirmed the car from earlier was gone. And I made a mental note to check my security footage in the morning. But right now, it was late. Stacey had texted me an hour ago asking where I was, and I knew I had some making up to do.

I slipped my key in the lock, turned it, and opened the door.

I went to step over the threshold but paused, my foot in the air.

There was something on the floor.

It had clearly been posted through the letterbox and I glanced down the street again to see if there was anyone there.

Picking up the small envelope, I flipped it over and pulled out the small glossy photograph from inside.

It was a photo of Stacey.

She was peering out of the window of the house. Her face was anxious.

The time stamp in the corner told me the photo was only an hour or so old. Taken around the same time that Stacey had texted me to ask where I was.

I flipped the photo over, wondering if it came with a note.

On the back, written in an untidy scrawl:

If you won't listen, maybe she will?

What the hell did that mean?

I could feel the panic starting to rise up. This was a message. A bloody important one. And yet, I felt like I didn't quite understand it.

Then my phone buzzed in my pocket.

Realising the front door was still open, I closed it and pulled my phone from my pocket, still looking at the words written on the back of the photo.

My eyes flickered to my phone screen and the WhatsApp notification that had popped up. It was from an unknown number:

You protect people, don't you? Funny how the ones closest to you keep ending up in the line of fire.

I had to read it twice as the adrenaline in my system roared in my ears.

Turning around, I yanked open the front door and ran down the few steps to where Jackson Yang, the young security guard who'd been part of Stacey's detail in Monaco, sat in his car.

Yanking open his driver's side door, I leaned down and said, "Who's been at the house?"

"N—no one," he stammered.

I held up the envelope, practically shoving it in his face.

"Someone delivered this to the house," I said. "They hand-delivered it through the letterbox. You've been sitting here the whole time, haven't you? Who the fuck has been to the house?"

"I—I don' know. Stacey let me in to use the toilet. No one's been here though."

I could hear the panic rising in his voice but right now I didn't care.

This was a big fucking problem. And there was only one person who'd be able to give me answers.

"Stay here," I said. "Call Sam. I need two of you on rotation for the remainder of your shift."

I didn't wait for his response before I was yanking the door to my car open and climbing in.

But first, I needed to swing by the office.

Chapter 92

Jason Hunter

London Office

Wednesday 6th July

The office was deserted.

As I pushed the door open, the building alarm sounded. I flipped the alarm panel open and keyed in the code.

The alarm stopped.

Letting out a small breath, I pulled my phone from my pocket and turned the torch on.

The place was eerie when it was empty.

I made my way across the room and opened my office door.

I don't know why, but I kept feeling like someone was going to jump out. There was no one here. I knew that. The alarm wouldn't have been set otherwise.

Dropping into the chair behind my desk, I leaned down and opened the bottom drawer. I didn't really need my torch. It was muscle memory that was propelling me forward.

Flipping up the false bottom of the desk drawer, my fingers wrapped around the cold metal of the illegal gun I kept there.

Chapter 93

CAMERON

CLUB DIONYSUS, SOHO

Wednesday 6ᵗʰ July

After Jason left, Cameron wandered through the club, greeting her guests. A few of her VIPs had arrived, and she'd escorted them through to their booths.

She'd retreated to her private office, knowing she would have to show her face again soon. But Jason's visit had rattled her.

Standing in the middle of her office, she watched the screens mounted on the wall. From here, she could watch the entire club come to life. The dancefloor was filling up fast, the DJ was in full swing, and the night's entertainment included dancers suspended from the ceiling on acrobatic hoops.

The bar was busy already, and all the booths on the main floor were full. The upstairs was still closed off, but it would open soon when the downstairs reached capacity.

Her thoughts wandered back to her conversation with Jason. She hadn't expected him to turn up to her club covered in blood.

And then the story had all come tumbling out while she'd been cleaning him up.

Evergreen Consulting was Britland's shell company.

It felt like a sucker punch.

Not only was Britland taking out the liabilities, but he was cleaning house, too. It didn't matter if he was doing it for himself or for someone else. He was literally erasing them from the world. Is that what he had wanted to do with Mickey?

She'd always assumed it was Alek Gromov who'd killed Mickey. After all, it was Gromov who'd been after the USB stick. But what if Gromov was acting on behalf of someone else? On behalf of someone who was pulling all the strings? What if Gromov had been working for Britland? What if they'd both been working for someone else?

Turning around, she headed over to the drinks cart and poured herself several fingers of whiskey into one of the crystal tumblers.

Every time she thought they were out the other side, something would happen.

Mickey's death haunted her daily.

It filled her mind with so many what-ifs.

What if she'd insisted on knowing more instead of burying her head in the sand? What if she'd pushed Mickey to tell her just what the hell was going on? What if she'd been able to do something? What if she'd been able to help him out of the sticky hole he'd found himself? What if... what if he hadn't died?

She lifted the crystal tumbler to her lips and took a large gulp, the liquid burning like fire as it slid down her throat.

What if...?

She placed the tumbler back on the drinks cart and opened her safe. Taking out what was inside, she slid it into her purse and then left.

There was someone she needed to see.

Chapter 94

Jason Hunter

Hampstead Heath, London

Wednesday 6th July

I drove through the wrought iron gates to Britland's house.

I'd never been here, but I'd seen the address written on all his paperwork, had reviewed the residential security assessments on the property, seen the floor plans and the photos. Which meant that, despite having never once set foot on the property, I knew it very well.

The building loomed into view at the end of the driveway.

It was a stunning house. Two marble steps led up to a wide front door flanked by two columns on each side and a pointed porch roof. Neatly manicured bushes lined the wall under the windows on either side of the door.

It wasn't that late, so I was surprised to see it so quiet. The place looked almost deserted, except for a soft glow coming from the window to the right of the front door.

I knew Britland knew I was there. The security assessments had shown an impressive surveillance operation, one that Britland was able to control from the comfort of his home office. If he didn't want me here, the gates wouldn't have opened.

Picking up the gun from the passenger seat, I climbed out of my car, closing the door quietly behind me.

Goosebumps rose on the back of my neck as I realised just how quiet the place was.

I climbed the two steps to the front door and knocked, the door swinging open ever so slightly from the contact.

I frowned. An unlocked door was never a good thing. It normally meant that someone unwanted had forced their way in.

Cautiously, I pushed the door open all the way.

"Britland?" I called. No answer. "Mr Mayor?" I said a little louder. Still nothing.

I clutched the gun in both hands. And the memory of holding a weapon like this settled something deep in my chest.

The entryway was dark and gloomy. Black walls and dark wood flooring made it difficult to see much. Someone could have been waiting in the shadows for all I knew.

I could just about make out a couple of doorways. But the soft glow I'd seen outside was coming from my right. It was seeping from underneath the door.

Moving carefully through the dark, I reached out and took hold of the door's handle. It wasn't locked, and the door swung open effortlessly.

Chapter 95

JASON HUNTER

BRITLAND'S HAMPSTEAD HOME, LONDON

Wednesday 6th July

Britland's study screamed wealth.

Everything from the dark walnut panelling to the floor-to-ceiling bookshelves. The room was long. The bookshelves lined the left wall, while the right was interrupted by two windows. A globe stood between them, about three feet high and bigger than a football.

At the far end of the room was Britland's desk. It was a huge thing and took up almost the whole width of the room. A leather chair sat behind the desk, and in it sat Britland.

He was facing the window, only his profile illuminated by the antique banker's lamp on his desk.

My heart lurched in my chest. And I lowered my gun.

Was he dead?

My mind raced as it tried to recalculate all the assumptions I'd made about Britland's involvement. First Halberd Group and then Evergreen Consulting. It had all pointed to Britland being his own mastermind. But the look on his face when he'd stood in my office yesterday flashed through my mind.

You're going to get me killed!

The panic on his face had been real.

My thoughts spiralled as I tried to work out what I'd missed.

"I suppose this was inevitable."

I flinched as I realised it was Britland who'd spoken.

The bastard was still alive. And I wasn't sure if I was relieved or annoyed.

"I only came to find out who's on my case," I said.

Britland chuckled and then turned his chair to face me, a cigar clutched in the fingers of his left hand, a tumbler of golden liquid – I guessed whiskey – in his right hand. He brought the cigar to his lips, puffed it slowly, and then let the smoke out.

"Take a seat," he said, gesturing to the lone chair opposite his desk.

"No, thanks," I said. "I don't plan on staying long."

"And what do you plan on doing?" he asked.

"Consider this a warning," I said, raising my gun.

Britland chuckled again.

"I fucking mean it, Britland," I said. "I'm done playing your shitty games. Tell me who's pulling the strings."

"But we have a contract," he said, a smug smile tugging at the corner of his lips.

"Not anymore. I don't work for crooks," I said.

The smile slipped from his face. "You want to be very careful about the kind of accusations you make," he said.

"Don't think I'm stupid, Britland. Your name was on that list."

Britland's eyes narrowed. The friendly mask was well and truly gone now, his expression cold.

"All you had to do was shut the fuck up, you know that, don't you? You just had to leave it well enough alone and this—"

Chapter 96

JASON HUNTER

BRITLAND'S HAMPSTEAD HOME, LONDON

Wednesday 6th July

The door to the study slammed open and I spun on my heels, gun raised, to see Cameron stood there, wearing the same glamorous outfit she'd been in when I'd visited the club just hours before. She was calm and composed.

Except for the handgun she was holding.

It was raised and pointed right at me.

"Cameron, what—" I started, but Britland cut me off with a hearty laugh.

"Oh, come on. What's this?" he asked.

"Did you kill Mickey?" she asked, her voice calm, the gun moving to point at Britland.

"Mickey? Oh that lowlife club owner?" Britland chuckled.

"Mickey was--" Cameron started but Britland cut her off.

"Blackmailing me," he said, his tone turning serious. "And he should have known better than that. What did he think was—"

She fired. The sound of the gunshot reverberated around the small space.

I recoiled, instinctively moving away from it and then pivoted to face Britland. A bullet hole in his head. His eyes were wide and glassy, as if he couldn't believe she'd pulled the trigger. Hell, I couldn't believe she'd pulled the trigger.

His hands hung limp by his sides, the glass tumbler rolling away on the floor.

Stunned, I stay frozen to the spot.

"Do you realise what you've just done?" I rasp, unable to tear my eyes away from Britland's lifeless body.

"You saw what he did to Mickey."

"But that doesn't make it right," I said, turning to face her, my ears still ringing.

"No," said Cameron, her expression hard. "It's called justice."

Chapter 97

JASON HUNTER

BRITLAND'S HAMPSTEAD HOME, LONDON

Wednesday 6th July

The room was silent. Cameron avoided my gaze, her eyes firmly fixed on Britland's body. I had no idea what to do. But I did know one thing— we needed to leave. Now.

I took one last look at Britland, scanning the room for anything that might be incriminating. I knew his security system was pretty high-tech, but I was desperately trying to think back to whether there were any cameras in his study.

I didn't *think* so, but I needed to be sure.

My eyes landed on a tiny little light, well-hidden between the books on the bookcase. Stepping closer, my stomach plummeted. It was a tiny webcam. And the light. That meant it was streaming live.

Fuck.

This was bad. Really, fucking, shitting bad.

I had no idea who was watching. And if I knew Britland, this was the absolute final nail in my coffin, not his.

Shit.

"Cameron," I said, finally snapping her back to reality.

She turned to look at me, and I pointed to the camera.

The colour drained from her face.

I reached up to the camera and yanked it from its spot on the bookcase, disconnecting the power cable at the back. Turning it over, I watched as the little white light dimmed.

Okay, that was one problem dealt with.

"What do we do?" asked Cameron, panic lacing her voice, the cool, calm exterior finally crumbling.

I glanced at the desk, knowing exactly what I was looking for. And sure enough, in the centre of the desk, covered in splatters of Britland's blood, was a closed laptop.

Opening the lid, the screen came to life. No password required. I frowned. Whatever was on this laptop, Britland would have locked down tight.

Except, the window that was still open told me why.

The livestream of the camera was open, the screen black. The label at the top said: *In the event of my death.*

Shit. Shit. Shit.

I scanned through the list of recipients on the right-hand side. There were at least a dozen names, but they were all anonymised. No clues as to who they were, just randomised numbers and letters, but I had a hunch, and I really hoped I was wrong.

The landline on Britland's desk rang, making me jump.

I looked at it, shocked. Who the hell had a landline these days?

It rang again.

I glanced at Cameron. Her eyes were wide as she looked between me and the phone.

It rang again. The sound loud and jarring.

I snatched the receiver up from the cradle and pressed it to my ear.

"You have less than 60 seconds before this place is swarming with people you don't want to meet."

The voice was deep and familiar somehow.

"Who is this?" I said.

"Jason," Cameron whispered. I looked at her to see that she was pointing a shaking finger at my chest. I looked down to see the red dot of a laser hovering over my heart.

"A friend," said the voice and the line went dead.

The red dot hovered for a few more seconds before disappearing.

And that's when I realised that I knew exactly who had called. The same man who had once sat in my living room and held me at gunpoint. I just didn't know why.

Now wasn't the time, though.

"We need to go. Now!" I said, grabbing Cameron with my free hand and tugging her towards the hallway.

Chapter 98

JASON HUNTER

BRITLAND'S HAMPSTEAD HOME, LONDON

Wednesday 6th July

Car doors slammed outside and I froze.

The hallway was too dark to see anything, so I blindly lunged for a doorway, dragging Cameron with me. We groped through the darkness, neither of us letting go of the other.

I heard the front door open as people entered the property. Whoever they were, they weren't being quiet.

I bumped into something soft and velvety; a sofa maybe? I guessed we were in some kind of sitting room. Less than ideal.

There were more feet stomping through the hallway and into the study, which meant we only had a minute or so before they'd expand their search. And that's when shit would really hit the fan.

I skirted around what I thought was a sofa and thought back to the floorplans I'd reviewed of the house. It felt like months ago and I was trying really damn hard not to let the panic cloud my mind. Panic made you sloppy, and right now I needed clarity.

I had a vague recollection of a room with two sofas and a table in between. But was that this room? There was only one way to find out and we were running out of time.

I took three steps forward and my fingers grazed another soft structure.

Bingo.

Slipping behind the sofa, I tugged Cameron down onto the floor and firmly clamped a hand over her mouth.

"Do. Not. Move," I whispered as quietly as I could. She nodded, her hands holding onto mine. Not to remove it, but to keep it in place.

That's when I realised the movement I'd heard before had gone and the house was once again silent.

A floorboard creaked as somebody moved. Then two more steps.

A beam of light swept through the room, missing us and giving me a clearer view of the room's layout. Shelving units lined the wall in front of us, and there was a door to our right. That's where we wanted to go. If we could move more towards the back of the property, we had a greater chance of being able to get out of this alive.

The light disappeared and the person retreated a few steps.

"Going right," I breathed in Cameron's ear. She nodded and I gently released her.

I listened for another moment, then squeezed Cameron's hand and pulled her to her feet as we ran for the door, both of us crouching.

We got to the kitchen. I let out a small sigh of relief.

Tall windows lining one side of the room let the moonlight filter in, illuminating the place.

The whole room was made up of marble countertops and white cupboards, and it was utterly spotless. Not to mention big enough to fit almost my entire house. This place was huge. Certainly much bigger than I'd realised.

We ran across the room, around the island that took up the centre of the room and towards the double doors at the far end.

I reached for the handle, grabbed it and yanked down but it didn't budge. *Shit*. A key jutted out of the lock under the handle, and I didn't hesitate in turning it. But the clunk sound it made as the locking mechanism in the doors retracted sounded a lot louder in the silent space.

Without glancing over my shoulder, I released Cameron's hand and yanked the door open.

A loud bang erupted and the glass in the door shattered alarmingly close to me. I grabbed Cameron and pulled her through the door with me.

We were on a huge terrace that overlooked the garden. Outside, it was still dark but I could just about make out the shape of the house, the edge of the terrace and the steps that led down to the wide rolling green below.

Another window shattered as more bullets chased us.

"Down the steps," I shouted, all attempts at being quiet abandoned. They knew where we were. We just needed to get out.

Cameron did as I said and raced down the steps two at a time. Impressive considering she was still in her stilettos. I followed, jumping down the last five steps.

I heard more glass shattering and the thumping of running feet as our assailants made it out onto the terrace and followed.

Shit. We'd run right into someone coming the other way. There was a split second where he seemed almost startled to see us. As he raised his gun, I punched him in the throat, and he gagged. I cupped a hand around the back of his head and pulled him forwards, kneeing him in the stomach at the same time. He doubled over, choking and gasping for air and I shoved him backwards towards the open doors on the lower floor of the house.

He stumbled and then I heard a splash as he fell into the indoor pool.

We needed a getaway, and fast.

Chapter 99

Jason Hunter

Britland's Hampstead home, London

Wednesday 6th July

We rounded the corner of the house, and I slammed an arm into Cameron's chest, jolting her to a halt.

The place was teeming with people. A mixture of black suits and full tactical gear.

What the hell was going on?

This looked like a clean-up crew.

My car was on the other side of the driveway, facing towards the house.

Idiot, I scolded myself. I should have at least turned it around.

Cameron's car, however, was facing away from the house. She'd clearly driven past my car and then parked as she turned it around. Better yet, hers was a 2017 Porsche 911 GTS which was a hell of a lot quicker than my 20-year-old BMW. Bright red, of course.

"Keys," I said.

Cameron slipped her car keys from the back pocket of her jeans and slapped them into my outstretched hand.

A bullet hit the brickwork a foot or so to my left and I winced as I felt something bury itself into my arm. Whatever it was, it stung like a bitch.

Looking back the way we'd come, I could see at least three men with weapons raised heading our way.

Raising my gun, I fired several shots, deliberately aiming wide but giving them enough of a warning to think twice about coming an closer.

"Now, or never," I said, grabbing hold of Cameron's hand again and darting forward.

We were halfway across the driveway when those out front noticed us.

Another step and I could see several of the suits pulling handguns from underneath their jackets.

I fired another shot that had them ducking for cover.

Fumbling with Cameron's keys, I found the fob and clicked the lock button.

The car locked, the lights flashing twice.

Shit.

We reached the car and ducked behind it as the suits started firing.

Cameron reached for her keys and between us we fumbled for the right button.

The car opened.

"In the back," I said to Cameron, raising my voice over the noise as I yanked the handle of the driver's door.

I slid into the driver's seat, threw the keys down into the centre console and started the engine. Another bullet slammed into the driver's door as I reached to close it. I instinctively flinched away and then reached for the handle again, pulling the door shut as I put the car into drive and slammed my foot down on the accelerator.

The wheels spun for half a second before gaining traction and the car lurched forward.

"Stay down!" I yelled as a bullet shattered the rear windscreen. And we sped away from the house.

Chapter 100

Jason Hunter

Shoreditch, London

Wednesday 6th July

I pulled over into a deserted lot and got out of the car.

My adrenaline was still running high, and I was trying to process what had just happened.

"What the hell were you thinking?" I said, turning on Cameron as she stepped from the car. Somehow, she looked composed, as if she hadn't just murdered someone and then ran for her life as masked men shot at her.

"You crossed a line," I said.

"He crossed it first," she said. Cool, calm, collected.

I looked away, frustrated.

This whole situation was so bloody messed up.

"We can't come back from this. You know that, right?" I said, turning to face her again.

"I never expected to, darling," she drawled with a smirk.

And there it was. The Cameron the rest of the world saw, not the friend I'd made over the last year.

She sauntered to the driver's door, opened it and then turned to look at me one last time.

"I had to," she said as she climbed into the car, and I watched as it drove away, wondering if that would be the last time I ever saw her. I hoped not. But there was no telling what the repercussions of tonight would be.

I'd gambled that the clean-up crew wouldn't follow. They didn't want anything public. That was the whole point. But if I wasn't on their radar before, I sure as hell was now. And so was Cameron. I'd need to watch my back. Keep my head down and keep quiet.

An old friend had mentioned that the port of Southampton was looking for a new security contract. Maybe that's what I needed, to get out of the city for a little while.

I let out a slow, steady breath and looked up at the stars.

It was quiet out here, peaceful.

So why did I feel like this wasn't over?

I rolled my shoulders once, twice, and winced. Looking down, I saw my shirt was torn and there was a wound on my arm from where a bullet had glanced off the house. It had bled a little, the red seeping into the shirt and turning it a bright crimson. It was a shallow wound. More of a graze than anything. Easy to treat. Easy to cover up.

Pulling my phone from my pocket, I opened up maps and typed in Sam's address.

I knew it wasn't far. And I was right. Just 15 minutes away.

I started walking.

Chapter 101

JASON HUNTER

LONDON OFFICE

Thursday 7th July

Sam hadn't been happy to see me on his doorstep last night. But I couldn't blame him, really. I wouldn't have been happy to see me either. And he was definitely pissed after I told him what had happened. Rightly so. He'd warned me about going rogue. And that's exactly what I'd done.

Instead of coming into the office today, he'd put himself on Stacey duty. Probably because he needed the space. Away from me. Who could blame him?

I walked into the office, my heart feeling heavy.

I'd been telling the truth when I told Cameron that there was no coming back from this.

I hadn't told Stacey yet; instead, I'd given her vague excuses about needing to be in the office first thing. But there'd be no hiding this.

And that's when I realised the office was empty.

I paused mid-step.

Where was everyone?

Lucy's desk was empty, her computer screen still on.

There was no hum of activity, no chatter of employees.

And that's when I noticed that someone was in my office. Specifically, someone was sitting in my chair.

I crossed the room as quickly as I could and flung the door to my office open.

Whoever he was, he was dressed in a well-tailored dark suit with grey hair.

"Mr Hunter, it's so nice to finally meet you."

"I'm sorry, I don't believe we've ever met," I said with a frown.

"No, no we haven't. This was a bit of a last resort really," he said.

I glanced over my shoulder at the empty office before turning back to the man who'd made himself comfortable at my desk.

"And what is it that you want?" I asked cautiously.

"A truce," he said.

"A truce?"

"Yes,"

"I don't have the memory stick," I said, my mouth going dry.

"Oh, I'm not worried about that. Our mutual friend, Mayor Britland, did enough of a clean-up for me that your Detective Inspector friend doesn't have a case to present to the CPS."

I felt the ground hollow out beneath me. Just who the hell was this guy?

"No," he continued. "I want to ensure you're not going to go chasing after ghosts because you have an unnerving way of pulling skeletons out of the closet."

"I don't know what you're talking about," I said.

"Of course you do. You see, I've seen the live stream of Cameron killing Mayor Britland in cold blood. And quite frankly, I don't want to get tangled up in his mess."

"So, what do you want?" I asked, my chest tight.

"A truce. I want us to co-exist peacefully. You won't go digging into things that don't concern you, and I won't go threatening the people you love."

I raised an eyebrow.

"Is that so? I don't take too kindly to being threatened."

"Oh, it's not a threat, Mr Hunter. It's a promise."

He stood from my chair and lazily strolled toward me.

"I can make your life incredibly miserable, Mr Hunter. And I really don't want to do that. Max and Lily wouldn't want that. And neither would your darling Stacey. Especially after all she's been through."

I felt sick.

Who the hell was this guy?

"Just keep to yourself. Run this little security operation you have going here," he said, waving a finger around in the air, "and all will be right with the world."

I watched as he walked out of my office, raising a hand over his shoulder in goodbye.

Jason Hunter

Home

Friday 22nd July

I'd been left reeling after my mystery visitor. He never did tell me his name. And, honestly, I didn't want to know. Not if it was going to cause more problems. I'd had enough. The last year and a half had taken its toll on me and on Stacey. She was my priority for the time being. Getting her back on the racetrack was all that mattered. Who knew if it would happen.

Her Sporting Director, Eden Schneider, had called and told her to take all the time she needed. He'd mentioned bringing her back in next season, but until then, she was just to focus on herself.

For the time being, Stacey needed me.

It had been a long and busy week at work. A good week, just busy.

Everything seemed to have settled since Britland's death.

It felt like the whole world had been shocked by it. It had been all over the news for days. A suicide, apparently. How the clean-up crew had staged it as a suicide, I had no idea. And I honestly didn't care.

My mystery visitor had been very convincing. And I was determined to keep my nose out.

Stacey lay sprawled on the sofa next to me, snoring softly.

We'd been watching a movie. Something light-hearted and fun and – in typical Stacey fashion – she'd fallen asleep almost instantly.

I looked down at her and stroked a lock of hair away from her face.

She looked so peaceful, and it made my heart squeeze just ever so slightly.

The credits rolled onto the screen and a soft buzzing interrupted the silence. I glanced down at my phone resting on the arm of the sofa and frowned.

It was a +27 number.

And I didn't need my phone to tell me where it was calling from. Cape Town.

I let the number ring out, not wanting to answer it. I didn't recognise the number. But there was only one person I knew who lived in Cape Town and if it was them calling me, it wouldn't be anything good.

I stared at my phone for a long moment before placing it face down on the sofa and finishing my beer.

Whatever it is, I'm not getting involved.

About the Author

I'm a book-loving, writing enthusiast. I love to travel, drink tea and pet every animal I meet. When I'm not elbow-deep in the writing world, you can usually find me helping other authors through my editing services.

I live in Hampshire, UK with my husband and young son.

Instagram: @writernatashaorme
Website: https://writer.natashaorme.com/
Sign up to my newsletter for exclusive updates, behind the scenes, and to be the first to hear about bookish news!

Acknowledgements

Although it's only me writing the words on the page, there's a whole host of people who have helped bring this book to life.

A huge thank you to my lovely friend Lauren who actually gave me the idea for this book – your enthusiasm and interest in my crazy ideas give me the motivation to keep going.

Huge thanks – as always – to my lovely editor Becky at Opal Grove Editing. Your magic red pen is the real hero in all of this. And to Malcolm, you're always able to understand my vision and create a cover that brings it to life.

To my friends and work colleagues who happily tolerate me talking about my fictional worlds (and always cheer me on).

Forever grateful to my mum who's always first in line to buy a copy, and to my dad who loves finding all my typos.

And finally, my wonderful husband Lee. Thank you for always supporting my little ideas, listening to my struggles and giving me the encouragement I need when sometimes I just want to give up. I couldn't do it without you.

Also in the Jason Hunter Series

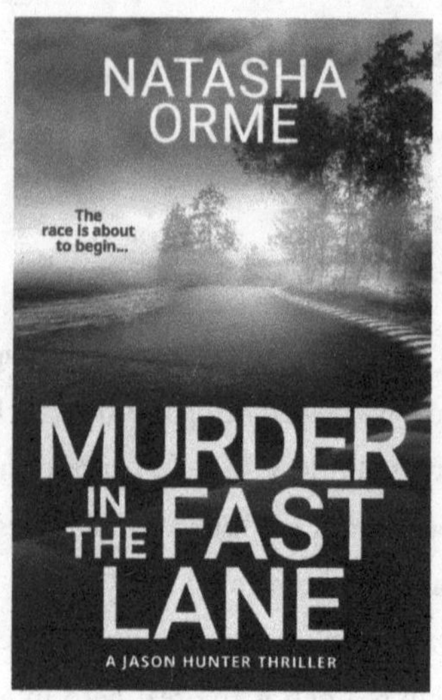

She wants to win the championship. He wants her dead.

Formula One racer Stacey James is taking the world by storm. But when her body double is killed on the Hungarian podium, things begin to spiral out of control.

Menacing phone calls, creepy photos and subtle threats. This guy just won't quit. The worst part? Everyone's a suspect but the police are no closer to getting answers.

Jason Hunter, personal security specialist and dad of two, has been hired to provide protection. But can he keep Stacey safe *and* catch the killer? Or is he out of his depth and putting more lives on the line?